Millionaire's (

by L

"Are you takin

Ethan sat back in his chair and regarded her with cold blue eyes.

Mary had never seen a man with more arrogance – or more presence – than this one. "I told you I'd agree to artificial insemination."

"I know what you told me." His sapphire gaze missed nothing, especially her intense desire to stop him. "But to make sure your end of the bargain is upheld, we'll do this the old-fashioned way."

"Not a chance in hell."

He looked amused. "You might even like it…"

Thunderbolt over Texas
by Barbara Dunlop

ᘖ ᑒᐸᑊ ᘊ

"You ready to walk down the aisle in a white dress, promise to love and honour me, then kiss me and throw a bouquet?"

As Cole outlined the scenario, an unexpected vision bloomed in his mind. Sydney in a white dress. Sydney in a veil. Sydney with a spray of delicate roses trembling in her hands. He could feel her skin, smell her perfume, taste the sweetness of her lush lips.

"We'd both know it was fake," she said.

Cole startled out of the vision and gave a short nod. "Yeah. Right. We'd both know it was fake."

"And that's what would matter. That's what would count." She squared her shoulders. "Knowing the benefits, I could do it."

"Then so can I," said Cole, just as he'd known he would from the second his brother conceived the plan. His family needed him, and that was all that needed to be said.

Available in June 2008
from Mills & Boon® Desire™

An Improper Affair
by Anna DePalo
&
Make-Believe Mistress
by Katherine Garbera

ᗡ✕ᗴ

The Billionaire's Baby Negotiation
by Day Leclaire
&
The Prince's Ultimate Deception
by Emilie Rose

ᗡ✕ᗴ

Millionaire's Calculated Baby Bid
by Laura Wright
&
Thunderbolt over Texas
by Barbara Dunlop

Millionaire's Calculated Baby Bid
LAURA WRIGHT

Thunderbolt over Texas
BARBARA DUNLOP

MILLS & BOON
Pure reading pleasure

*First published in Great Britain 2008
by Harlequin Mills & Boon Limited,
Eton House, 18-24 Paradise Road, Richmond, Surrey TW9 1SR*

The publisher acknowledges the copyright holders of the individual works as follows:

Millionaire's Calculated Baby Bid © Laura Wright 2007
Thunderbolt over Texas © Barbara Dunlop 2006

ISBN: 978 0 263 85905 8

51-0608

*Printed and bound in Spain
by Litografía Rosés S.A., Barcelona*

MILLIONAIRE'S
CALCULATED BABY BID

by
Laura Wright

Dear Reader,

The truth is I love the alpha male. I love reading about him, writing about him and being married to him. I believe this obsession started in school, where in my senior year I realised that the guys who grew up to be driven, highly intelligent, take-charge, sexy alpha males were not the popular school boys I'd hoped would notice me. No, those guys were peaking too soon. Our men, our Mr Darcys, were the quiet ones, intense and driven in their pursuits.

In the first book of my series, NO RING REQUIRED, we meet the alpha of all alphas: Ethan Curtis. "Driven in his pursuits" takes on a whole new meaning for this self-made millionaire, who has only one unfulfilled goal left to pursue – to have a blue-blooded child. Ethan will do anything to get what he wants, and if he has to blackmail a beautiful blonde in the process, so be it…

Enjoy!

Laura

LAURA WRIGHT

has spent most of her life immersed in the world of acting, singing and competitive ballroom dancing. But when she started writing romance, she knew she'd found her true calling! Although born and raised in Minneapolis, Laura has also lived in New York, Ohio and Wisconsin. Currently, she has set down her bags in Los Angeles, California, and although the town can be a little crazy at times, Laura is grateful to have her theatrical production manager husband, two young children and three dogs to keep her sane.

During her downtime from writing, Laura loves to paint, play peek-a-boo with her little boy, go to movies with her husband and read with her daughter. She loves hearing from her readers and can be reached at PO Box 57523 Sherman Oaks, CA. 91413, USA.

For Lucca Elliott, my sweet baby boy...

Prologue

One hour ago Mary had expected to lie back on the king-size bed in the most exclusive bed-and-breakfast in Long Lake, Minnesota, and let Ethan Curtis make love to her, with no emotion, zero response from her body. At that very same time, she'd wondered if he'd be rough, cold, like the unfeeling bastard she'd met in her family's former offices a week ago—the offices he now controlled and ran like a well-oiled, profit-gouging, soul-sucking machine.

His mouth moved over hers, slowly, seductively coaxing her back to the present. Every time his skin brushed against hers, every time his teeth raked lightly over her neck or back or shoulder, she mewled so loudly with desire she was sure the entire inn heard her and knew exactly what she was doing.

Ethan Curtis might've been a bastard, but he was anything but cold.

Moonlight spilled into the room, making it impossible not to see Ethan's face as he pushed into her again, his cut cheekbones, hard mouth, and tanned neck taut with exertion and damp with sweat. His cobalt gaze slipped from her eyes to her mouth, and he lowered his head. Mary's heart hammered in her chest as she tried to force back the rush of desire in her blood when his full mouth found hers and nuzzled her lips open.

The reality of why they were here in bed together, so that her father was now free from any threat of prison, scratched at the door of her mind. She wished she could crawl out from underneath Ethan and leave the room, but her body continued to betray her. Maybe it was because she hadn't been with a man in two years. Maybe she just craved the weight and the closeness and the surge of adrenaline, but she wanted this man so badly she ached with it.

Ethan drifted lazily from her mouth to her cheek, then to her ear. She felt the tip of his tongue against her lobe and shivered, her back arching, her hips arching, her body taking him deeper. Her ears were surprisingly sensitive, and she hated that he knew it, that he was having this power over her—yet loved it at the same time. His tongue flicked back and forth as though he were tending to more than just the lobe of her ear, and she trembled again with sudden spasms she couldn't control. Outside their door, she heard voices, heavy footfall in the hallway, then a door closing. Had they heard her as she moaned with desire, her body begging him for more?

The urge to touch Ethan, grab his lower back and buttocks, sink her fingers and nails into his muscular flesh was almost overwhelming and she fisted the sheets at her sides. It was the one thing she'd promised herself—not to touch him. But the pledge was hurting her far more than it was hurting him, she imagined. His tanned, thickly muscled chest and shoulders had erotic voices of their own and were calling to her as he rose for a moment, then settled back against her breasts.

How could you sleep with a man like this? she heard herself say, though the only sound her throat produced was a deep moan of satisfaction as he lowered his head to her breast and suckled deeply on one hard, pink nipple. *How could you desire a man like this?*

He's a demon.

Shuddering with the electric heat, she wrapped her legs around him and arched her back, pumping her hips furiously. She was close, so close. It had been two incredibly quiet years since she'd been with a man she'd dated for only a few months, two long years since she'd faked release before breaking it off and wandering back into hermit territory and remaining there as the eternal businesswoman. She'd felt the real charge of climax only in her dreams—those dreams of faceless strangers pleasuring her body until she woke up sweaty and frustrated. But there was no faking anything tonight.

Again her thoughts were seized and cast aside by Ethan's touch. He slipped his hand between them, his fingers inching downward until he combed through the pale curls between her spread thighs. As he stroked her, flicked the tender, aching bud, Mary gulped for air. She didn't want to give in to him. He didn't deserve her desire, her complete and utter surrender. But her head fell back anyway as the heat of his hand and the skill of his fingers took her over the edge. She knew how loudly she cried out as he played her, as he sank deeper, but she didn't care. Wounded, desperate and totally unaware of time, she clawed at the white sheets, pretending they were his skin.

Ethan watched her, his gaze feral yet brushed with uncharacteristic concern. Then with a growl of hunger, he pushed deeply inside her, his rhythm steady, his breathing anything but. The force of his release made him shake, made his body hard as iron, and when he dropped gently on top of her, he buried his head in the damp curve of her neck.

It was only moments before Mary's skin started to cool and her rational mind returned, along with her anger. No matter how much her body craved this man, in the light of day this had been little more than a transaction.

A wave of nausea moved through her as she recalled the day Ethan Curtis had made her an offer she hadn't been able to refuse.

"You're one arrogant son of a bitch, you know that, Curtis?" she had said to him.

Ethan had sat back in his leather chair and regarded her with cold eyes. "I think we've established that. Are you going to take the deal or not?"

With his short black hair, sharp blue eyes and hooked nose, Ethan resembled a hawk more than a man. Mary had never seen a man with more arrogance or more presence.

She had stood in his massive office of glass and metal, with its hard, uncompromising edges, and tried to be as much of a hard-ass as him. "I told you I would agree to artificial insemination."

"If I felt that you would actually honor—"

"Honor?" she said, appalled. "We've leaped way beyond that now."

"True." His sapphire gaze had missed nothing, especially the intense desire she had to thwart him in any way possible. "But to make certain your end of the bargain is upheld, we'll do this the old-fashioned way."

"Not a chance in hell."

He'd looked amused. "You may even like it."

She'd given him a derisive glance. "Maybe. But we'll never know. I'm not going to bed with you, Mr. Curtis."

The look of amusement had disappeared and he'd replied gravely, "You want your father cleared of all charges. I want a child. It's very simple."

Simple. The word now crashed around in Mary's brain as the man who'd uttered it one week ago rolled off her in one gentle movement. Nothing was simple about this situation. She ventured a quick glance at him as he sat up, his back to her, ropes of thick muscle flexing as he moved. Was it possible to despise someone yet be intrigued by them at the same time?

His voice cut through her silent query. "Do you want me to go?"

Despite her efforts to remain indifferent, she felt anger bubble up within her. At herself and at him. "Yes."

His jaw tight, he let out a slow breath. "I *will* see you again tomorrow."

Without answering, she got up from the bed and headed straight for the bathroom. She wasn't about to turn over and lie there, sheet pulled up to her chin like a naive girl who'd just been taken advantage of. She'd known exactly what she was doing and why, and had admittedly enjoyed herself.

She turned on the shower to drown out any sound of him getting dressed and walking out, then threw back the shower curtain and stared at the water as it dropped like rain onto the virginal white surface of the porcelain tub. She placed one foot over the tub, but quickly stepped back on the mat. Why the hell wasn't she getting in there, getting clean, getting rid of any sign of him? What kind of woman didn't want to wash off the scent of a man she had sworn to hate—a man who wanted her only to procure a blue-blooded child? Not any kind of woman she would respect.

Mary let go of the curtain and went to stand in front of the full-length mirror on the bathroom door. With nervous fingers, she ran a hand down her torso, over her belly. Had they made a child tonight? A shiver of excitement went through her, accompanied by an intense feeling of dread. A baby. She sighed. There was nothing in the world she wanted more than to build a family of her own, but not this way.

Feeling ashamed, she looked away. Her priorities were what they had always been, ever since she was a child: to fix the lives of others before her own. And right now having all charges dropped against her father was the most important thing. She wasn't getting a family out of this deal, she was keeping her father out of prison.

Her hands splayed on her belly once more and she shook her head. Impossible. The whole damn deal. She was a fool for thinking it would work, just as Ethan Curtis was a fool for thinking that if she did get pregnant, the baby would ever be raised by anyone but its mother.

One

Four Weeks Later.

"Whose idea was it to install a kitchen in the office?" Tess York inquired, the words slightly muffled by a massive bite of eggs Benedict.

Olivia Winston flipped a yellow dish towel over her shoulder and walked her petite, though incredibly curvaceous, frame over to the table with the grace of a movie star. "Ah, that would be me."

"Well, you're a genius, kid."

Beneath a rim of shaggy brown bangs, Olivia's gold eyes sparkled. "This I know."

Tess laughed at her partner's mock display of arrogance, her long mass of red curls hopping about her back like marionettes. "All I want to know is where my mimosa is."

"No drinking before ten o'clock." Mary Kelley sat across from Tess, her wavy blond hair falling about her face as she absentmindedly drew slash marks through the hollandaise with her fork. "Unless disaster strikes."

"I'd say a two-week dry spell qualifies," Tess said slyly, making Olivia laugh.

"It's August." Mary looked from one of her partners to the other. "We're always a little slow at the end of the summer."

"Slow, sure," Olivia retorted, holding a piece of perfectly cooked bacon up like a white flag. "But we're bordering on drought."

Barring these two weeks in August, No Ring Required was normally buzzing with activity. The premier wife-for-hire company in the Midwest had zero competition and one hell of a brilliant staff. With Mary's creativity and business sense, Olivia's culinary skill and Tess's wise budgeting and decorating style, NRR was a highly successful company. The problem, Mary had to admit, was that all three of them were such intense workaholics who cared nothing for a private life that they had no idea what to do with themselves on their downtime. And each time the end of summer came aknocking, the women panicked in their own ways.

"Well," Mary continued, putting down her fork and dropping her napkin over an untouched plate of food. "Clearly this is no time to be picky about clients."

"Yeah, Olivia," Tess murmured with a grin.

Olivia raised her brows questioningly. "And what is that supposed to mean?"

"I think she's referring to your problem with trust-fund clients," Mary offered, laughing when Tess cleared her throat loudly.

Olivia scowled, then reached down and grabbed Mary's plate. "I don't like them, and nothing's going to change that. Trust-funders are boorish, brainless, self-obsessed jerks, who think they not only own the world, but everyone else along with it."

Tess flashed Mary a grin. "Tell us how you really feel."

"Yes," Mary agreed. "I'm not entirely clear on your opinion regarding the rich."

As her partners chuckled, Olivia sighed. "It's not the rich, it's— Oh, forget it." Clearly looking for a way to end the current conversation, Olivia glared at Mary's untouched plate. "Mary, you're not on a diet, are you?"

"What?" Mary said, sobering.

Olivia tossed her an assessing glance before she turned and sashayed back to her beloved Viking range. "You know that I feel as though diets are a total affront to all those in the culinary world."

"I do know that."

"Besides, there's not a grapefruit or bowl of cabbage soup in my fridge, I'm afraid."

As a shot of nerves zipped through her, Mary shook her head. "No diet, Olivia. I guess I'm just not very hungry."

Tess paused long enough to swallow. "As much as I hate to side with Olivia, that's been going on for a while now."

"Yep," Olivia agreed.

"And, well," Tess began awkwardly, "we're here if…well, you know."

Mary nodded and forced a smile. "I know."

Among the three of them, talking about business was an easy, playful and spirited adventure, but when the conversation turned to anything emotional or personal, the women of NRR seemed to transform into the Stooges—a bumbling, uneasy mess. From the inception of No Ring Required there had been a sort of unspoken rule between the partners to keep personal matters to themselves. Odd, and perhaps against every female cliché, for three women to abstain from discussion about history and feelings, but there it was.

"So, what's on the agenda today, ladies?" Tess asked, pushing away from the table and a very clean plate.

"I have a meeting with a potential client," Mary informed them, her gaze drifting over to the clock on the wall. Okay, five minutes were up. The test was done. The zip of nerves from a moment ago turned into a pulse-pounding elephant-sitting-on-her-chest type of situation.

"Maybe not such a dry spell after all," Olivia remarked gaily, her good mood returning. "I also have a client coming in at two whose fiancée ditched him a week before the wedding and he wants help with what he referred to as a "screw her" dinner party."

Tess laughed. "Should be fun."

Mary hardly heard them as the muscles in her legs tensed painfully, as though she was on the verge of a charley horse. The pregnancy test was hidden behind fifty or so rolls of the insanely soft Charmin Ultra that

Olivia insisted on buying. Would there be one line or two? One line or two?

"Big name or big business for you?" Tess asked, staring at Mary expectantly.

"Ah…both actually."

"Sounds great." Olivia set her own full plate down beside Tess, then promptly rearranged her silverware, napkin and water glass to their proper places, now ready to partake in her own breakfast.

Her heart slamming against her ribs, Mary stood and grabbed her purse. "I just have to hit the little girl's room and then I'll be on my way."

"Good luck," Olivia called.

Tess nodded. "Yeah, good luck, kid."

If they only knew the double meaning in her good wishes, Mary thought, each step toward the bathroom feeling as though she was walking in quicksand. She had no idea what she wanted to see when she tossed aside all that toilet paper and pulled out the test. If it was positive, she'd have to make plans to get away from Minneapolis eventually, away from Ethan—that man would never let her walk away with his child. If it was negative, her father's life was over. She felt a sickly sour feeling in her stomach. She had lives to protect, and she wasn't altogether sure how capable she was.

She locked the door behind her, sat on the floor and opened the cabinets under the sink. The mountain of white rolls pushed aside easily as she reached inside and felt for the thin stick. Her pulse pounded in her ears. God, what did she want here?

Her fingers closed around the test and she yanked it back. With one heavy exhale she stared at the results.

It was three twenty-seven and Ethan Curtis was growing more impatient by the second.

He wasn't used to being kept waiting. People arrived early for meetings with him, fifteen to thirty minutes on average. They would sit in his massive lobby until he was ready to see them. For six years it had been this way. He knew his employees thought he was an arrogant ass. He liked it that way.

He punched the intercom button. "Marylyn, when Miss Kelley arrives, have her join me on the roof."

There was a slight pause on the other end of the line. Marylyn had never heard such a request, but she recovered quickly. "Yes, sir. Of course."

Ethan glanced at the clock. Three thirty-one. Where the hell was she? He stalked over to the elevator and stabbed the button. Mary Kelley was a strong-willed, business-first, no-nonsense type of person—not unlike himself. But if she worked for him, she'd be fired by now.

He was not generally a nervous man. He didn't pace, worry or stress before a deal was done. If a client didn't perform or comply the way he wanted them to, he finessed the situation, made it work to his advantage. However, as he rode his private elevator the short distance to the roof, his gut continued to contract painfully, just like it had the day his father had informed him that his mother had taken up with a new man and wasn't coming back.

Ethan walked out of the elevator and onto the rooftop, for which he had hired a world-renowned landscape architect and two botanists to transform into his escape three years ago. The courtyard opened to a Moroccan-tiled fountain and several ancient sculptures, while to the left was a sun terrace, complete with bar and circular planters filled with flax, pyracantha and perennials to keep the urban scene colorful year-round. Red bougainvillea covered several of the arched trellises, and cherry trees flanked the central walkway. It was a strange mixture of ease and exotic, and it suited Ethan perfectly.

He sensed her, smelled her, before he saw her. Fresh, soapy—yes, he remembered. The lower half of him contracted as his mind played the ever-present film of those nights in July over again. Ethan saw himself lying on top of her, buried deep inside of her, his mouth on hers as he breathed in her scent and she moaned and writhed like a wildcat.

He glanced over his shoulder to see her walking toward him. She was average height, average build, but Mary Kelley possessed two things that would make any man stop dead in his tracks and stare. Long, toned, sexy-as-hell legs that he could practically feel wrapped around his waist at this moment, and pale blue eyes that turned up at the corners, like a cat's. "You're late."

She didn't respond. "What's all this, Mr. Curtis?" she said, looking around the garden seemingly unimpressed. "Your bat cave?"

As well as the legs and the eyes, she also had a sharp tongue.

"A sanctuary."

Her brows drew together as she sat in the chair opposite him, the skirt of her pale blue Chanel suit sliding upward to just a few inches above her knees. The late-afternoon sun hit her full force, her blond hair appearing almost white. "And what do you need sanctuary from? All the people you've screwed over this week?"

Yes, a very sharp tongue, though he remembered that it could also be soft and wet. "You think I thrive on making life difficult for others?"

"I think it may be your life's blood."

There was no disputing the fact that she disliked him. No, he could see that clearly. What he couldn't make out from her attitude was if she was carrying his child or not, and that was the one thing he desperately wanted to know.

He walked over to the bar. "Drink?"

She nodded. "Thank you."

"Anything in particular? Martini, soda?" That would give him his answer.

"Something cold would be nice. It's pretty warm."

"You're going to make me work for this, aren't you?"

"Would you really appreciate it any other way?" she said brusquely.

"Martini?"

"Lemonade would be great if you have it. I'm driving."

"Mary—"

"Do you think you deserve an easy answer, Mr. Curtis?" she interrupted coldly. "Think back to how we got here."

He had done nothing but, for the past four weeks, though not in the same way as she, clearly. "We made an agreement."

She laughed bitterly. "Is that what you'd call it? You blackmailed me and I gave in. Maybe gave up is a better way to put it."

Ethan abandoned the drinks and went to stand before her. Her cat eyes were blazing hatred, and her claws were out, but he didn't give a damn if she was angry. He wanted one thing and one thing only, and he would go to any lengths necessary to get it.

"Are you pregnant?" he asked bluntly.

It took her a moment to answer. Several emotions crossed her face, and her breathing seemed shallow and slightly labored before she finally nodded. "Yes."

Ethan turned away, his heart pounding like a jackhammer. He'd wanted this but had never believed it possible. He had no idea how to react.

"You'll drop all charges against my father," Mary said, her tone nonemotional.

He stood there, his back to her. "Of course."

"And you won't interfere in my life until the baby is born."

He opened his mouth to agree, then paused. He turned to face her again. "I don't know if can do that."

"That was our agreement," Mary countered, coming to her feet, her gaze fierce. "Do you not even have one ounce of honor in your blood, Mr. Curtis? Where the hell did you grow up, under a rock?"

She didn't know where he came from, couldn't know,

but her words struck him hard and he frowned. "I will keep my word."

Seemingly satisfied, Mary grabbed her purse and started for the elevator. "Good."

"But there's one condition," Ethan called after her.

She whirled around, held his gaze without blinking. "There were no conditions."

"This has nothing to do with my child, Mary. This is business."

"I was under the impression that the child was business," she said dryly.

Despite the dig, Ethan pressed on. "I want to hire you."

She looked confused for a moment, then broke out laughing bitterly. "Never."

"You'd turn away business so you don't have to be around me? I thought you were way tougher than that."

"I have enough business. I don't need yours."

The foolishness of that statement made him smile. "Being the heads of two successful companies, we both know that's not true."

"Look," she began impatiently, "my deal with you is done. Unless you plan to go back on your word and not drop the charges—"

"No," he cut in firmly. "But perhaps you also want that sculpture your father risked so much to retrieve?"

"I couldn't give a damn."

"No, but your father does." He gestured to the court-yard and the small sculpture of a woman and child that Hugh Kelley had almost gone to jail for. It had been a gift from the Harringtons, part of their courtship when Ethan took over the company. They'd hated him for buying controlling shares in Harrington Corp., but the company was floundering under their care, and because they still wanted to be involved, they'd forced themselves to act nicely. If Ethan had known the rare sculpture belonged to a family member, he probably would've rejected the piece. For as much as he wanted to be accepted and welcomed into the old money of Minneapolis, he hated family drama. He hadn't been too keen on having Hugh Kelley arrested for wanting the sculpture back, either, but he also wouldn't allow breaking and entering at his company for any reason.

"Why are you doing this?" Mary asked, her cat eyes inspecting him as though he were a pesky rodent. "Why would you care if my father has that sculpture back? You have what you want."

A pink blush stained her cheeks. She was so beautiful, and her temper and passion only made her more so. She was kidding herself and him if she thought they were done with each other. Two things had come out of their nights together: a baby and the desire to have her in his bed again. Both would take time, but he'd get what he wanted.

"I want to be there," he said simply. "I want to be around you and see what's happening to you. I want to see this child grow. That's all." When she said nothing, he moved on. "I have several parties to give and to attend over the next month. And one trip—"

"Trip?" she interrupted.

"To Mackinac Island."

"Not a chance."

"You don't travel with clients?"

"You're not a client."

"Listen, if it were simply a business meeting, I'd go alone, but I have to stay a few days and I'm planning on throwing a party as well."

"And you could find someone to help you with that anywhere," she said. "Some woman you know? And I'm sure you know several."

His mouth twitched with amusement. "I do."

"A girlfriend."

"No."

"How about a call girl then?" she suggested, flashing him a sarcastic grin.

"I want the best. A professional—and NRR has a sterling reputation. And, quite honestly, it wouldn't hurt having a Harrington by my side to—"

"Right," she said quickly, then shook her head. "I don't think so."

She was so damn stubborn. "Do you know the circles I run in?"

"I could guess."

"The kind that are really good for your business."

She shrugged, shook her head again.

He stepped closer, studied her, then grinned. "You're afraid of what might happen if you're around me."

"Try concerned." She walked away, over to the bar where she poured herself a glass of iced tea. "Listen, Mr. Curtis, I won't deny my attraction to you, just like I won't deny my abhorrence of you, either."

"I appreciate your honesty. But that's still—"

"A no."

"Well your refusal doesn't take away from the fact that I need help. I could ask one of your partners—"

She fairly choked on her tea. "No."

Ethan hesitated. It was the first time he'd seen her ruffled during their conversation. Sex didn't shake her up emotionally, and neither did money, business or the subject of her father, but just mentioning her partners at NRR had her sweating.

"You have two partners, isn't that right?" he asked casually.

"They know nothing about you…or this," she said in a caustic tone. "And I want it to stay that way."

"I see."

She put down her glass and stood at the side of the bar. "You want your eyes on me all the time…"

"For starters."

She nodded slowly, as though she were thinking. "All right, Mr. Curtis. You get what you want once again. I'll take the job." She turned away then, and walked to the elevator. "But understand something," she added as the door slid open. "What happened at the lake will never happen again."

"Whatever you say, Mary," Ethan said with a slow grin as the elevator door closed.

It was seven o'clock on the nose when Mary walked into the little Craftsman house at 4445 Gabby Street. She'd grown up there, happy as any girl could be with two parents who adored her and told her so every day. With two such gentle souls guiding her, she should have been a softer, sweeter personality, but clearly there was too much Harrington in her. Instead of hugs, she loved to argue and battle and win. Today at Ethan Curtis's office she'd done all three fairly well. She'd won her dad's freedom, though she'd paid a high price for it.

Mary walked through the house, then out the screen door. She knew where her father was. During sunset, Hugh Kelley always sat in the backyard, his butt in dirt and under a shifting sky, he patted the newly sprung string bean plants as though they were his children. He was sixty-five, but lately he looked closer to seventy-five, far from the strapping man he used to be. Today was no different. He looked old and weathered, his gray hair too long in the back. For the millionth time Mary wondered if he would ever recover from her mother's long illness and death and the arrest that followed. She hoped her news would at the very least remove a few layers of despair.

He glanced up from his beans and grinned. "Never been late in your life, have you, lass?"

Her father's Irish brogue wrapped around her like a soft sweater. "If there was one thing you taught me, Pop, it was punctuality."

"What a load of crap."

Mary laughed and plunked down beside him in the dirt.

"Watch yourself there." Hugh gestured to the ground. "That suit will be black as coal dust by the time you leave."

"I'm all right, Pop."

He snapped a bean from its vine and handed it to her.

"And you know I haven't been on time a day in my life. Neither had your mother. Not you, though. Born right on your due date, you were. Neither your mother nor I ever understood where your timeliness came from. Well, no place we'd admit to, certainly."

Hugh wasn't being cryptic, just matter-of-fact. The rift between Mary's father and her grandparents was old news—though old news he loved to drum up again and again. Not that she blamed him. The Harringtons had never approved of him, and had made him feel like an Irish peasant from day one. Mary just wished things could've been different all around. Bitterness and resentment were such a waste of time.

She took a bite of her bean as the late-summer breeze played with her hair. "So, I have some news."

"What's that, lass?"

"Ethan Curtis has dropped the charges."

Hugh didn't look surprised. "So my lawyer informs me."

"You already knew?"

"Yep. Teddy called me half an hour ago."

Mary studied his expression. Unchanged, tired, defeated. She shook her head. "Why aren't you happy, relieved, something?"

"I am something." His pale blue eyes, so like her own, brightened with passion. "I'm pissed off."

"What? Why?"

"I know you, lass. I know you better than anyone. What did you do to make this happen?"

Her heart jumped into her throat, but she remained

cool as steel on the outside. "I don't know what you're talking about."

"Mare."

"Pop, I talked to the man."

Hugh snorted. "Ethan Curtis is no man. He's a devil, a demon with no soul."

Mary was all set to agree when a memory of the cozy room on Lake Richard flashed into her mind. Ethan was a demon, yes, but there was another side to him—a deeply buried side that held a surprising amount of warmth and tenderness. She'd seen it when he'd talked about his child.

She closed her eyes. *His child*.

"Well he's decided to let it go," Mary forced out. "He agreed that the sculpture wasn't really worth his time and is even willing to give it back to you. After all, it was just a gift from Grandmother, with zero sentimental value to him and—"

"A gift that old woman had no right to give," Hugh pointed out gruffly.

Mary gave a patient sigh. "I know, Pop."

The basket beside him strained with vegetables. No doubt he'd been out here picking for a few hours. Lord only knew what he was going to do with it all. "Promise me you're not in any trouble."

Mary's chin lifted. She'd lied, yes, but she'd done what she had to do. She was no more pregnant than a box of rocks, but her father was free, and protecting him was all she cared about right now.

"I have nothing to fear from Ethan Curtis," she said

tightly. As long as he didn't find out the truth, she amended silently, as she picked up the basket of vegetables and walked inside the house.

Two

Mary wondered for a moment if she'd fallen asleep and was, God forbid, snoring. Every once in awhile NRR got a client who was so dull one or all of the partners would actually find themselves nodding off while discussing contracts.

Today it was Mary's turn to down a third cup of coffee and pry her eyes open with toothpicks. She shifted in her chair and focused on Ivan Garrison, a new client who had hired her to design a menu for a party he was throwing aboard his yacht, *Clara Belle*. For the past thirty minutes the forty-year-old wannabe boat captain had been sorrowfully telling Mary that he'd named the boat in honor of his dead wife, who he'd married for her "outstanding boating skill and formidable rack."

It had taken Mary a good thirty seconds to realize that Ivan was referring to his wife's chest and another ten seconds to contemplate passing him on to Olivia, since the job mainly consisted of culinary planning. But he was one of those trust-fund jerks who made Olivia's skin crawl, and the risk of having her abide by NRR's seventh vow, Do No Harm might be asking too much.

Who knew? If he took Olivia for a ride in his yellow Lamborghini and insisted she call him Captain like he did everyone else, Olivia just might bop him on the head the night before the party and serve him to his guests with an apple in his mouth the next day.

"The date for the regatta gala as you know is the twenty-fifth," he said, touching the brim of the snow-white captain's hat he had worn to both meetings. "I'll have my secretary send over the guest list. Please make sure to refer to me as Captain on the invitation. That's how my friends and business associates know me."

Aye aye, sir! Mary nodded. "Of course."

"I'd like to really pack this party. We always get enough entrants for the race, but the galas aren't as well attended."

"We could make it as a charity event," Mary suggested.

"I'll think about that." He leaned back in his chair and sighed. "Now, have I told you how I came to be called Captain?"

"No." If Ivan was going to come around every week, she'd have to invest in some NoDoz.

"As you know, it's not my given name," he said. "When I was six—wait, no, closer to eight, my nanny, her name was Alisia and she was the one who bathed me—"

"Excuse me. I'm sorry to interrupt."

Mary glanced up and smiled thankfully at her partner. "No problem, Olivia. We were just finishing up here."

Olivia acknowledged Ivan with a quick nod. "Hello, Captain." Then she turned back to Mary. "Your next client is here."

"I don't have—" Mary stopped herself. What the heck was she doing? Her savior, Olivia had clearly noticed her drooping eyelids and coffee-stained teeth, maybe even heard the beginning of the creepy nanny-and-the-eight-year-old's-bath story and was giving her a way out.

"We can discuss the rest on the phone, Captain," Mary said, standing and shaking his hand. "Or if you'd prefer, we could e-mail."

The captain sighed wistfully. "My Clara Belle loved the e-mail. Did I tell you she had twelve computers, one for every bathroom? She wanted to stay connected. I haven't had the heart to remove them."

After one more minute of commiserating about the impracticality of expensive technology in damp places, Mary told Ivan where to find the little captain's room and walked toward the lobby with Olivia.

Mary released a weary sigh. "Thank you so much."

"For what?" Olivia asked.

"The 'your next client is here' save. I'm thankful for the business, but sadly Ivan is only eccentric and strange in an uninteresting way. There's nothing worse."

Olivia looked confused. "Mary, I'm always happy to help with tedious clients, but in this case, you really do have someone waiting." She nodded toward the man sitting in one of the lobby's artfully distressed brown leather chairs.

Mary's breath caught at the sight of him, and she wanted to kick herself for the girlish reaction, but she walked toward him instead. Ethan Curtis wasn't the kind of handsome you'd see on the pages of a *Businessman Weekly*. No three-piece suits or slicked-back hair, no calm, refined demeanor. He looked edgy and ready to pounce, his severe blue eyes alert and ready for a battle. Dressed in tailored pants and an expensive, perfectly cut black shirt, his large frame ate up the leather chair as around them the air crackled with a potent mixture of desire and conflict.

"We didn't have an appointment today, Mr. Curtis," Mary said in a gently caustic tone.

Amusement flashed in his eyes. "Yes, I know. But this is urgent."

Obviously she wasn't getting rid of him anytime soon. "Let's go into my office."

"No. I need to take you somewhere."

"Impossible," she told him sharply.

"Nothing's impossible."

"I can't." Didn't he see that Olivia was still lurking around? If she overheard them, she'd get the wrong idea…well, the right idea, and Mary didn't want that. "I have insane amounts of work—"

"This is work."

Mary pressed her lips together in frustration. She felt caught in a trap. If she refused, made even the smallest of scenes, Olivia would be out here, wondering what was up. That could bring Tess, too. She eyed Ethan skeptically, lowered her voice. "You say this is work?"

"Of course." He spoke the right words, but he stared at her mouth while he said them.

"Better be." She tossed him a severe gaze before heading into her office for her purse.

Mary stepped into the world of trendy layettes and custom chintz toddler chairs and felt her heart sink into her shoes. It was the last place in the world she wanted to be. The fact that not only was she lying about being pregnant but that it would be a long, long time before she came into this type of store for any real purpose weighed on her like an anchor. She eyed the blue and pink bookcases and dressers with cute custom airplane and unicorn knobs.

"This is a baby shop, Mr. Curtis," she said quietly, sidestepping a beautiful whitewashed Morigeau-Lepine changing table.

Ethan dropped into a pale-green gliding chair. "Can we drop the 'mister'?"

"I don't think so."

He raised one brow in a mocking slant and whispered, "Hey, I've seen that tiny raspberry birthmark right below your navel."

A wash of heat slipped over her skin and she could only mutter, "Right…"

"Come sit down." He motioned for her to take the yellow duckie glider beside him. "You never seem to get off your feet."

"I'm fine. I'll stand."

"Ethan."

"Fine. Ethan," she ground out. "Now, are you going to tell me why we're in a baby shop?"

He picked up a lovely piece of original artwork from a nearby table and studied the drawing of two frogs sailing a boat. "I'm thinking we could add one more item to your workload."

"Like?"

"A nursery in my house."

Mary's pulse escalated to a frenetic pace. "You want me to design a nursery for the...our..."

"Baby, yes. I may have unlimited resources, but you weren't far off when you suggested I grew up under a rock. It was a trailer park actually. Dark, dirty and decorated with the curbside castoffs of the rich people on the other side of town. So, I have zero taste. And as you can see, I'm a guy."

She stared at him, not sure how to feel about what he'd just revealed to her. She hadn't meant to insult him with the "rock" comment. Well, maybe she had a little, but now she felt pretty damn snobby. Although, his need to be accepted by the Minneapolis bluebloods, have a child with one, made way more sense now. Not that his actions were in any way forgiven. "Look, I'm sorry about what I said...the rock thing—"

He waved away her apology with his hand, his jaw a little too tight. "It's not important. What is important however is that my child has a place to sleep. So? Is this agreeable to you?"

This wasn't a bizarre request for an NRR client. She'd designed over twenty nurseries and children's rooms over the past five years. Single fathers, gay fathers who had to admit they had no taste, even busy moms on occasion.

"I thought you might enjoy this," Ethan said, coming to his feet.

"Did you?" He wanted her to decorate her own child's room. A child that didn't exist.

She turned away from Ethan and closed her eyes, took a deep breath. What was she thinking? What was she thinking lying to someone about something so important, something as sacred as having a baby? This was getting out of hand. Yes, she'd had to protect her father, and now that he was out of danger, wasn't it time to tell Ethan Curtis that he was not going to be a daddy, suffer his censure, his threats, and get on with her life?

Fear darted into her gut. But what if he refiled charges? That was entirely possible—maybe even probable given how angry and spiteful he'd be if he learned the truth. Her father couldn't survive another arrest. No, there was no way she was allowing that to happen.

Mary fingered a swatch of green gingham fabric. It would work wonderfully for a boy or a girl. Tears sat behind her throat. She wasn't the most maternal person in the world, but she wanted a child. Someday. With a man who loved her...

"Mary?"

She turned and looked at Ethan. "Okay."

"Hello, there." A very perky blond sales clerk appeared before them, her round brown eyes wide with excitement. "So, when's our baby due?"

Before Mary could even open her mouth to say that they were just looking around, Ethan chimed in with "Early to mid April."

Mary's head whipped around so fast she wondered if she'd given herself whiplash.

Ethan shrugged. "I did the calculations."

"A spring baby," the salesgirl said, beaming at Ethan as though he were a candidate for father of the year already. "How about we start with a crib?"

Ethan gestured to Mary. "The lady's in charge."

The girl looked expectantly at Mary. "Traditional? Round? Any thoughts?"

"No thoughts," Mary said, feeling weak all of a sudden. "Not today."

The girl looked sympathetic and lowered her voice. "Mom's tired."

You have no idea, lady.

"I tried to get her to sit down," Ethan said with a frustrated shake of the head.

The girl nodded as if to say, I've seen many a pregnant woman and understood their moods. "We can do this another day."

Mary nodded. "Another day is good." Another year might be good to.

Ethan checked his watch. "It's after one." He eyed Mary with a concerned frown. "Have you eaten lunch?"

Mary shook her head. "Not yet, but I'll get something back at the office—"

"You need to eat now. You wait here. I'll go get the car."

"I have my car," she said, but he was already halfway out the door.

To make matters worse, the salesgirl sidled up to Mary, clasped her hands together and sighed. "You're so lucky."

"Why?"

She looked at Mary as though she was crazy or just plain mean. "That man is going to make a great daddy."

"If he can stop ordering people around long enough," Mary muttered to herself.

"Excuse me?"

Mary smiled at the girl, shook her head, then followed Ethan out the door.

"You know, there was an iffy-looking Thai place next to that baby store," Mary said, sipping lemonade and munching on perfectly tender chicken picata and fresh spinach salad.

Across from her, Ethan waved his fork. "This is better."

Mary shrugged, a trace of a smile in her voice. "Well, sure, if you like quiet, great food and a killer view."

Under the guise of work, Ethan had taken her to his home for some lunch. Worn-out from the experience at the baby shop, and more than a little bit curious about what kind of home a man like this one would choose, she hadn't put up much of a fuss. And her curiosity was well rewarded.

She had expected Ethan's home to mirror his office—glass and chrome and modern—but maybe she should've taken a clue from his rooftop garden instead.

There was absolutely nothing modern about the estate. It was enchanting and secluded, complete with a charming wooded drive that led straight up to the massive French-country style home.

Inside was nothing less than spectacular, but not in a showy, uptight way. Though it was sparsely furnished, the rooms were warm and rustic with lots of brick and hardwood.

Mary sipped her lemonade, taking in the soft summer afternoon on the sprawling deck that nestled right up to the edge of a private lake.

"I thought you should see the space you'll be working with," Ethan said, finishing off his last bite of chicken.

Mary nodded. "You're nothing if not helpful, Mr. Curtis."

A breeze kicked up around them, sending pre-autumn leaves swirling over the edge of the deck into the water.

"Hey, I thought we talked about this back at the baby shop. You were going to call me Ethan—"

"I only agreed to that to get you to stop talking."

"What?" he said, chuckling.

"You were bringing up the past and I wasn't interested in going there."

"The very recent past."

She attempted to look confused. "Was it? Feels like ages ago, like it didn't happen at all."

He glared at her belly. "Oh, it happened, Mary."

Heat flooded her skin, but she forced her expression to remain impassive.

His gaze found hers again and he studied her. "You've got quite an attitude on you."

"With you, yes."

"I'm sure I'm not the only one," he said, one brow raised sardonically.

"Don't you have a room to show me?"

He sighed. "Come on, Mary, can we make peace here? Maybe even start again? Friends?"

Inside the confines of his office, where she could remember who and what he was, Mary felt safe. She had her walls up, double thick. Even on his rooftop or at the baby shop, he still seemed arrogant and ever the dictator. But here, in his home, with nature and softness surrounding him, it was different. His skin seemed bronze and highly touchable, his eyes glistened like two inviting lakes beckoning her to jump in, and his clothes seemed highly unnecessary. Mary felt her defenses slipping. Forget being friends; she wanted him to kiss her again—just once so she could prove to herself that it wasn't as good as she remembered. Sure, he had more depth than he let on, but she could make no mistake about it—Ethan Curtis was a selfish, misguided man, who was solely out for himself.

She put down her napkin and tried not to stare at the lush curve of his lower lip. "I won't pretend that we're friends, or even friendly."

"Fine, but can you really despise me? For wanting a child?"

She laughed, shocked at how obtuse he was being. "Is that a serious question? Of course it's understandable and wonderful to want a child—blackmailing a woman you know nothing about to get one is not."

He leaned forward and with a trace of a growl said, "True."

"You have no excuse for your behavior?"

"None whatsoever."

They stared at each other in stubborn silence, sparks of heat, of desire, flickering between them.

Finally Ethan spoke, "Let's go see the room."

They walked side by side through the house and up the curving staircase to the second floor. Ethan had run these stairs a hundred times, alone of course. He hadn't invited many people to his home, and the ones that had made it past the foyer had never been allowed upstairs. He normally took women back to their place after a date. Less complicated that way.

These upcoming parties were going to be the first time he'd invited a large group to his home, and the thought alarmed him somewhat, though he knew it was the right business decision. If a person was going to switch insurance companies for their billion-dollar business, they would want to see the man who'd be taking it over in his natural habitat—simple as that.

"I chose the room next to mine," Ethan explained as they walked down the long hallway. "If he or she needs me in the middle of the night…" He paused at the door to the nursery and looked at her. "That's how it goes, right? They wake up at night and you go to them?"

"I wouldn't know." Her skin had taken on a grayish

pallor as she stared into the empty room with its beamed ceilings and white walls.

"Your womanly instincts must tell you something—" Ethan began, but was quickly cut off by Mary's soft laughter. "All right, I'm a little nervous about this whole thing. I want a child more than anything, but I know absolutely nothing."

"You'll get help."

"I don't do therapists."

She released a heavy sigh and turned to face him. "No, Ethan. Not that kind of help."

"What? Like a nanny or something?"

"Or something."

He shook his head. "All this child will need is me."

"Two seconds ago you were saying you didn't know a thing."

"I'll learn."

"Maybe you won't be able to give a child everything. I mean…"

"What? What do you mean?"

She gritted her teeth. "Well, you were just talking about womanly instincts. I mean, don't you think that a child needs a mother?"

Ethan felt his whole body go numb at her query and tried to shake it off, but the more he tried to control the feeling, the anger building inside him, the harder it attacked him. He heard himself mutter a scornful sound, then say, "Not from what I've noticed."

Mary's face was impassive, except for the frown lines between her brows. "What have you noticed?"

His head was swimming, his thoughts as jumpy as his skin. But why, dammit? Why was he reacting this way? The truth was he'd done just fine after his mom ran off. Sure he got into trouble with the law, but he'd gotten a hold of himself, and look at where he was today—no thanks to a mother. No, he and his kid would do just fine.

Mary felt the conflict start deep in her gut. She didn't want to give a damn about Ethan or his past or his feelings on his family, but the stark pain etched on his face was very telling and intriguing. She would never have imagined seeing the hint of a suffering boy behind the overconfident glare of the man. "Ethan," she began softly. "I'm not going to push you on this, but—"

Turning away from her, he lifted his chin and stared into the nursery. He was not about to discuss his past with her. "What do you think of the room?"

"It's great," she said in a soft voice. "Perfect. Any kid's dream."

"I'd like to get started on it right away."

"Sure."

He looked down at her once again, his eyes so dark blue and impassioned she felt her breath catch. "Mary?"

"Yes?"

"Would you mind..." He broke off, shook his head.

"What?"

"Can I touch you?"

Her self-control, always to be counted on, melted like the last bits of snow on a warm spring day. "We agreed—"

"No." He moved closer, until they were nearly touching. "Your stomach."

"Oh."

He cursed darkly. "I know it's ridiculous. Way too early. All of that. But, I…"

Her gaze dropped to her belly. "It is early."

"I know, but I just…" His mouth was close to her ear, that sensual, cynical mouth.

"All right," she heard herself utter foolishly.

Mary closed her eyes, afraid of what she might say or do when his hand gently cupped her stomach. Heat surged through the light cotton fabric of her shirt, and she was flooded with emotions. There was no child here, yet there was an ache so intense she thought she'd collapse if he didn't move his hand up toward her breasts or down between her thighs. Frustrated weakness overtook her and she wobbled against him.

"Are you all right?" he asked, holding her steady.

She had never run from anything in her life, but at that moment she had to get out of his house, away from that room, far from him. "I have to get back to the office."

"I'll drive you back."

She ignored the concern in his voice and pushed away from him. "I followed you over here, remember?"

"Maybe you should sit down for a minute. You seem—"

"The first party is Friday, correct?" she said, running her fingers through her hair, as if that would help quiet her shaking body. "If you can send me the guest list."

"Of course." He attempted to touch her again, but she moved away.

"Thank you for lunch, Ethan." Brushing past him, she walked quickly down the hallway, down the stairs and out the front door, only remembering to breathe once she was safely inside her car.

Three

"What's Olivia making?" Mary asked when she returned to the office later that day. Even in her sorry mental state, the scent she'd encountered when entering the lobby of their office building five minutes ago had made her taste buds come alive. Mouthwatering aromas wafting through their building weren't an unusual occurrence during the week, they just made her want to run up the four flights of stairs to get to the source instead of taking the very slow elevator.

Poised at the front desk, with a full plate of beautifully arranged golden spheres, Tess tried to smile. Unfortunately, her mouth was full and she could only manage a chipmunk-like grin. "Scones," she said on a sigh, pointing at the plate. "Cranberry. Have one."

"I've actually just come back from lunch, so I'm pretty stuffed."

"Seriously? Too full for one of these?"

Tess rolled her eyes, then grabbed one. "Devil."

"Don't blame the addict, kid," Tess replied, reaching for another. "Blame her supplier."

"Where is Olivia?"

"Trying out another scone recipe. Chocolate this time."

"Great."

"She has a high tea to plan. That angry groom wants something beautiful and classic to celebrate the loss of his fiancée."

"How strange, yet lovely."

"He has over sixty guests."

"Lovely for us, too, then."

Tess laughed. "So, where were you?"

Obviously Olivia hadn't told her about Ethan.

"That new client Olivia was telling me about?"

Or not. Mary glanced through the mail on the desk. "Yes. Ethan Curtis. CEO of Harrington Corp. and old-money wannabe."

"Harrington Corp.? Isn't that your family's insurance company."

Mary nodded. "Was. Before Ethan Curtis took it over."

"Interesting that he'd hire you," Tess said nonchalantly, taking another scone, but only fiddling with it on her plate.

"I've got the blue-blood background he's looking for," Mary explained. "In many respects.

"Olivia said he was pretty good-looking."

"I suppose he is."

"A clean-shaven Colin Farrell with the body of a construction worker, is what she said, I think."

"That's incredibly specific. She saw him for like five seconds."

"Just be careful," Tess said, her tone serious.

Such a strong warning from a woman who rarely got involved in the personal matters of her partners made Mary's defenses perk up. "He's just a client, Tess."

"Of course. Sure. But you know, it's always better to be safe, kid. Expect an agenda and you won't get hurt." She picked up her scone and pointed it at Mary. "You never know the true character of a person or what they're really after."

Whenever Tess spoke in this cryptic way, Mary had the burning desire to ask her what she meant by it, and maybe where the cynicism was coming from. But the women of NRR kept their pasts in the past. As for Tess's concern over Ethan Curtis's character, Mary wasn't flying blind—she knew exactly who he was and what he wanted. But her partner's advice was sound. After what had happened today, how she'd felt standing so close to him, as though she were frozen solid and he was a very inviting campfire, she had to be careful—adopt the all-business facade she normally wore with such ease and comfort.

"I'll watch my back." She tossed her partner a reassuring grin. "But in the meantime, Mr. Curtis has given me five days to plan a very swanky event. I'd better get on it." She paused over the plate of scones. "Damn that Olivia," she grumbled, grabbing one and heading toward her office.

* * *

In the past Ethan had used a local catering company for his parties. A boutique-type place, very upscale and guaranteed to impress. Their food had always been good, though at times unrecognizable. But, in his opinion, the menu and service had always felt cold and impersonal, not really his speed. For years he'd gone along with the very fancy, tasteless hors d'oeuvres, prickly flower arrangements and silent waitstaff because, well, he'd been to several events with just that type of vibe and everyone had seemed to enjoy themselves.

Then he'd asked Mary Kelley to plan his event.

When she'd come to him with the menu and details of what she had planned, he'd worried. Would his stuffy clientele appreciate her vision?

Ethan glanced around his home. Clearly, he'd worried for no reason. In five short days she'd transformed the entire first floor of his home into a relaxed, candlelit lounge, and outside on his deck and lawn, she'd created a beautiful Asian garden. It was anything but showy. In fact, the feel of the whole party was classic and elegant and totally comfortable. Smiling, helpful waitstaff milled about with delicious alcoholic concoctions like wet-cucumber and ginger-passionfruit margaritas, and Asian-French treats like miso-braised short ribs, coriander-crusted ahi tuna and Vietnamese sweet-potato fries with a chili cream dipping sauce.

Surrounded by several clients and potential clients, Ethan felt in his element and ready to do business, but he couldn't stop himself from wondering where Mary was. Earlier in the night she'd slipped away to change and reappeared right before the first doorbell chime.

Ethan had been having a difficult time keeping his eyes off her since. His gaze scanned the crowd and found her chatting with two couples, looking at ease and incredibly sexy. Her makeup was smoky and sophisticated, and she'd slicked her blond hair back into a very chic ponytail. But it was the clothes she was wearing that really made his entire body jolt. She looked as though she'd just stepped off a runway in New York. The black crisscross halter top and white pencil skirt showed off her long, slim figure to perfection. Soon she wouldn't be able to wear clothes like this, he mused thoughtfully. Her body would grow with their child, blossom with curves.

He continued to watch her as she gestured to one of the waitstaff carrying those very popular pale-green wet-cucumber margaritas. After serving the couple, Mary made her way over to Ethan and his insurance friends, her light-blue cat eyes bright with success and confidence. "Good evening. Is everyone enjoying themselves?"

The people around Ethan nodded and offered their host and hostess several enthusiastic compliments, then chuckled with amusement when Ethan declared he had to have what appeared to be the last piece of ahi and he was going to seek it out. Feeling oddly possessive in the large crowd of married and single men, Ethan led Mary out on the deck, where guests were waiting for a boat ride around the small lake.

"You haven't said anything about—" she gestured around the room "—all of this."

"Looks good," he said distractedly. The light out on the deck was even more intimate than the candles inside the house. Her neck looked soft and white and he played with the thought of leaning in and kissing her, right where her pulse thrummed gently.

"Looks good?" she repeated. "Is that all I'm going to get from you?"

"Nice choice of words," Ethan muttered, closing the gap between them so they were nearly touching, his chest to the tips of her breasts. Heat surged through Ethan's blood, and Mary must've seen the desire in his eyes because she quickly restated her question.

"What I meant was, is everything satisfactory?"

Ten feet away, around the side of the house, there was an alcove, just dark enough for them not to be spotted. He wanted to take her there, watch her pale-blue eyes turn smoky as he removed her skirt. "The food is amazing, the house looks perfect...yes, all satisfactory."

"Good."

"Great party, Curtis. Really top-notch." Downing a plate of short ribs as though they were going out of style, Ed Grasner, one of Ethan's biggest clients, walked by, no doubt headed for the boats and his wife.

Like a brick to the head, Ethan remembered why his guests were here. It was not to facilitate a seduction— he could do that on his own time. He turned back to Mary, his game face on. "The success of this evening isn't based on how much everyone eats and drinks or how great the house looks, it's based on acquiring several new clients."

Mary looked confused, as though she was watching a chameleon change colors. "Of course."

Ethan nodded toward a couple in their late thirties, sitting at one of the candlelit tables by the water. "Isaac and Emily Underwood. The St.Paul Underwoods. Very old money."

"Yes, I've heard of them."

"They own twenty-five exclusive inns around the Midwest. Get to them, get to the rest of their family. Can your efforts tonight reel in prize fish like that?"

"Is this a business party or the hunting and gaming channel?"

"I want what I want. And ninety-nine percent of the time I get it."

She shook her head at him.

He raised a brow. "I sound arrogant?"

"Arrogant, presumptuous, lacking in finesse."

Her derogatory adjectives caused him to stiffen. "Do you ever not say what's on your mind?"

"Once or twice. But it's a rarity."

Ethan had never been spoken to like this. At least not in the past fifteen years. He wasn't used to it, but for some reason with her, it didn't bother him all that much. In fact, her honesty and candor appealed to him.

"Mr. Curtis?" The pair that Ethan had just been talking about were walking toward him. The Underwoods were a handsome couple, very blond and tanned. Understated wealth oozed from them. They also appeared very much in love, their hands tightly clasped, only releasing each other when Ethan and Mary reached out a hand to greet them.

Emily gave Mary a warm, beautifully white smile. "I hear that you are the one responsible for this party?"

"I am," Mary said pleasantly. "Are you enjoying yourself this evening, Mrs. Underwood?"

The woman looked confused. "Have we been introduced?"

"Not yet. But I've heard much about you and your husband, and of course your lovely inns, from my grandparents."

"Your grandparents?"

"The Harringtons."

The casual warmth from a moment ago morphed into a look of understanding and respect. "Of course. I should have noticed it before. You have your grandmother's eyes. The shape."

Mary smiled, but her stomach churned lightly as it did whenever someone found a similarity between her and her grandmother. She didn't despise the woman like her father did, but growing up she had always been compared with her and had desperately wanted to be compared to her mother instead. But they'd looked so different it was almost impossible to see.

Ethan's hand came to rest on her back and she instinctively leaned into him. "Have you had a boat ride?" he asked, gesturing toward the lake. When they nodded, he asked them if they'd tried the food.

Chuckling, Isaac spoke then, "The food is amazing,

Curtis. Really. Both Emily and I have taken full advantage of your hospitality." He turned to Mary. "We must have the name of your chef. There are a few things we'd love to add to our menus."

"Of course," Mary replied. "The chef is my business partner, Olivia. I'll make sure to give you her name and number before you leave. But first, I see that the waitstaff are bringing out the desserts. You must try the pistachio crème brûlée with orange ice cream."

"Sounds delicious," Emily said with childlike enthusiasm.

Lowering her voice, Mary said conspiratorially, "Heavenly actually." She gestured toward the house. "Let's make sure you both have at least one."

Emily giggled. "At least. Come along, Isaac."

Before Mary could disappear, Ethan grabbed her arm. "Why are you sending them away? I wanted to speak with them about—"

"Relax, Curtis," she said softly, her eyes bright with mischief. "They'll be back. And because they want to, not because they've been hooked, yanked onto a boat and gutted."

Equally shocked and impressed, Ethan studied her. "Very nice."

She inclined her head. "Thank you."

Ethan's gaze followed her hungrily as she walked off to feed crème brûlée to his guests.

Some men resembled excessively tall penguins in their tuxedoes. Some looked awkward and uncomfortable. But Ethan Curtis wore his like a second skin. As he stalked his estate, he looked like a predator in search of his next prey—and he seemed to take his targets down with amazing speed and assuredness. By the end of the night, several potential clients had verbally signed on to Harrington Corp.'s already thick roster, and as Mary had predicted, the Underwoods had come back to him in a sugar haze, asking for a meeting at his office the following Monday.

When Mary found Ethan he was in the kitchen, looking very pleased with himself, his bow tie undone and falling against his open white shirt. Beer in hand, he chatted with the on-site chef, Jean Paul, as the man prepared to leave.

Mary shut her eyes against the sudden and unbidden image of Ethan out of that tux, his heavily muscled, tanned skin pressing down into the cushion of a woman's body—her body. She despised her reaction to him and to the memory of those nights together. Why couldn't she get it through her thick skull that those moments were over? Yes, sometimes he looked at her with a flicker of desire in his eyes, but the moment was over in seconds and he was back to business. He hadn't even commented on how she looked tonight, and she was really working it.

She grabbed her purse from the counter by the fridge. What did it matter? She was the one insisting that nothing romantic ever happen again. She faced him and spoke in her most professional voice. "Well, we're done here. If there's nothing else…"

Jean Paul discreetly returned to his knives, and Ethan regarded her with open respect. "I owe you a very big thank-you."

"You're welcome. It was a success, I think."

"Completely." He came to stand before her, his dark-blue eyes glittering with the satisfaction of a tiger who'd just bagged several hunters for dinner. His sensuous mouth turned up at the corners as he grinned at her, stealing her breath. "In fact, many of my guests are wondering what you'll come up with next."

"They'll just have to wait and see."

"I'm wondering, too." One of his dark brows lifted. "Do I have to wait?"

If he came any closer, she was going to lose it. Feeling irritatingly light-headed, she reached out for the granite countertop to steady herself. "We could discuss the menus and themes at any time."

"How about now? I didn't get one of the boat rides."

"I don't know if the guys are still out there."

His grinned widened. "I think I can manage to take you for a ride myself."

"Ethan Curtis, where have you been?" The slow, whiskey-smooth female voice came from behind Mary, and she turned with a jerk to see a five-foot-nine Playboy playmate, dressed in an orange tank dress.

"Allison, where did you come from?" Ethan asked, sounding more annoyed than surprised.

"Didn't you say eleven? I don't wear a watch, but I could swear I'm right on time." Her voice and body language just screamed sex.

Mary heard Ethan curse, but she didn't dare turn back to face him, not with her neck turning red as she knew it was. He had a date. An after-party date. Of course he did. Why not?

"Wait for me by the pool, Allison," Ethan said, his voice soft but commanding. "I'm not quite finished here."

Finding her nerve at long last, Mary forgot about her red neck and gave the hot blonde a hotter glare. "Allison, is it?"

She smiled. "Two Ls and two Ns."

Brilliant and beautiful, Mary mused dryly. What a combination. "You don't need to go anywhere. Mr. Curtis and I are finished." She turned to Ethan and gave him a fake smile. "I'll call you in a few days, sir—to discuss the next function."

Anger burned in her stomach and, as she walked swiftly through his house and out the front door, she called herself fourteen kinds of fool for even considering him in a romantic way. He was an egotistical, spoiled player who had no idea what he really wanted.

"Mary, slow down." Ethan caught up with her on his driveway and grabbed her hand as she tried to open her car door.

She brushed him off. "I have work waiting for me at home and you have a Barbie twin waiting for you by the pool."

"I made that date weeks ago. Before...well..." He pushed a hand through his hair. "This is awkward."

"Damn right," she retorted in a sharp voice. "So, I'm going to go now before it gets any more awkward."

"No."

"I'm not into threesomes, Curtis."

"I didn't even know you were interested in a twosome."

Gritting her teeth, Mary stared at him. "Ditto."

He took a moment to process her meaning. "If you think I don't want to go to bed with you again, you're wrong."

"Who the hell could tell?"

"What does that mean?"

"You hardly looked at me tonight," she said with a scowl. "Then the cover of *Sluts-R-Us* magazine walks in and your eyes pop out of—"

"I see you, Mary," he interrupted hotly. "I remember every damn detail."

"But?"

"Weren't you the one who said that what happened those nights at the lake would never happen again?"

She hated when the truth was tossed in her face. "Yes." She wrenched open her car door.

"And it's complicated, isn't it?" he continued. "What we did? What we made? Who I am."

"Who you are? I can't figure it out."

"The bastard who blackmailed you…basically."

His words shocked her. The easy admission of something so base and vile. She got in her car and slammed the door. "So, what? You feel guilty?"

"No."

"Of course not. You see nothing wrong with what you did."

"I don't feel guilty, that's true. But I do feel…" He

cursed. "Conflicted. Protective." He shrugged, as if the truth surprised the hell out of him. "Isn't that the damnedest thing?"

"Protective? Of whom?"

"You."

"You're protecting me from you?"

"Maybe. I don't know."

"Well, stop it," she said caustically, gunning her engine. "Sex doesn't have to be any more emotionally significant than a really charged football game."

The words exploded into the air like fireworks, but she didn't believe them, and she knew that he knew she didn't believe it. What was she trying to do? Why couldn't she abandon this idea of him and her, one more time, or two or three? What was she? A masochist?

"Mary—"

"Go prove my point to Allison in there," she said bitingly before shoving the car into Reverse and taking off down the quiet, wooded drive.

Four

Mary sat in Little Bo and Peep's baby shop, up to her eyeballs in terry cloth, stretch cotton, bouncy seats and black and white mobiles. For the past twenty minutes, she hadn't been able to pick out a single thing for the nursery. She knew exactly what clothes she loved, what crib and bassinet she wanted, she even knew the drawer pulls she would pick out if this were all real. But designing a nursery for a child that didn't exist was next to impossible. She felt like a total fraud and she wanted to give up.

The doorbell over the shop entrance jangled merrily, and Mary watched a young couple come through the door with excited grins. They oohed and aahed as they moved from one quaint set of nursery furniture set to the next, hands clasped tightly, the woman's round stomach looking like a sweet watermelon. She wanted that. A real relationship, a real baby...something impossible to have with Ethan Curtis. Mary's mind rolled back to the party and how it had ended. For the past two days she'd thought of nothing but him and that blonde, and her own irrational need to be with him again. She'd wondered what had happened after she'd left. Had Ethan met her by the pool? Did they go for a swim together? Allisonn—two Ls, two Ns—hadn't seemed like the kind of woman who thought swimsuits were all that important.

Beside her, the young mother pointed at a tiny Minnesota Twins baseball cap and squealed with delight, catching Mary's eye in the process. Mary forced a smile, then moved on to look at bathtubs and safety accessories. Why the hell did she care what Ethan did? Or *who* he did, for that matter? She had to get over this.

The saleswoman walked by her again with that look all salespeople give a person when they think you're lingering without purpose.

Are you stealing or just indecisive?

"Right, I get it," Mary grumbled under her breath as she abandoned the bath supplies and headed to the front of the store. Nothing was going to happen today. She wasn't about to do any work on the nursery in her state of mind. If Ethan asked her how she was progressing, she'd just have to stall and—

"Mary?"

Coming into the shop just as Mary was exiting was a very elegant woman in her midseventies, dressed in a thin crepe navy blue suit, her white hair swept off her mildly wrinkled face in a tightly pinned chignon.

"Grandmother? What are you doing here?"

Grace Harrington surveyed her granddaughter, her perfectly arched brows lifting at the sight of Mary's plain black pantsuit and slightly scuffed heels. To Grace Harrington, clothes were like Ziplock baggies, only good for one use.

"Pearl Edicott's granddaughter is expecting twins," her grandmother said in a pinched tone. "Pearl has the most horrific taste. It's a very good thing she knows it."

"Very good thing," Mary repeated, smiling in spite of herself. Grace Harrington was an over-the-top snob, and if Mary had any sense, she'd probably detest her. After all, Grace wasn't all that warm either, more days than not she found something wrong with Mary's clothing or hairstyle, and she treated her help like they didn't breathe the same air as she did. And then there was the fact that she had cut Mary's mother out of her life when she'd married Hugh.

Yet, with all of that, Mary felt a connection with her, a strange admiration that went far beyond her wealth. Grace was smart, well-read and a stickler for speaking her mind. Mary could really respect that. She and her grandparents were rarely *simpatico*, but they were her blood, and had always wanted to be a part of her life, and strangely Mary's mother had never discouraged her from seeing them.

Grace picked up two twin chenille baby robes that cost a hundred dollars each and eyed them closely. "And what are you doing here, my dear?"

"Designing a nursery for a client."

"Ah, yes, your business. How is that going?"

"Great."

Grace forgot about the robes for a moment and focused on Mary, her lips pursed. "This isn't for one of those two-father homes, is it?"

"Not this time."

"A couple, then?" She didn't give Mary a chance to answer as she clucked her tongue disapprovingly. "A mother who doesn't want to create her own child's room. How modern."

Mary was about to ask her grandmother if she herself had actually designed her own daughter's nursery or if she'd hired three or four interior designers to make it happen, but she knew she'd probably get an answer that resembled something like, "It was my vision. As usual, the help was only there to execute it."

"The nursery is for a single father actually," Mary told her.

"Anyone I know?"

Mary's brow lifted. "Now how many single fathers do you socialize with, Grandmother?"

Grace gave her a blank look. "None…that I know of." Spotting a beautiful pink-and-blue blanket draped over one of the handcrafted armchairs, Grace turned her back on Mary. "Well, this chenille is lovely. It reminds me of the very one your mother carried around for years. If the maid even spoke of washing it, she would…" Grace stopped abruptly and cleared her throat.

Mary was grateful not to have to see the woman's

face in that moment. Turning toward a row of onesies, she quickly changed the subject. "Babies are really no bigger than dolls, are they?"

"For a short time, yes," Grace replied softly. "But before you even realize it they are grown and deciding what they will wear and who they will marry without any input from you."

"There you are." A booming male voice broke through all the femininity. "I called your office and Olivia said you'd be—"

"Ethan?" In the heaviness of her conversation with Grace, Mary hadn't heard the bell over the door. If she had heard—and seen—who was about to enter the shop, she would've been out the door in a matter of seconds. This was not good.

Ethan spotted Grace and changed instantly from casual guy to cynical business mogul. "Mrs. Harrington. What a pleasant surprise."

"I doubt that," the older woman said dryly.

Before her grandmother could connect the single father with Ethan, Mary said quickly, "I'm organizing several functions for Mr. Curtis."

"Is that so?" Grace said, pursing her lips as if she'd just gotten a whiff of rotting fish, or as if the thought of her blue-blooded granddaughter working for the upstart who had basically stolen her family's company made her want to throw up. "When did he hire you?"

In other words, how long has this been going on and why was I not informed?

"Just a few weeks ago," Mary replied.

"And he has a meeting with you in a baby boutique?"

"No."

No doubt sensing that Mary was floundering, Ethan jumped in to save her. "We were supposed to meet at the restaurant next door, but I saw your granddaughter in here and wanted to start early. As you know, Mrs. Harrington, I have little patience and zero time. I was in the neighborhood seeing a client and there was something I needed to discuss with Miss Kelley that couldn't wait. Luckily she agreed to meet with me."

"Luckily for you she agreed to take you on as a client, Mr. Curtis," Grace said frigidly.

He nodded. "Your granddaughter is very talented."

"A fact of which I am well aware."

"Knowing that your granddaughter is planning the event, maybe you'll reconsider the brunch on Saturday."

"Perhaps," she said tightly, then turned to Mary. "I have to run, my dear."

"But the gift for the twins…"

"This shop is a little too new money for my taste, and you know how I despise that." She didn't have to look at Ethan to get her point across. "Your father is out of harm's way now, I hear."

"Yes," Mary said, surprised her grandmother would bring something like that up, much less care.

"Nasty business, that. But we were in no position to help, unfortunately." After two air kisses to Mary's cheeks and nothing whatever for Ethan, she left them.

"That woman couldn't hate me more if I spit on her shoe," Ethan muttered.

"Oh, yes she could, but I wouldn't advise trying it."

"You'd think I stole the company right out from under their noses."

"Didn't you?"

He gave her a haughty look. "Harrington Corp. was in trouble. Your grandfather was really slipping. Clients weren't getting serviced the way they had in the past and many were threatening to walk. I didn't steal anything. If anything I saved that damn company."

"Pretty much the same as stealing it, to my grand-parents." Mary took her cell phone out of her pocket and showed it to him. "Now, you have my phone number, right?"

"Yes."

"Couldn't you have called me instead of tracking me down?"

"Why? Did I embarrass you?" he asked coldly.

"Don't be so thick, Curtis. I'm in a baby shop. I had to dance fast with my grandmother about why I was here, then why you were here—"

"*I* danced fast on that one," he interrupted.

She ignored him. "You know I want to keep this quiet. I thought we both did."

"I never said I wanted to keep anything quiet—"

"Hello, there." The saleswoman who had been watching Mary for the past thirty minutes in annoyance joined them, completely smiley-faced and enthusiastic at the sight of Ethan. "Daddy's here."

Ethan looked pleased with the comment and nod-ded. "He is."

"Would you and your wife like some lemonade before you get started?"

Mary snorted derisively and said, "I'm not his—"

"Yes, we would," Ethan said, cutting her off before following the saleswoman to a small refreshment area.

For the next twenty minutes Mary sat beside Ethan and watched as the saleswoman laid blankets and rugs, hats and booties, washtubs and soothing lullaby CDs at Ethan's feet as though he were the sultan of Bruni.

Feeling close to exploding if she stayed in the shop one more minute, Mary leaned in and whispered to Ethan, "I have to get back to the office," then grabbed her purse and headed for the door.

He caught up with her, placing his hand on her arm. "We need to talk."

"About?" she asked, trying to ignore the heat of his fingers searing into her skin.

"The brunch."

"Call my office and we'll set something up for to-morrow—"

"No, I'm the client. You can come to my office." His jaw hardened, letting her know there was no denying his command. "Today, four-thirty."

As she struggled to maintain her calm exterior, Mary fought the desire that simmered beneath. "Fine. Four-thirty."

"You look exhausted."

Not exactly the first thing a woman wants to hear

when the man she finds overwhelmingly attractive opens his office door.

"Thanks," Mary uttered sarcastically.

Ethan grinned, gestured toward the chocolate brown leather couch. "Sit down."

"I'm fine."

"We're not going to discuss the brunch while you stand. This could take a while."

"How long are you estimating?"

"Why? Do you have a date or something?"

Standing on either side of the coffee table, like two gunslingers, they stared at each other.

"Not the best joke I've made this week."

"No."

"Come on, have a seat," Ethan said, dropping onto the plush leather and grinning.

On a weary sigh, she plunked down on the couch. "Okay, I'm sitting, now let's start with the menu. I think we should go for a southern theme. Olivia has this New Mexican menu— Wait, what are you doing?"

Before Mary could stop him, Ethan had taken off her shoes and placed her feet in his lap. "I'm helping you to relax."

"Why?"

"Why not?"

"I'll tell you why not. I'm here for business not for pl—" She came to screeching halt, which made Ethan's eyes glitter even more wickedly.

"If this helps," he began. "Rubbing your aching feet is business. Technically."

"I can't wait to hear this."

"It's my job, my duty—my business, if you will. Or so I've read."

She looked surprised. "You've been reading books on…"

"Pregnancy? Yep."

"Seriously?"

He nodded. "Pregnancy, baby care, labor, postpartum, breastfeeding—"

"Okay, that's enough," she said, relaxing back into the couch as Ethan's strong hands worked the tired knots in her arches. "Five minutes max."

He laughed. "I've learned many useful things."

"Like?" she asked, trying to keep her eyes open and the soft, cozy sound out of her voice.

"Like nausea and strange cravings are very normal in the first trimester."

"Uh-huh."

"So are leg cramps and exhaustion."

"Yep."

"And an unusually high sex drive."

Her eyes flew open and she sat up, swung her legs to the floor. It took her a moment to tamp down the tremors of need running through her. She felt the urge so strongly, all she wanted him to do was continue touching her. She wanted his mouth on hers, nudging her lips apart with his tongue… "All right," she said breathlessly. "Southern food, maybe Southwest or Cajun. What about having an autumn-barn-dance theme for your brunch?"

"A heavy sex drive is nothing to be ashamed of, Mary."

She tilted her chin up. "I've never been ashamed of it."

What she was saying dawned on him almost immediately, and his eyes lit with mischief, his lips parted sensuously.

"Now, can we get back to this?" she asked coolly.

He wouldn't allow her to look away. "Nothing happened with Allisonn."

Her heart skipped and she swallowed nervously. She wanted to tell him that she couldn't care less about blondie, but he wouldn't believe her. "This doesn't sound like brunch discussion."

"Mary..." he began, his voice the husky baritone she remembered from those nights at the lake.

"Listen, Curtis, what you do in your house, bedroom, pool, etcetera is your business. Let's just get on with this."

"Why are you so hard?"

"Bad genes," she responded succinctly which made him laugh. "Not from my parents. They were angels. But they say attitude skips a generation."

Shaking his head, he stared at her for a moment, then he stood up and reached for her. "Dance with me?"

"You've got to be kidding."

"We'll make it business related. Show me what you're talking about with this barn concept. There's got to be some dancing involved on my deck, right?"

"Yes, but there's no music."

"I could turn some on, but I don't think we need it," He touched his temple with his index finger. "It's all in here."

Laughing, she took his hand and let him pull her to her feet and into his arms. "You have country music playing up there?"

He pretended to be insulted by her query. "Blues, baby. Only the blues for me."

Her toes sank into the plush carpet and she sank into Ethan's embrace. His hand gripped her waist, then slid to her back to pull her closer. She felt feminine and unsure, but she didn't want him to release her.

"I don't know how to dance," she admitted.

"I'm not that great at it, either," he said. "But I can manage a few turns and the side-to-side swaying."

His eyes were so expressive, so full of life. They could leap from anger to lust to boredom to amusement in mere moments, but it was these times that made her toes curl, the times when he stared at her with unabashed longing.

As he rocked back and forth, as his hips brushed hers and his palm pressed possessively against her hand, Mary experienced a feeling so powerful, so new it made her heart thump painfully in her chest. She was enjoying herself, with Ethan Curtis, the man who had forced her into— A man she should never enjoy herself with.

Her thoughts dropped away suddenly as Ethan quickened his pace, twirling her first to the right, then the left. With a sinful grin, he grasped both of her hands and gave her a gentle push back, then he turned her and pulled her into his body, so her back was pressed against his chest.

She glanced over her shoulder at him and smiled at the amusement in his eyes. "Tell anyone about this and I'm never dancing with you again."

Laughing with delight, Mary let him sway them both to the right and left, then squealed when he dipped her. When he rolled her out toward the couch, she released him and dropped back on the brown leather cushions. Chuckling along with her, Ethan did, too. For a moment neither of them spoke, then they both turned to look at each other.

"We'd better be careful," Ethan said.

"Why?" Mary asked breathlessly. "What do you mean?"

He reached over and brushed a strand of honey-colored hair from her cheek. "If we don't watch our step we might have fun together—or worse, actually start liking each other."

To Mary's delight, the brunch fell on a glorious late-August day. The trees were starting to contemplate change, their green leaves making room for rich golds, ruby reds and pumpkin oranges. Mary had nixed the Cajun idea, but the pre-autumn Southern barn theme was there and looking fabulous. As she meandered through the guests, who had almost doubled in size since the last party, she took in her handiwork with a proud grin. The deck and surrounding land was decorated with an odd but interesting, contemporary rustic charm; hay bales in glass troughs like funky centerpieces, scarecrows dressed like runway models, Tom Sawyer-style rafts in the water, and on and on. Then there was the food. Pumpkin and sage soup in miniature pumpkins, fried catfish with a spicy green tomato relish, mustard greens with pancetta, watermelon and pecan pie tartlets.

Everyone seemed relaxed, the stuffy atmosphere of this crowd's customary Saturday cocktail party forgotten. Diamonds still sparkled from ears, wrists and fingers, but the backdrop was denim and Ralph Lauren plaid.

Mary spotted five-star-inns' Isaac and Emily Underwood coming toward her and smiled welcomingly. She knew that, as of last Monday, the couple were now Ethan's clients. "Well, hello, there. Are you two enjoying yourselves?"

"Your creativity is astounding, Mary," Isaac said, gesturing to the backyard.

"Thank you."

"Yes, amazing," Emily added.

Isaac dropped his voice to a conspiratorial whisper, "Even though we don't have to work, the feeling of success can bring great rewards, don't you think?"

Mary's brows drew together. Contrary to what the Underwoods believed was reality, Mary had to work for every penny. The Harringtons didn't help her one bit, never had, nor had she ever asked them to.

"This is a great success," Emily said, two-carat diamond studs sparkling in her ears. "Especially for Ethan. Invitations to his parties will be sought-after now."

"Now?"

Heat spread across Emily's face and she stumbled to explain. "Well, what I mean to say is…"

Isaac quickly covered for her. "Curtis is brilliant,

and he has the client list to prove it, but as far as social-
izing…well, he's not really one of us, you understand."

She certainly did, and she had to resist the urge to
grab the pumpkin out of Isaac's hand and dump the
contents over his head. Lucky for her and for them, the
Underwoods spotted another group of snotty elitists
over by the bar and excused themselves. Why did Ethan
want to be a part of this world? she wondered, heading
inside the house. She scanned the room looking for him,
expecting to find him in the center of a group of wealthy
people who were looking for free advice, but he wasn't
there. She sidled up to one of the waitstaff. "Have you
seen Mr. Curtis?"

"I think he's in the kitchen."

"Alone?"

"No, there's a full kitchen staff in there, Ms. Kelley."

"I mean, was he with anyone? A guest?" she asked
tightly. Like maybe a Tiffany—one F, two Ys?

The man shook his head. "Not that I saw."

As she walked toward the kitchen, the sound of
clanging pots and hustling staff was interspersed with
a shrill, critical voice that Mary instantly recognized as
her grandmother's.

The door opened and as a mortified-looking waitress
rushed out with a plate of food, Mary heard the older
woman's voice again. "You can take my family's company, hire my granddaughter to act as your wife at
parties and invite the top shelf as your guests, but that
will never make you one of us."

Interrupting the conversation didn't sound like a

good plan. She didn't want to embarrass Ethan any further. So Mary watched through a crack in the door. The room was busy with waitstaff, chefs and to Mary's horror, not only her grandmother, but two of her grandmother's closest friends. Grace Harrington stood a few feet from Ethan, who had his back to the sleek Wolf range, her friends behind her like a scene from one of those movies about exclusive high school cliques.

"Breeding cannot be bought," Grace continued, her tone spiteful and cruel. "Where and who you come from is in every movement you make. Make no mistake about it, Mr. Curtis, you wear your trailer-park upbringing like a second skin."

The room stilled. The chefs stopped chopping, the waitstaff looked horrified as they tried to stare at anything but Ethan.

White-hot fury burned in Ethan's eyes. "I know exactly where I come from, Mrs. Harrington, and I'm proud of it."

"Is that so? Then why try so hard to impress us all?"

"My work makes enough of an impression to satisfy me. These events are a way to gain more clients. After all," he said with a slow smile, "before I came along, Harrington Corp. was not only hemorrhaging money but about to lose seventy percent of their client base as well."

Grace's jaw dropped, and she looked as though she couldn't breathe. Ditto with the geriatric sentinels behind her. Mary had never seen her grandmother bested before, and she felt oddly sorry for her, but knew the older woman had it coming to her. Grace Harrington could dish it out, and maybe now she would learn to take it.

Mary watched Ethan grab a beer from the counter and tip it toward the threesome. "Good afternoon, ladies. I have every confidence that you can find the front door from here."

And then he was coming her way, in ten seconds he'd bump right into her. Mary dropped back into a small alcove off the hallway and waited for him to leave the kitchen and pass by her. His jaw tight, his stride purposeful, he walked past her and in the opposite direction of the party. After waiting a moment for her grandmother and her friends to leave, Mary followed Ethan. She had a good idea where he'd be.

She climbed the stairs and walked down the hall, unsure of what she was going to say to him when she found him. The door to the nursery was closed, but that didn't dissuade her.

Without knocking, she entered the room. Ethan was lying on his back on the floor, staring out the enormous bay window. Sunlight splashed over his handsome face, illuminating his pensive expression.

Mary sat beside him. Maybe he'd been right that day in his office, after their musicless dance, maybe they were becoming friends. God only knew why, after their history. But the fact was she understood him a little better now, understood what drove him. Her mother had felt some of the same feelings of not being good enough, not knowing where she belonged or who really cared about her for herself and not how much money she had.

"She's right."

Ethan's words jarred her, brought her back to the present. "Who's right?"

"Your grandmother. I'm not worth much more than the trailer I was born in."

"That's not exactly what she said." Mary knew that she sounded as though she were defending Grace, when that's not what she was trying to do at all. She knew her grandmother had been cold and cruel, but Ethan could be that way as well.

"That's what she said, Mary. I've heard versions of that diatribe many times. From my ex-wife, from my own mother. Doesn't seem to matter how hard I work." He shrugged. "I'll never escape it."

"This self-pitying thing has to stop, Ethan."

He sat up, stared at her with cold eyes. "What?"

"Why do you care?" she demanded.

"What?"

"Why do you care what any of them think?"

The anger dropped away, and he shook his head. Just kept shaking his head. "I have no idea."

"Why can't you be satisfied with the life you've created?"

The double meaning wasn't lost on either of them, and in that moment, Mary knew it was just a matter of time before she confessed the truth about her pregnancy. She didn't want to care about him. He'd forced her to make some abominable decisions...and yet...

She put a hand on his shoulder, and in less than an instant he covered it with his own. "Under that layer of pride and arrogance," she said softly, "is a pretty decent guy. I can't help but believe that."

He leaned in until his forehead touched hers. "Even with everything that's happened?"

"Yes."

He tipped her chin up and with a soft groan his mouth found hers in a slow, drugging kiss. Mary opened to him, even suckled his bottom lip until he uttered her name and pulled her closer, his tongue mating with hers.

She protested when he pulled away from her, whispering a barely audible no.

With his face still so close to her own, he regarded her intently. "Are you pitying me, Mary?"

She wanted his mouth, his tongue, his skin against hers and no more questions. "Does it matter?" she uttered huskily.

A long moment of silence passed, and then Ethan groaned, a frustrated, animal-like sound. "No," he muttered, closing his eyes, nuzzling her cheek until he found her mouth again.

Five

Despite the open window, the air in the room had become stiflingly warm. Mary's limbs felt heavy, and she clung to Ethan for support. His mouth was hard on hers, his breath sweet and intoxicating. For a moment she wondered if she was drunk, but then realized she had been sipping seltzer water all morning. Mouth slanting, Ethan unleashed the full strength of his need, his tongue against hers, caressing the tip until Mary was breathless and limp. Whatever he wanted to do, she was a willing participant.

Without a word, Mary started unbuttoning her white blouse, her fingers shaking. Her skin needed to breathe, needed to be touched. As Ethan chuckled softly against her lips, she tugged away at her shirt, wishing she could just rip it off.

"Let me," he uttered hoarsely.

"And this," she practically begged, struggling with the hooks on her pale-pink bra.

"Tell me what you want, Mary."

"You."

"My weight on top of you? My chest brushing against your nipples?"

"Your mouth."

His head was in the crook of her neck, his forehead nuzzling her, his teeth nipping at her skin. "On your mouth? On your breasts? Do you want me to suckle them like I did your tongue?"

"Yes," came her ragged whisper.

Gently he pulled the straps over her shoulders, eased her bra to her waist. She felt as though she were falling, sliding down, down, until she landed against plush, fuzzy white carpet. Her back to the floor, Ethan poised on top of her, his dark blue eyes hungry, almost desperate, Mary struggled to catch her breath.

"Ethan," she rasped.

Ethan paused, his body pulsing with heat. He'd never heard her say his name like that—desperately.

His body tight to the point of pain, Ethan slid his hand up her torso to her rib cage and gently cupped one breast. Instantly hungry for more, he brushed his thumb over her nipple until it stiffened into a rosy peak. His mouth watered. He'd tasted her before, but the memory had been little comfort over the past weeks.

"You are so beautiful," he whispered, leaning forward into the warmth of her body, her skin, his mouth grazing the tender bud.

Gasping, she arched her back, her chest rising and falling rapidly, one hand fisting the carpet. Her skin was so hot, electric, and he couldn't help himself, he covered her with his mouth and suckled deeply.

"Oh..." she uttered breathlessly, cupping her other breast. "Oh, Ethan, please."

Ethan rooted between her ribs to her other breast, over her fingers until he found the sweet, taut peak in the center. Her body danced beneath his, her hips pumped as though he was inside her, and how he longed to be.

So caught up in the moment, Ethan gently sank his teeth into the pink flesh surrounding her nipple as he continued to flick the tight bud. Her breath quickened, and he could hear her heart pounding in her chest. He wanted to make her climax, just with his mouth on her breast, and she was close, so close. But then outside the window came the sounds of people laughing and talking, some loud enough to hear.

"Where do you think Curtis ran off to?" one said.

"Back to the office?" someone suggested, chuckling.

The conversation wasn't lost on Mary or Ethan, and they stilled, looked at each other, their breathing labored. Then after a moment, Mary let out a frustrated sigh and rolled away from him.

Feeling like an ass, Ethan didn't say anything as he watched her dress, but when she finally looked at him, pink-cheeked, slightly disheveled and, judging by her eyes, still on the verge of orgasm, he couldn't stop himself.

"No farther?" he asked gently.

She shook her head, deep regret in her eyes, but from what, he wasn't sure. "We have to get back to the party."

"God, why?"

"They're leaving."

"I don't care—"

"Yes, you do," she said, coming to her feet, smoothing her blouse. "We need to make an appearance, say goodbye to those who remain. You don't want people thinking that you completely disappeared."

"I don't give a damn what they think." Desire still raged through him. He wanted to play caveman and drag her off to his bed and lock the door behind him. "I want to finish this."

"Another time."

He was about to tell her that he didn't want to wait, but he knew that determined look on her face, knew better than to try to sway or push her. "I'm holding you to that," he grumbled.

By the time they returned, separately of course, to the party, most of the guests had gone. There were a few stragglers milling about, and while Mary thanked and paid the staff, Ethan showed his face to the last of the guests.

He was in his office when Mary found him a half hour later.

"Well, the general consensus is that everyone had a good time," she said.

"Everyone?" he asked pointedly, his gaze intense.

She bit her lip, which made his groin tighten painfully. "I should get going."

"Stay until the end," he said.

"This is the end. Everyone's gone, even the wait and kitchen staffs have taken off."

He sat back in his chair. "I meant stay until the end of the night...when it gets light outside and my housekeeper serves breakfast."

"Ethan..."

"You could stay upstairs in my bed. Because you want to...this time."

She sighed, let her eyes fall closed for a moment. When she opened them again, he saw the same look in her eyes as he had upstairs. She wasn't finished with him or what they'd started, but she also wasn't about to agree to stay with him, either. She shook her head. "I'm sorry." Then turned and left the room.

Her ancient Betty Boop bedside lamp clicked on and Mary uttered a tired, "Man..."

Her father's face, bed-worn and confused, stared down at her. "What are you doing here, lass?"

"Sleeping."

"Why?"

She glanced at her matching Betty Boop clock, both it and the lamp presents from her parents for her twelfth birthday. "Because it's four in the morning."

Hugh sat on the bed and dragged a hand through his rumpled hair. "Why are you here and not in your apartment?"

Right. Mary glanced around her old bedroom. Not a thing out of place since she'd found her own apartment at nineteen. Same red-checked curtains and white dresser. She smiled halfheartedly when she spotted her *Xanadu* album in the corner by the old turntable.

Her father cleared his throat, and Mary looked at him sheepishly. "All right, I ran away."

"Did you indeed?" he said, his shaggy brows lifting.

"From a boy." Actually from a man, a gorgeous, fever-inducing man, who wanted her in his bed almost as much as he wanted the nonexistent child in her belly. Mary shook her head. What a mess. She burrowed deeper under her old, white down comforter.

"You won't be telling me why you're running from this boy, will you lass?"

Her lips pressed tightly together, she shook her head like a stubborn toddler. How could she possibly? Her dad wouldn't understand what she'd done—the lengths to which she'd gone to protect him. Or worse yet, he'd understand perfectly, feel incredibly guilty and fall deeper into the chasm of despair he was already stuck in.

"You just need a bit of the old family house, do you?" he asked finally, shooing a tiny insect away from the lamp.

She gave him a grateful smile. "If you don't mind, Pop."

"You know you're always welcome here, lass." He paused for a moment, his eyes concerned. "I just don't want you to be running away from your problems too often. You'll never have time to sit down and take a breath if you do."

"I know."

"I love you, lass."

"I love you too, Pop."

When her father left the room, Mary lay back against her pillow and stared out at the same moon she'd watched change from sliver to crescent to full so many times when she was a kid. What had started out as the only foreseeable way to keep her father out of jail, or from a trial at the very least, had become a nightmare that she wanted to wake up from. She and Ethan had a meeting next week, and no matter how difficult it would be, she was not going to run away from the truth. She was going to tell him everything.

The wind off the lake whipped her hair from side to side, as though trying to make up its mind which direction to go. It was Sunday morning, a day Mary usually reserved for the newspaper, coffee and as many Danishes as she could eat without exploding, but when Ivan Garrison had called and asked her to see his boat, she'd readily accepted. The fact was, she was dying for some impersonal work to take her mind off Ethan.

After seeing his eighty-four-foot yacht, and having a quick discussion about where he'd like everything set up for the gala, the captain had asked her to take a sail on the very boat that he would be racing that day. Mary had been on very few sailboats in her time, and had been a little afraid of seasickness, but after popping a couple of Dramamine, she'd hopped aboard and found life on the water rather magnificent.

After they'd rounded the lake twice, Ivan headed back to the marina. Over the wind and the lapping of the water, Mary called, "This is great! I think your guests will be very impressed, Captain."

Ivan grinned at her. "Not just by the gala, I'm hoping."

Confused, she said, "I'm sorry?"

"I've decided to take your advice and make this a charity event."

Mary nodded. So, the captain did have a soul after all. Shocking, he wasn't just a Lamborghini-driving playboy. She'd have to tell Olivia.

"So all the entry fees will go to charity?" she called as Ivan maneuvered around in the marina, approaching the dock at a very slow speed.

"My financial advisors have told me that this will be a great tax write-off."

So he wasn't exactly Mother Teresa, but at least he had agreed to do something worthwhile. Maybe she wouldn't mention this to Olivia.

"Have you decided which charity appeals to you?" she asked him.

"Cancer's pretty popular."

"True."

Ivan slowly entered the slip, then placed the transmission in neutral and let the wind blow the boat back. "But which one to choose?" he called, securing the boat's front dock line first. "Children? Lung? Breast?"

Mary removed her life vest and placed it beside her on the bench. "Well, how about the Cancer Research Institute? They pretty much cover it all."

"Perfect." Staring onto the dock, Ivan squinted, then frowned. "Is he waiting for you or me?"

Mary glanced up, saw what Ivan was seeing and felt her pulse jump inside her veins. Standing there, arms crossed and looking murderous, was Ethan. "That would be for me."

Six

Ethan's body tightened at the sight of Mary walking down the dock toward him. A white T-shirt, pink shorts and bare feet had never looked so dangerous on any woman. Visions swam in his mind, images of soft skin against his mouth and long legs wrapped around his waist, cute round buttocks cupped in his hands. This intense physical reaction was becoming way too familiar, and he wondered if the only way he was going to get rid of it was to take her to bed again.

Ethan had known many women in his time, but his need for them had faded quickly. Why wasn't it the same with Mary Kelley? Why had the desire to taste her, fill his nostrils with her scent, open her thighs and bury himself deep inside her only intensified over time? Was it the baby or something else, something more?

Her pale-blue eyes mocked him as she came to stand before him, a grin tugging at her mouth. "You are officially stalking me now, Curtis."

"Well, one of us has to protect the baby," he muttered grimly.

"What in the world are you talking about?"

He gestured to the water. "Out there on the open water, no life jacket, no nothing."

"Open water?" she repeated, laughing. "Come on. This is a lake, calm as a sleeping kitten. There's no danger here."

Ethan eyed the man coming up behind her. "Isn't there?"

"Oh, for God's sake," Mary said as her sailboat buddy walked by with a smile and a wave. She waved back and called, "I'll call you on Thursday," then returned her attention to a very annoyed Ethan. "I was wearing a life jacket, and the captain—he's just a client."

"*The captain*," Ethan drawled with derision. "Please don't tell me that he makes you call him that?"

Mary regarded him incredulously. "Let's not get into crazy demands from clients, shall we?"

"Fine," he muttered darkly, following her down the dock and toward the parking lot.

As she dug the car keys from her purse, she asked, "Now, what's brought you all the way out here?"

"Do you have a doctor?"

She stopped, turned to look at him. "Why? Do you have a medical emergency?"

Her joke was lost on him and he scowled. "Be serious for a second."

"I have a doctor, Ethan."

"For the pregnancy?"

Her gaze flickered to the ground then back up, and he wondered if that was too intimate a thing to ask her.

"Yes, I have a doctor," she said finally. "A family-practice type thing. Why?"

He shook his head. "That's not good enough. You need an Ob/Gyn."

Exhaling heavily, she walked away from him toward the lot, but he was on her heels. "I'm serious, Mary."

"I'm going to come to your house and take every one of those books away from you. Foot massage is one thing, buddy, but—" she fumbled in her purse again for her keys "—you're getting way too knowledgeable on *Girlfriends' Guides* and *Mothering and You*, and frankly, it's making me feel a little weird."

Ethan paused. He didn't have those two books, but he made a mental note to get them. "Listen, I have a client whose wife is Deena Norrison."

"Never heard of her."

"She's only one of the best Ob/Gyn's in the country."

When Mary reached her car and still couldn't find her keys, she looked ready to explode. Undeterred, Ethan continued, "She's agreed to see you."

"I have a good doctor, Ethan," Mary assured him, her

hand stuffed inside her purse again, perspiration beading on her brow.

"Good is not great, and Deena's the best. Doesn't our child deserve the best?"

"Aha!" Mary held up her keys triumphantly, but her glee was short-lived when she noticed the stern look on Ethan's face. She sighed. "When is this appointment? This week is swamped for me, and next week we leave for Mackinac Island."

"How's today?"

"Today," she repeated, the blood draining from her face.

"Right now." He took her cool hand in his. "There's no reason to be nervous. I'm sure everything is fine."

"Now?"

"I know. Isn't that great? She's a pretty cool lady. She'll fit you in at four. Ultrasound and everything."

Mary shook her head. "But—"

Ethan didn't give her time to refuse. Once she saw the kid's heartbeat and heard from the best doctor in the country that everything was just as it should be, she'd relax. "Come on," he said, gently guiding her toward his car. "I'll drive."

Dr. Deena Norrison's reception area looked like a photograph straight out of the pages of *Victoria* magazine. Surrounded by cabbage-rose wallpaper, clients sank down into soft and cushy deep-pink sofas with rolled arms. The love seats and chairs, Mary was certain, had down pillows.

Mary sat on one of the love seats, her purse perched on the Queen Anne table before her. The scent of flowers was dizzying and made her feel as though she was trapped inside an English garden at the height of summer.

"Are you okay?" Ethan asked beside her.

"No. I don't know." The deodorant she'd put on this morning had disappeared, and she felt wet and uncomfortable.

"I can get you some water or something?" Ethan suggested.

The woman at the front desk stood, smiled at them and said in a polite whisper, "Mrs. Curtis?"

"Oh, jeez," Mary muttered.

"We can correct that later," Ethan assured her, then turned to the receptionist and said, "She's right here."

"We'll be taking you back soon," the woman informed them.

Mary saw it all in her mind: an examination table covered in a crisp old English linen sheet with exquisite crocheted trim and white slip-covered booties on the stirrups. She giggled a little hysterically.

"You need to relax," Ethan suggested gently.

"Easy for you to say," Mary uttered as the receptionist held out a clipboard with a flower pen attached.

"If you can just fill out this paperwork."

Sensing that Mary was not about to move, Ethan retrieved the papers for her and placed them in her lap. "I could do this if—"

"No, it's fine."

As Mary filled out the forms, the words blurred

together, and she had to stop and take a deep breath. The front door to the office opened and a woman came in. She was really far along in her pregnancy and looked exhausted. She dropped down in the chair beside Mary's love seat and exhaled heavily. When she spotted Mary, she smiled. "Long way to go yet, huh? When are you due?"

"What? Oh…ah…" It was all she could get out. Her heart pounded furiously in her chest, and waves of nausea were hitting her every few minutes. She needed air, needed to breathe something other than that damn flower smell. Suddenly panicked, she stood, dropped the paperwork on the table and ran out of the office. She spotted a stairwell to her left and ran to the door. Down the stairs she flew, her shirt spotted with sweat, her breathing labored. She heard Ethan behind her, calling her name, but she didn't stop. Once she made it to the lobby, she swung the front door open wide and ran to a grassy spot where a few nurses were eating their lunch.

Breathing heavily, she wanted to collapse on the grass, but instead she started pacing.

"Mary?"

She didn't look at him, didn't stop moving. "I can't do this."

"It's okay." His voice was soothing, and she hated him for his concern. He was the one who'd gotten them into this mess in the first place, damn him. "You don't have to see her," he continued. "Use your own doctor. I just thought it would be—"

"It's not the doctor, Ethan."

"Then what?" When she wouldn't stop pacing, he grabbed her shoulders and held her against him, his tone worried now. "What the hell is wrong?"

His chest felt so strong and she wanted to sink into it, disappear inside of it, but he wouldn't allow her to hide. Easing one hand from her shoulder, he tipped her chin up so she had to look at him.

"Tell me what's going on, Mary."

Miserably, she shook her head. "There is no baby."

"What?"

"No baby, Ethan."

He went white. "Did something happen...that boat ride..."

"No." She stared at him, into those beautiful dark-blue eyes she'd believed for so long were soulless. What a damn mess. This whole thing. "I just wanted my father to be okay."

He still looked confused, but after a moment, re-alization dawned and confusion was swapped for a fiercely accusing gaze. "You were never pregnant?"

Shame coiled in her belly and she shook her head. "No."

"You were never pregnant," he repeated.

"I'm sorry."

Ethan stared at her, his eyes wide in fury. "Yes, you will be," he uttered, his jaw knotted with the force of emotion.

"Ethan."

"I should've known."

"Ethan, please, I—" But her words fell on deaf ears. He had already turned his back on her and was stalking toward his car. Feeling as though she'd just assaulted someone, Mary dropped onto a hard picnic bench and watched his BMW leave the parking lot, tires squealing.

Seven

Twenty minutes later, Ethan entered the crumbling stone gates of Days of Grace Trailer Park. As he drove past the shabby office, muscle memory took hold and his BMW practically steered itself to the curb beside number fifty-three. The one-bedroom mobile home his father had sold just before his death looked as though it had been remodeled, as though someone were really trying to make the place a home, with fresh paint, a nice carport and fenced garden.

"About damn time," Ethan muttered, opening his window a crack before killing the engine.

It was ironic. At sixteen, he couldn't have gotten out of this park fast enough. He'd had big dreams, big plans, and he'd sworn to himself he'd never be back. But here he was, drawn to it like scum to bathroom tile. How was it that he felt infinitely more comfortable parked outside his father's trailer than at his home or office? Why was it that he could breathe here? The air was stale and slightly mildewed; nothing had changed.

He shoved a hand through his hair. He should have expected Mary to lie to him. People were never honest, never to be trusted—including himself. Why the hell hadn't he learned that in all this time? Maybe because he'd thought himself worthy of a family, good enough to make a child with a Harrington.

A large man in his early thirties wearing a baseball hat and ripped jeans came out of the house. When he spotted Ethan, he lifted a hand in a wary hello. Wasn't the first time the guy had seen Ethan parked there, but he'd never called security. No doubt the guy knew he could've handled the situation himself if things got out of control. After all, he was pretty big.

Not looking for any more trouble today, Ethan gunned the engine of his sports car and took off back to his self-made world.

Mondays were usually Mary's best day. She was well rested, coffeed-up and excited to get back to work. Today, however, she felt as though a semi had been driving back and forth over her body all night long. She felt jittery and exhausted at the same time—a wicked combination.

As she walked into the office, her hand shook a little around the double espresso she carried. The first person she saw was Olivia. The startlingly pretty brunette was sitting at the receptionist's desk—something she liked to do before Meg, the receptionist, got there at nine. "Hey there, Miss Kelley," she said in a chipper voice. "You're here early."

"And I'm not the only one."

"I have some phone calls to return. I wanted to get to them early." Olivia's eyes narrowed as she stared hard at Mary. "Did you get any sleep last night?"

Mary sighed, placed her plastic coffee cup on the reception desk. "I think somewhere between four and six I dozed off."

"Work…or—" Olivia hesitated, bit her full bottom lip "—something else?"

For a moment Mary contemplated blowing Olivia's mind with the entire story of Ethan Curtis and her. She just wanted to unburden herself with a girlfriend for a few minutes, emotionally puke and have Olivia figuratively hold her hair back. But for good or bad, the partners of NRR just didn't go there with each other—though Mary wondered if any of them wanted to but were afraid to ruffle the feathers of their business.

"I was working late," Mary said at last. "The captain is very demanding."

Olivia laughed at that, her dark eyes filled with mirth. "He seems like a semidecent guy, despite the millions and the bawdy reputation."

"He is, actually. Did I tell you he's donating all the proceeds from the regatta gala to charity?"

"Would it be uncharitable of me to say that he should?"

It was Mary's turn to laugh, though the sound felt a little forced. "Ivan's all right. Not much going on upstairs, though."

"What a shocker," Olivia said sarcastically. "Inherited wealth?"

"Yes."

Olivia rolled her eyes as she stood up and headed into the kitchen. "Do you want something to eat? I made blueberry muffins, and, not to toot my own horn or anything, but both attorneys offices downstairs came up to ask where that amazing scent was coming from."

Mary's stomach rolled rudely at the thought of food and she headed toward her office. "Maybe later."

"Okay. Oh, hey, Mary?"

"Yeah."

"Mr. Curtis called."

Mary felt a tremor of nervous energy move through her, and suddenly she felt unable to breathe. She hadn't spoken to him since Saturday, since her breakdown in the parking lot.

She poked her head out of her office and gave Olivia a weak smile. "Let me guess. He no longer requires my services."

Wielding a saucepan in one hand and an egg in the other, Olivia looked perplexed. "No. Actually, he asked if you could come by his house today at four-thirty."

"What?" There was no way she had heard Olivia correctly.

"Four-thirty," Olivia repeated. "His house."

"Oh. Okay." Well, sure. Why should he make the

trip to her office to can her when he could do it in person? Her heart pounded so hard in her chest the movement actually hurt.

"Is he an inheritance jerk, too, Mary?"

Mary shook her head. "No, self-made all the way."

Olivia nodded. "I thought so. He always sounds down-to-earth when he calls. That's pretty refreshing."

Mary went back into her office on unsteady legs and dropped into the chair behind her desk. She had to be ready to hear whatever he had to say. There was no doubt he was going to fire her, but what if he wanted to tell her that he was bringing her father back up on charges?

The queasy, dizzy, anxiety-ridden feeling she'd been having since yesterday came back full force, and she put her head down on her desk. Her eyes remained open, and even in the semidarkness of her self-made tent, Mary saw what she'd collapsed upon. The plans for Ethan's nursery—a nursery she hadn't even begun. With a groan she pushed the plans off her desk and into the trash can.

Ethan's housekeeper, Sybil, who Mary had only seen twice before—right before the staff and caterers arrived for a party—answered the door with a vexed expression. "Hello, Ms. Kelley."

"How are you, Sybil?"

The woman released a weighty breath. "Mr. Curtis is in the game room. Let me show you the way."

"Game room?" Mary repeated, following behind the housekeeper. She'd been in Ethan's house several times and she'd never seen a game room.

Glancing over her shoulder, Sybil rolled her eyes. "It's where he goes when he's brooding."

Brooding? Mary tried not to register the shock she felt. First of all, she couldn't imagine Ethan showing anyone his emotions—it just wasn't his style. And second of all, did he know that the woman he paid to run his household talked about him this way? She'd bet not.

They passed the dining room and library, then rounded a curve into a hallway that Mary had never ventured down, or even remembered seeing. When they came to a door, Sybil knocked once, then said to Mary, "Here we are."

"Should I just go in?" Mary asked when she heard no answer.

Sybil nodded. "He's expecting you."

After the woman walked away, Mary gripped the knob and pushed the door open. For a good thirty seconds after entering the large room, Mary thought she'd just stepped into kid's fantasyland, Chucky Cheese. But since she didn't smell pizza or see a large, furry gray animal with whiskers, she knew she must be in Ethan's game room.

The room was a perfect square, with one wall devoted to windows that faced the backyard and lake. It was as if the room was meant to have a screen or drape down the center as a divider, as the right side was completely devoted to every arcade game imaginable. Being a fan of arcades from way back, Mary recognized skeet ball right away and smiled wistfully. There was also basket-ball, air hockey, pound the squirrel, racecar games and many more she saw but wasn't familiar with. Then there was the left side of the room, which couldn't have been more different. It was an office, with a very modern desk and furnishings in charcoal gray and chrome, and in the middle of it sat Ethan, reading the newspaper.

She had an urge to turn around and leave before he saw her, but instead she walked into the room and parked herself beside the foosball table. "Quite a setup you got here."

Still hidden behind the *New York Times*, Ethan muttered a terse, "These are all the things I couldn't afford when I was a kid. I wanted to have them now."

Mary Kelley was no genius, but she sure understood his meaning: he'd had nothing growing up and was hoping to give this to his child. The child he'd thought was coming. The child he'd blackmailed a woman into creating with him.

She got it, and she felt Sybil's pain, and she, too, rolled her eyes. Why couldn't he have been in his library beside the bar drinking like any normal pissed-off male?

She fiddled with the handles on the foosball table. "Do you play?"

"I rarely play games," he said, still masked by the *Times*.

Neither did she, and she was having quite enough of this one. "Listen, you wanted to see me."

"Yeah." The paper came down with a snap, and Mary saw his face for the first time since they'd stood outside the doctor's office and she'd told him the truth. As he stood and walked over to her, he looked like a determined, really angry devil, his black hair slightly spiky and his blue eyes fierce with a need to hurt. He stood close, stared into her eyes and said in a punishing voice, "I have never felt such disgust with anyone in my life."

It was a strange thing—in that moment, spurred on by those words, Mary's nerves suddenly lifted and she was no longer afraid of what he was going to do about her and her father. The only thing she felt in the moment was the need to strike back. "I know that feeling. I had it about a month ago. But we were standing in your office, not your playroom."

His eyes blazed. "What you did was beyond low."

"You're right."

"And you have nothing to say."

"Just this. Need I remind you that you basically forced me into—"

"I never forced you to do anything," he interrupted darkly. "It was your choice—"

"Choice?" she repeated. Was he kidding? "What choice did I have? Tell me that?"

"You could have walked away."

"And left my dad to…what? Go to jail. Never." She glared at him. "But you don't understand that kind of devotion, do you? You've never loved anyone that much— so damn much that you'd make a great sacrifice for them."

His gaze slipped to her belly.

She shook her head, not about to pity him. "No, Mr. Curtis. That wasn't a sacrifice. That was a *need* to be met, a blue-blooded medal to hang around your neck to make you finally feel worthy." His nostrils flared, and he looked dangerously close to exploding, but Mary wouldn't back down. "At least the child would've belonged to the old-money club, right? And maybe you, too, by association? No, it doesn't work that way." She was yelling now, frustrated at him, at herself. "They don't care about association, they only care about blood. Can you get that through your thick skull?"

When she stopped ranting, they both stood there, face-to-face, breathing heavily. His eyes had lost some of their heat and she wondered if she'd finally gotten through to him. But he didn't answer her, not that she expected him to. He had too much pride. Instead, he did as all highly successful business persons do—he went for the jugular.

"You're wondering if I'm going to file charges against your father now, aren't you?" he said evenly, his tone cool.

Mary wasn't about to deny it. "Of course."

"I'm not."

Shock slammed into her and she actually stuttered. "Wh-why?"

With a casual shrug, he left her and wandered over to the air hockey table where he picked up a paddle and examined it. "I've decided to close that chapter."

Mary couldn't contain her relief. Her father didn't have to worry about court or jail ever again. She wasn't about to thank Ethan, but she could feel the tension drain from her body and she sagged against the foosball table.

"But I do want something from you."

Ethan's words sent a shock of alarm through her tired limbs. "What?"

"Mackinac Island."

Oh, no. The trip to the beautiful Michigan island. She was supposed to have planned a party there, served as hostess, but how could that ever happen now? "You want me to recommend someone to take my place, right?" she asked hopefully.

"No."

"You can't be seriously considering—"

He slammed the paddle down and glared at her. "Believe me when I say I would rather bring a python with me on this trip. But your reputation has preceeded you, and I need that party to go off without a problem."

No way. She couldn't. There was too much between them. She shook her head. "No."

"You owe me."

"I owe you nothing," she assured him, straightening up, forcing her legs to hold her weight and not buckle.

His voice dropped and his lips thinned dangerously. "Don't think I wouldn't reconsider opening that paternal book again if I have to."

She shook her head, knowing she was cornered. "You're really good at blackmail."

He lifted one sardonic eyebrow. "I'll protect my business any way I have to."

"Clearly."

"Just as you would, Mary. Mine is administrative business and yours would be personal business."

The idea that they were in any way alike made Mary's blood jump in her veins, but she knew when her choices were few. "This will be our final business endeavor together."

He nodded. "After the last guest has left my party, Ms. Kelley, you and I can pretend that we've never met each other. How's that?"

"Perfect."

Eight

The airport was packed, but Mary maneuvered her way through the crowds with the fierce determination of a woman going to war. According to the itinerary Ethan's secretary had sent over yesterday morning, the plan was to fly to Chicago, then to Pellston Airport in Michigan, then take a cab to the Mackinac Island ferry. After their declarations of mutual disgust for each other, Mary was more than a little shocked that she and Ethan would be traveling together. She could've easily caught her own flight and met him at the hotel, but he'd insisted they make the trip together.

After checking in and making it through security without a body search, Mary headed over to the gate to wait for Ethan. She winced as she slid her carry-on bag off her shoulder and onto one of the hard plastic chairs.

The captain's regatta gala had been successful yesterday, raising a huge amount of money for the Cancer Research Institute, but Mary had forgotten to apply a liberal coat of sunscreen and had managed to give herself quite a sunburn in the process. And the painful moments just kept coming as she spotted Ethan walking toward her, looking anything but the stuffy business traveler in a long-sleeved white shirt and jeans, his large frame and hawklike gaze sending people out of his way without a word from him.

"Ms. Kelley."

Her body instantly betrayed her, her insides jumping with awareness at the sound of his voice. "Mr. Curtis."

"You look well," he said, barely glancing at her striped polo shirt and white cropped jeans.

"Ah...thanks," she muttered with a touch of sarcasm.

Ignoring her tone, Ethan handed her a large envelope. "I've taken the liberty of providing a dossier on the potential clients we're going to see. Their likes, dislikes, food preferences and hobbies."

"Great." Mary couldn't help but notice all the wistful stares Ethan was getting from women walking past. No wonder he could be so arrogant.

"As far as staff to hire for the party goes," he continued brusquely, "I have the name of the best—"

"I've already been in touch with several staff-for-hire agencies on the island," Mary informed him proudly. "I know who I'm going to hire and have already spoken to most of the staff."

The only sign that Ethan might be impressed by her actions was the slight lift of his brows. "You're nothing if not on top of matters, are you?"

Mary couldn't tell if his words were meant as a back-handed compliment or sexual innuendo, but she flashed him a defiant glance regardless. "I'm good at what I do, how about that?"

"Make-believe," he muttered.

"Excuse me?"

"A wife-for-hire agency, Mary?" he stated, as if that said it all. "What is that but pretending to be someone else?"

Mary was silent for a moment, her ire moderated by observation. "You know, I think there's hope for you yet, Curtis."

"I guess it's my turn to say, excuse me?"

"If you can recognize the phony in me, you'll be able to see it in yourself soon enough."

Before Ethan could even react to her words, a woman approached them with a plastered-on smile. "Mr. Curtis, you may board now if you wish. The first-class cabin is ready."

"Thank you."

Ready to follow him, Mary shouldered her bag. "Should I go with you or are we boarding separately?"

A slow grin touched Ethan's mouth, and he nodded at her boarding pass. "Better check your seat assignment first."

Confused, Mary looked down at the ticket in her hand. When she looked back up, Ethan was already on his way toward the gate. How lovely, she mused. While he got pampered with warm towels and chocolate chip cookies in first class, she was going to share a bathroom with forty other passengers in coach.

"What's wrong with your neck?" Ethan asked her once they were aboard the ferry and headed for Mackinac Island.

"It's nothing," she grumbled.

"Nothing my ass," he countered as they walked the length of the deck and back again. "You're moving like a robot."

Ethan was just full of compliments, and she felt like socking him. "It's just a pulled muscle. No big deal."

"You can't meet clients like that."

"It'll pass, okay? Relax."

"How did it happen?"

The wind off the water whipped Mary's hair around her neck as she tried to pick up her pace and shake off the stiffness in her limbs. "Do you really care? Why don't you go inside and have a cup of coffee or a bourbon or something and let me work out these kinks myself."

"I care, okay?" he said dryly. "What the hell happened on the flight?"

She sighed, stopped in her tracks and faced him. "A very large man decided to take a nap on my shoulder, and no amount of pushing and prodding and poking would wake him up. I was stuck in this insanely awkward position for two hours. I wonder if they have a chiropractor on the island."

Ethan stared at her.

"What?" she asked.

"You poked someone?"

She sighed with heavy patience. "It was just with the eraser end of a pencil." But, oh, how she had wanted to do so much more. "Little good it did. It only made him snore harder. And don't even get me started with the lady on my right."

"Did you poke her, too?"

"No, but I thought about it." Mary pressed a hand to her lower back and stretched out her spine a little.

"Wanted to tell you her life story?"

"No. But that would've been okay, life story I could've handled. I can work up a good conversation with a stranger." Her memory of the woman was pretty fresh and a wave of nausea hit her full-on. "No, this was a lack-of-deodorant thing."

Amusement played behind his eyes. "I'm not going to feel sorry for you."

"Who asked you to?" she returned playfully, using every ounce of will to make herself start walking again.

"You belonged in coach."

She gave him a mock bow. "I know that, Mr. Curtis. I'm an employee, and I'm cool with that. In work and in life I know who I am and where I belong, and I fully accept it." She couldn't help herself, the words just fell out. "Unlike other people."

"What's that supposed to mean?" he asked as they reached the railing.

Only wanting to make a quick dig, not have a full-on fight, Mary glanced over the edge to the choppy sea below and tried to deflect. "Look at that water."

Ethan wasn't having any of it. Not that she expected him to. "Don't go all female on me, Mary."

Mary considered. "I don't think that was as much female as it was passive-aggressive."

"Whatever it was, just say what you've got to say," he said impatiently.

She exhaled and turned to face him. "This is just a thought, but maybe if you'd stop trying to be something you're not, you could actually enjoy your success. Maybe you wouldn't have to resort to blackmailing people into doing what you want. They might come willingly."

He grinned then, his gaze moving lazily over her. "If I remember correctly you came very willingly."

"Don't be crude."

He shrugged, looking like a bad little boy. "I was talking about coming to work for me. But I like where your dirty mind goes, Ms. Kelley."

"If you remember correctly, working for you was something I fought tooth and nail."

"I remember you giving in pretty quickly, actually, as though you wanted to be as close to me as I wanted to be to you."

Were they always going to end up here? Mary wondered. Bantering back and forth, both wanting to outsmart and outplay the other. And to what end…? It was only a few more days. "All I'm saying is that if you'd accept who you are and where you came from maybe you could be happy."

"Who says I want to be happy?"

"Everyone's looking for happiness, in some form or another."

"Not me."

She ignored him. "The problem is you're going about it the wrong way."

He gave his back to the water and lounged against the railing. "And you know the way to true happiness, Mary?"

No, but... "I'm trying. I'm sure as hell trying." She cocked her head to the left to look at the island as it came into view and felt a searing pain in her neck. She groaned.

Ethan cursed softly. "You can hardly turn your head."

"I'm fine. Nothing that a hot shower and a massage won't cure."

He touched her shoulder. "You know, I'd offer to help you with both of those forms of physical therapy, but—"

"But you pretty much hate me right now," she answered, trying to ignore the heat from his hand.

"Nope, that logic doesn't matter so much for a guy."

She tried to look shocked, but laughter quickly bubbled in her throat. "Okay, so what is it, then? You can't help me take a shower because *I* can't stand *you*?"

He considered this for about two seconds. "Ah...no. A guy can get past that sad fact, too."

She laughed again.

His voice lowered to a sexy timbre. "And you don't hate me, Mary."

His arrogance and unflinching confidence could be a real pain in the ass sometimes, especially when his assumptions were right on target. "Well, so what is it, then? Don't tell me you won't assist my shower time out of some misplaced sense of duty."

"No." He faced the coming island and looked pensive. "I'm just afraid it might make me happy, and as I said, I'm not looking for that."

The Birches was an authentic 1890s Queen Anne Victorian, and when Mary first stepped inside the entryway, she thought she'd fallen asleep and woken up in a dream—or at the very least a movie. The nine-bedroom, six-bath original Victorian had beautifully restored hardwood floors, luscious paneled ceilings, three fireplaces, extensive property, and from the wraparound porch, a panoramic view of the Straits of Mackinac, Round Island, Mackinac Bridge and the Grand Hotel.

She couldn't even imagine how much it cost to rent such a place. Harold, the real estate agent Ethan had used for their trip, gestured gleefully around himself. "Here we are, Mr. Curtis. Beautiful home, isn't it."

"Nice," Ethan said unenthusiastically as he checked his Blackberry.

Poor Harold looked so dejected that Mary felt compelled to offer up her best smile. "Well, I think it's lovely."

He gave her a grateful look. "It was rumored that Rudolph Valentino and Nita Naldi stayed here at one time."

"Really?"

"Right after *Blood and Sand*."

"Wasn't Valentino married?"

Harold nodded and said conspiratorially, "To two women, actually. He hadn't yet divorced the other."

"I hate silent films," Ethan muttered, checking his e-mail.

Mary rolled her eyes at Harold. "So, where am I staying?"

Before Harold could even open his mouth, Ethan jumped in with, "I arranged for you to have the house next door."

"What?" Mary looked from Ethan to Harold and back again. "A whole house? Come on, Curtis. I thought I'd just get a hotel room close by."

Harold cleared his throat, his neck growing as red as a ripe tomato as he tried to make eye contact with Ethan. "Actually, sir, we had an emergency, and the family staying there had to remain on. But," he said, brightening, "we have a lovely suite for Ms. Kelley across town at the Mackinac Inn."

"That will be fine," Mary said pleasantly, but she could feel Ethan already shaking his head.

"No, it won't," he informed her. "We have work to do, and you need to be here. Across town..." he said in a tone that sounded as though she were going to stay somewhere in Paris. "You can't even get anywhere around here without a horse or a bicycle. It'll take forever."

"Sir," Harold attempted deferentially. "I assure you that on an island so small, transportation is quick and very easy to—"

Ethan ignored him, his gaze hard and fixated on Mary. "You'll stay with me."

She was getting awfully tired of Ethan Curtis's demands. "No way."

"This house is large enough for ten people," he said.

"Again. No way."

He scowled. "You're acting like a child."

"I'm acting like a professional. Forget for a moment how it looks and feels to me, but how would it look to your clients if the woman you hired is also staying in the home you rented?"

He shrugged. "Practical."

"No." She lowered her voice as Harold pretended to inspect a wall sconce. "Like she's also being hired for another purpose."

They stared at each other, a haze of lust blanketing Ethan's expression. Mary felt helpless, weak for a moment as a quick shiver shot through her. She tried to control the sudden pounding of her heart, until finally the look on Ethan's face dissolved.

"You're being paranoid," he said roughly. "This is business. I'll have offices here and so will you. You can take the entire second floor and I'll remain down here. Barring business, we never have to see each other."

Mary sighed. She didn't want to argue the point anymore, and poor, miserable Harold had all but tried to crawl up inside the wall sconce and disappear. She would figure out her situation on her own. "All right, Harold. Can you show me upstairs?"

The man released a weary breath and started up the

stairs. "There are some beautiful rooms to choose from and incredible views of the water."

Before she followed him, Ethan put his hand on her shoulder. "Make sure you get that shower. You're still walking like a robot." Then he leaned in, whispered in her ear, "And if you need any help…"

Yes, she'd have to find another arrangement as soon as possible. Just the warmth of Ethan's hand made her want to curl into him, nuzzle his neck and remove his shirt, but she detached herself anyway, and followed the agent up the stairs. "Hey, Harold, how old is this house did you say?"

"It was built in 1891, but everything's been updated for your convenience."

"Like the plumbing?"

"Of course."

"And locks on the doors?"

"Every one of them, miss."

She heard Ethan chuckle below, and the sound shot to every nerve, every muscle, every spot that ached for his touch.

Nine

Good thing he'd checked the house's extensive property, or he might not have found her.

The historic barn was only about sixty feet from the main house and featured three horse stalls, food storage areas, tack room, carriage storage room, hay room and small living quarters upstairs. That last bit of information had tipped Ethan off when Mary hadn't come downstairs after a shower and change.

Ethan scowled at her. "You're the most stubborn person I have ever met."

Wearing a white terry cloth robe that showed absolutely nothing except for her feet and about an inch of neck, Mary stood at the barn door, blocking his entrance. "Thank you."

"That agent told you about this place, didn't he?"

"His name is Harold."

"Yeah, well, Harold clearly isn't looking for a good word from me to his boss."

"Don't take it out on Harold," Mary said, trying to force her hair into some type of halo style on top of her head with a couple of pins. She looked like a damn angel and Ethan had an intense urge to be saved.

"Are you going to show me around?" Ethan asked wryly.

Defiance glimmered in her pale-blue eyes, but she took a step back and allowed him to pass. "Do you promise to be good?"

"Are you kidding? Don't you know me at all?"

She laughed, a soft, throaty sound that made him think of the nights they'd shared, the sound that would erupt from her throat every time she climaxed. Blood thrummed in his temples as he followed her past the neat tack room and unused stalls, up the short set of stairs to the loft. There he took one look around and sniffed derisively. "This place is microscopic and—"

"And perfect for one person," Mary finished for him.

The walk upstairs had caused the ties on her robe to loosen, and the lapels were gaping slightly—just enough for him to see a curve of one pale breast. His mouth watered, and he tore his gaze away and glared at the bed. Warm light infused the room, kissing the pale-blue coverlet. It was a soft space, and he felt way too hard to belong there.

"I think it's the best of both worlds," Mary said, mistaking his tense jaw and piercing gaze for annoyance instead of desire. "Seeing how we feel about each other."

How they felt about each other. The idea made Ethan want to laugh. One minute he wanted to shake her, and the next he wanted to kiss her. What he did know was that he didn't want to hate her—not anymore—didn't want to feel pissed off at her. "I don't like this."

She sighed. "We're close enough to work and far enough not to…"

"Not to what?" he asked, wondering how long it would take him to remove that robe. Two seconds? Five? Or maybe he'd want to do it slowly, just a shoulder first. Or maybe he's start at her feet, work his way up to her calves, thighs… "Fall into bed again?"

Pink suddenly stained her cheeks, and she moistened her bottom lip with her tongue. "Something like that."

"It seems like a whole lot of trouble for nothing."

Her chin lifted. "I seem to remember you comparing me to a python. Aren't you glad that the python isn't living upstairs?"

He didn't answer. He walked over to the window and stared out. "There's no view of the water from here."

She sniffed. "I think I'll live."

"You'll be up here day and night…alone."

"Why do you care, Curtis?"

"I don't," he said through gritted teeth. He didn't want to.

"Business won't suffer," she assured him. "I can be up at the house in under five minutes."

If he didn't get the hell out of here right now, he was

going to find out the answer to that robe question of his, and then Mary Kelley would have the upper hand on him and he couldn't have that. He turned away from the window and stalked across the tiny space. "Thirty will be fine."

She studied him, her brows slightly knitted. "What's the plan for the rest of the day?"

"We have a few hours of good light left. Maybe… scouting a location for the party?"

She looked surprised. "I would've thought you'd want it at the house."

"I'm not sure what I want," he said tightly. "I'd like some options."

Her expression now impenetrable, she nodded. "All right. Well, I'm finally going to take that shower I've been looking forward to since this morning, and I'll meet you out front in thirty minutes."

The thought of Mary naked under a waterfall of hot water had Ethan sucking in oxygen, but not enough: his lungs constricted with pain. *She* was going to take off that robe, not him. *She* was going to touch her skin, not him. Women could be masters at torture, but this woman had it down to a science. His gaze shot to the small bathroom to his right. So white and clean and sweet.

His entire body charged with electricity, Ethan turned away and headed back down the stairs.

"We could always walk into town," Mary suggested as she sat in the back of a small black buggy, outside the gates of their rental house.

Glaring at the docile horse, Ethan slowly shook his head. "Nope."

The carriage driver looked straight ahead, smart enough not to get involved, but Mary wasn't afraid to incur the wrath of Ethan Curtis. The late-afternoon sun was starting to mellow into a stunning orangish pink and if they didn't get a move on they'd be scouting locations for the party in the dark.

"Are you going to climb up here or not?" Mary asked as she watched Ethan sidle up to the chestnut mare.

"Just give me a minute," he uttered crossly, reaching out to stroke the animal's mane as he whispered something to her Mary couldn't hear.

When he finally climbed into the buggy and dropped down beside Mary, she was curious as hell. "So, what's up with you and Shirley?"

"It was personal."

The driver clicked his tongue a few times and they were off down the dirt road. "Did you ask for her hand in marriage?" Mary asked, grinning. "Oops, sorry, I mean her hoof?"

"We were just having a little discussion, that's all."

"About?"

"Manners."

Mary laughed. "Did you have a drink before we left the house?"

Ethan crossed his arms over his chest and reclined back in his seat. "I don't want her throwing us, that's all."

"The driver said she's as docile as they come."

"That's what they'd like you to believe," he muttered dryly.

"They?"

"The driver and…Shirley."

Again she laughed. "What in the world are you talking about?"

"I'm not all that into horses, okay?"

"Oh, c'mon. Everyone loves horses. How could you not like horses? It's un-American."

"Okay, they don't like me," he grumbled.

"You need therapy," she said as they passed another horse and buggy on their way to town. The air had chilled considerably since their arrival, and Mary scooted just a little closer to Ethan. "All right, I'm listening. Tell me the whole sad story."

"What story?"

"Give me a break." She inched even closer to him so their legs were touching. "You've got to be freaked out for a reason—what's the story?"

On a curse, Ethan lifted his arm, dropped it around her shoulders. "I was ten. It was Sammy Bishop's birthday party and this sweet and supposedly ancient horse named Izabo was there giving rides to all the kids. With everyone else, she walked slower than a turtle, it was almost funny, the parents were actually referring to her IzaSlow. But as soon as *I* got on her back it was Kentucky Derby time." He lifted up his left forearm. "I fell and broke my arm in three places."

Mary let her head relax against his arm, knowing full well how totally inappropriate they were both being.

"That was a fluke thing and it happened one time. You can't hold that against—"

"Then when I was fourteen," he said as the buggy took a deep hole and they bumped against each other. "My girlfriend dragged me to the circus. Everything was fine until the horse and rider came out. Jezebel the Great freaked out halfway through her routine and stormed the stands."

"No way."

"Oh, yeah. And who do you think she headed straight for?"

"Okay, I'm beginning to see a pattern," Mary said, laughing, the scent of lake water heavy in the air.

"I broke two ribs."

Without thinking, Mary reached over and ran her fingers down the length of his rib cage only stopping when she heard his sharp intake of breath. "Feel fine to me."

His heavy-lidded gaze held hers. "Well sure, they've healed now."

It was a good thing that the driver stopped then, or Mary believed Ethan might've leaned in and kissed her, and she also believed she would have kissed him back. They got out in front of a fudge shop and started walking up Main Street, which had a similar architectural feel to New Orleans, though the scents in the air were totally different. As they passed shops, restaurants and art galleries, Mary missed Ethan's arm around her, the strength of him, and she silently wished he'd take her hand, lace her fingers with his.

"You know what?" she said as they walked to the

west end of downtown where the pedestrians were fewer. "I don't think it's really about the horses not liking you."

"Oh, this should be interesting."

"I think it's a sex thing."

A dark brow lifted over one eye. "Come again?"

"Izabo, Jezebel and Shirley," she pointed out. "It's a female thing. Females have this reaction to you."

Ethan processed this for a brief moment, then burst out laughing. "How the hell did I get mixed up with you?"

She tossed him a taunting smirk. "Do you really want me to answer that?"

They continued down the street, passing a lovely old church, a library and a quaint soda shop—which Mary considered for the party, then quickly deemed too informal. Several blocks down, closer to the water, Ethan pointed to a lovely, small, intimate hotel called the Miran Inn. "What do you think of this place?"

Cocking her head to one side, Mary looked the inn up and down. "It's beautiful, but hotels have been done to death. Not to mention the fact that three of the ten potential clients we're throwing this party for own inns on the island."

"Right."

"Don't you want something interesting and surprising? Something the spouses actually want to come to?"

"Yes."

Mary had been contemplating something since they'd arrived here, and she wanted to pull it out now. "Let's go." Grabbing his hand, she tugged, urging him to follow her.

"Where?"

"Just follow me."

Mary led him off the main street and down a short hill to a bluff, onto the sandy beach. Overhead the gulls were calling on each other to share their fish, and several tourists were taking pictures of a beautiful lighthouse in the distance. Releasing his hand, Mary walked down to the water's edge and lifted her hands to the fading sun. "Perfect," she called, turning back to face him. "A barbecue on the beach. Intimate, casual, great food— and no horses involved."

Ethan glanced around, then slowly nodded. "I like it."

"Great," she said excitedly. It would be her first beachside barbeque and she was going to make it a day to remember.

Ethan came to stand beside her, a look of admiration in his eyes. "I have to admit, you're great at what you do, you know that?"

Her hair whipped around her face. "Thank you."

He tucked one thick blond strand behind her ear, then let his thumb retreat across her cheek. "Very smart, very intuitive. There's just one problem."

Her expression froze. "What's that?"

"You're too beautiful for your own good. A man couldn't get you out of his mind no matter how pissed off he was."

"Don't you mean 'is'?" He was too close. She could feel the heat off his body, and there was no denying the desire in his eyes.

His fingers left her cheek and slid down her neck,

pausing at her collarbone. He didn't move for a moment, and his face looked rigid, as if he was contemplating what he'd just done. Then he dropped his hand and shook his head helplessly. "I'm sorry. I...I have to get back."

Electricity was shooting through Mary's body like fireworks, but she fought for control and nodded once. "Of course."

"I have a dinner meeting."

"And I have a guest list to study."

They walked side by side, up the bluff and back to Main Street to catch a cab.

"You'll be all right on your own tonight?" Ethan asked as one pulled up in front of them.

Mary climbed into the cab and this time sat close to the door. "Have been for the past twenty-some years," she uttered softly.

"What was that?" Ethan asked, not having heard her muffled answer.

She released a heavy sigh. "I said, I'll be just fine."

At night on Mackinac Island something wonderful happens. As the sun sets slowly and exquisitely against the water, the sounds of nature hum rhythmically through an invisible speaker. Forget expensive sound machines to soothe you to sleep, opening a window and stretching out on the bed was all Mary needed for a relaxing evening.

Well, that and some food...and a glass of wine.

With several pillows behind her head, Mary grabbed the delivery menus she'd garnered from the buggy driver and flipped through them. Beside her on the table was the guest list she now knew backward and forward, and she was ready to chill out. She paused on the page of an Italian menu that sounded pretty good and grabbed her cell phone off the bedside table. But before she had completed dialing the number, there was a sharp rap on the door downstairs.

She glanced at the clock. Would Ethan really be done with his dinner meeting by eight-thirty? Maybe it was Harold, come to discuss the history of each barn stall and let her know that Man O' War once sired a foal here. Laughing at her idiocy, Mary loped down the stairs and hauled back the barn door.

Ethan Curtis leaned against the door frame looking incredibly handsome in jeans and a black long-sleeved T-shirt, his sharp jaw dusted with stubble.

"Everything okay?" Mary asked, amusement in her voice.

"Yeah," he began, then took it back. "Well, no. There's a problem up at the main house."

"Seriously? What is it? Did a pipe burst or something? These older houses are notorious for plumbing problems no matter how new the pipes..."

"No. It's not the pipes."

"Fireplace smoking?"

"No."

She just loved it when he was forthcoming. "Well, what is it? Can't figure out which bed to sleep in?"

His eyes darkened. "Something like that."

Instinctively she took a step back, but only managed

to knock her heel against a bucket and feel like a clumsy oaf. "How did your meeting go?"

"Good, fine, boring," he said, his gaze moving over her. "They're looking forward to the barbecue."

Mary nodded, her mouth suddenly numb. If he would only just grab her, make this easy on both of them.

"Oh…" Ethan pulled a plastic bag from behind his back and handed it to her. "I thought if you hadn't eaten…"

"Thanks. I was just about to order something."

"Now you don't have to."

Many different ways of asking, "Would you like to share this with me?" popped into Mary's head, but she rejected all of them. After all, he'd just come from dinner with clients. "Well, I'm going to go and enjoy this."

"Okay." He didn't move.

She raised a brow at him and tried to apply a professional tone. "Do we need to discuss anything or can it wait until morning?"

He walked past her into the barn, his hand brushing over hers as he took the takeout bag from her. "You know what? I don't think it can wait."

Ten

Ethan hadn't been kidding about the dinner he'd just had with two potential clients. The food had been ordinary, the conversation bland, and somewhere around the caprese salad, he'd hoped for a fire in the kitchen so an immediate evacuation would send him back to The Birches.

Mary followed him up the stairs to the loft, her tone warily playful. "Something tells me that inviting you in may turn out to be dangerous."

"Perceptive," he said over his shoulder.

"So if you come in, can we talk about the menu?"

"I'm already in, but sure." At the moment, Ethan could care less about the menu for the barbecue. He was in Mary's room, surrounded by moonlight and the subtle soapy scent of her. Hell, at this moment, he couldn't care less about work, clients or good manners.

Her back to the wall, Mary gestured around the room. "Not many places to sit."

Ethan glanced at the bed, then back at her. "No."

Looking suddenly self-conscious in her pink tank top and matching boy shorts, Mary eyed the bathroom door. "I should throw on a robe or something."

"Don't go to any trouble for me."

"I think I'm already in trouble," she muttered, walking over to the bedside table and grabbing a yellow legal pad. "So, the caterer thinks—and I agree with her—that an all-American barbecue would be best. Ribs, burgers, barbecued chicken, sweet-potato fries, salads, pecan and apple pies. And maybe some local flavors like fresh cherried whitefish."

Didn't she get it? Ethan wondered, dropping the takeout bag on the window seat. She could move across the room, across the yard or all the way across the island and it wouldn't make a damn bit of difference. He'd still come for her, he'd still seek her out—his need for her was that strong.

"Some of the local menu items are interesting," she continued, her breathing slightly labored as she spoke, as though she'd just ran the loft stairs. "We could have a tasting if you'd like."

"I'd like that."

His tone and meaning were clear as the night sky outside the window, and Mary shook her head, her pale-blue eyes uneasy. "We can't."

"We won't."

Mary's skin suddenly felt very tight, as if she'd spent weeks in the sun without protection, and she tossed him a look that said, "Yeah, right." They were leading up to something here, something inevitable, proven even further by the fact that Ethan was walking toward her right now.

"I swear I won't even go near the bed," he said. Ethan brought his hands up and cupped her face, the warmth of his skin melting all of her resolve in an instant. She leaned toward him as he dipped his head and covered her mouth in a series of soul-crashing kisses.

He was so warm as his mouth and his chest brushed teasingly against her breasts that Mary's knees nearly buckled, and she wrapped her arms around Ethan's neck for support. His body responding at once, Ethan groaned at the nearness and gently pressed her back against the wall, cradling her neck in his hand as he explored her mouth with teasing, drifting kisses until she opened for him, gave him a sweep of her tongue.

Mary tried to keep her head, tried to recall what they had said to each other just the other day, the rotten things they'd said, but each thought faded away like fog in the sun. She felt his hand delve under her shirt, felt his palm on her stomach and sucked air through her teeth, her back arching as she silently begged him to explore higher.

Pressing closer to her, Ethan reached around her with his free hand and unhooked her bra, setting her free while holding her captive with his mouth. Mary could hardly remain still. Her skin itched to be touched, and when his hand raked up her torso and covered one full breast, when he slowly rolled the hard peak between his thumb and forefinger, she cried out into his mouth.

The sound had Ethan backing off for a moment, his hungry gaze fixated on her. Thinking he was about to scoop her up and deposit her on the bed, Mary shook her head wearily. "You swore you wouldn't—"

"Go near the bed," he finished for her. "And I'm not."

"Then…what are you—"

She never finished the sentence as Ethan lifted her shirt over her head and artfully cast aside her lacy bra. She stared at him, at his face, marveled at the need there as the lower half of her contracted and hummed.

"I wasn't hungry until now," he mumbled, dipping his head and nuzzling up one pale slope until he found the sustenance he required. His tongue circled her taut nipple slowly, desperately slowly, and Mary could only arch her back again and again, thrusting herself in and out of his mouth until finally he took her between his lips and tongue and suckled deep and hard.

"Oh, Ethan," she whispered breathlessly, her knees weak and the small curve at the top of her inner thigh wet with desire.

Ethan drank from her, his tongue flicking the swollen bud back and forth until her hips began to move, to thrust forward and back looking for his hand, his mouth, something to ease the building tension within her—or maybe to build it even further. His mouth moved down, gently sinking his teeth into her belly and hip bones as his hands brought her shorts and underwear to her ankles, then off completely.

Mary felt a moment of embarrassment, being fully naked in front of him, standing there in slashes of moonlight, her breasts free, one nipple still wet from his mouth, and the lower half of her open and ready for whatever he was willing to give.

On his knees, Ethan spared her one wicked, hungry glance before taking what he wanted. "Open your legs," he said, his warm breath so close to her sensitive flesh that Mary found it almost impossible to hold on to the climax she felt building just inches from his mouth.

She widened her stance and let her eyelids drift closed, tried to calm her body, ease the electric charges running through at a sprint, but when he spread the soft folds back with his thumbs, she couldn't control anything anymore. When he lapped at her with his tongue, Mary groaned and pressed herself against him. When he suckled and nuzzled the tender bud beneath, she cried out his name, "Ethan, please, I can't…"

She had no idea what she couldn't do, if it was hold on to her climax or give in to him or both, her mind was adrift on a sea of all-consuming pleasure. Then his hands came around to her buttocks, squeezing the flesh as he found his rhythm, his tongue flicking the tiny nub over and over as Mary rocked her hips.

"I can't hold on…" she uttered, her limbs weak, her body charged with electricity as the waves crashed and she stiffened—every part of her but her hips. She cried out and rocked wildly against his mouth, shuddering, giving in to release.

Mary sagged against the wall, her hips still bucking,

but slowly now as she sucked air through her teeth and tried to force back rational thought to her mind. When Ethan left her to stand, she felt slightly cold, but he took her in his arms and held her against him, his heart thundering so powerfully she could feel it against her chest. More than anything, she wanted him to take her to the bed, rise up over her and sink down between her legs. For a moment she thought about pushing him back onto the bed and straddling him, taking what she wanted as he had just taken from her.

But she never got the chance. She was still shaking from head to toe when Ethan moved away from her. He walked into the bathroom and came back with her robe, which he gently placed around her. Then he found her gaze and uttered a gentle, "I'll go."

"You don't have to," she said boldly, not really giving a damn that she sounded needful and not the littlest bit desperate.

He ran a hand through his hair and looked uncomfortable, shaken…or was that angry? She couldn't tell. "I really do."

She quickly slipped her arms through the holes in the robe, then nodded at Ethan. What the hell else could she do? "So, tomorrow…"

"Ten. On the porch." It was all he said before heading down the stairs and out of the barn.

Mary went to the window, watched him walk across the yard, her knees still trembling with aftershocks of her climax, the relaxing sounds of nature now replaced by the hum in her body—the need for more. If she'd had her way—and Ethan could've handled it, if he had the same unrelenting desire that she felt for him—he'd be poised above her right now, spreading her legs again, but this time for an entirely different purpose.

The image caused such intense shots of electricity to run through her body that she had to sit down on the edge of the bed.

Mary left City Hall with permits for the party and walked through town, hoping to arrive back at Ethan's place just before their scheduled meeting time. She'd been up since five that morning, planning the party and keeping her mind focused on Ethan's business goals as well as her own—basically anything except what had happened last night. As she passed Ticklers Fudge Shoppe, her cell phone rang, making several passersby frown at the disturbance.

She flipped open the phone and pressed it to her ear. "Hello?"

"Hey, it's Tess," came the voice of her partner. "And Olivia," chirped the other. "We're conferencing you."

Mary had been on several trips, business and otherwise over the past five years and had rarely missed hearing from her partners. This morning, however, she felt incredibly comforted by the sound of their voices. "Hey, there. How are things back home?"

"Same old, same old," Olivia informed her. "And how is Mackinac Island? Insanely beautiful and romantic?"

"She's not there for romance, Olivia," Tess said, a bite of irritation in her tone.

"Of course she's not. I just meant—"

"It's lovely," Mary said with a laugh, passing the small church that was about three-quarters of a mile from The Birches, making her heart jump nervously at the thought of seeing Ethan in a few minutes. "Lovely and incredibly picturesque."

"Well, in that case," Tess began, her business tone smartly in place. "Make sure you take plenty of pictures for our book."

"I will," Mary promised. "So, besides checking on the beauty of the island, anything you two want to discuss—anything going on I should know about?"

"Well," Olivia said excitedly. "We wanted to tell you that we've gotten three calls from men who were at Mr. Curtis's party last week. Two older gentlemen whose wives have passed and who have no idea how to run a social or home life. By the way, they were very impressed with what you did and are desperate to hold similar events for their companies. One of them is selling his home and moving to a waterfront estate— he's terrified because his wife handled all of that type of detail."

"Sounds right up our alley," Mary said, very pleased that her efforts had brought NRR several more clients. "And what about the third?"

Olivia snorted. "One very arrogant thirty-something trust-fund baby."

"Oh, your favorite," Mary said, grinning.

"And Tess palmed him off on me," Olivia added sourly. Mary heard Tess groan in frustration, as though she'd had this conversation ten times already. "He needs your culinary skills."

The wind picked up around Mary, bringing the scent of overcast morning and lake water to her nostrils. "What's his name?"

"Mac Valentine," Olivia told her.

Mary racked her brain for a mental picture of him, then recalled the handsome man Ethan had introduced to her at the first party. Oh, yes. Everything Olivia despised. Family money, total playboy, gorgeous and knew it.

Olivia sighed. "It'll be fine. Just like the rest of you, I refuse to get sucked in by clients. Do my job and do it well, and that's it."

As she walked down the country lane, Mary spotted her "just a client" on the porch of the old Victorian home, mug in hand, and felt a shiver of awareness move through her. If the girls only knew what a mess she'd gotten herself into over this particular client, they'd probably kick her out of the business. "Got to go, ladies."

"Oh, one more thing," Tess said quickly. "Your grandmother has called here three times since you've been gone."

"Why didn't she try my cell?"

"She said she misplaced the number, so I gave it to her again. She sounded pretty agitated."

That's what came from not checking her messages at home or at the office. "She always sounds that way. Agitated is normal. Now if you said she sounded blissful or pleased, I'd be worried."

Both women laughed.

"Thanks for the call. I'll talk to you both later." Mary dropped her phone into her purse and walked through the yard toward Ethan. A scant bit of sunlight had broken through the clouds and was taking up residence on the porch, playing with the coffee-brown highlights in Ethan's dark hair. He looked serious and sexy, dressed in all black, the features in his face all angles and sharpness with a tigerlike stare. Her heart in her throat, Mary climbed the porch steps and sat beside him on the bench.

"Taking a walk?" he asked, his tone rigid.

"Just back from City Hall and a meeting with the caterer and waitstaff. They're really thrilled with the barbecue." She tried to ignore the way his gaze moved over her in a possessive, animal-like way. "The tasting you requested is today at one-thirty. If that works with your schedule."

He shook his head. "I don't need a tasting. I trust your instincts."

"Last night you said—"

"I wasn't talking about food last night, Mary."

His words stunned her, and his reckless, impenetrable gaze had heat coiling through her. Since he had wanted so much to avoid talking about their situation last night, she'd thought to grant him the same courtesy today, but he looked anything but calm, cool and forgetful, so she lifted her chin and said, "Do we need to discuss what happened last night?"

"Only if you want to continue where we left off," he said with a bluntness that matched hers.

Mary's nerves dropped away completely, and the no-

nonsense businesswoman with an attitude took over. She had been open to him in more ways than one last night, and he was the one who'd walked away. She didn't want to play games anymore, back and forth and want and don't want—it was b.s. "All I want right now is to do my job. The best damn job anyone's ever seen."

His eyes glittered with ire. "I have no doubt you'll succeed in that."

"And after I've finished this job, I want to leave here. I want to go back home and…" She paused, unable to finish her sentence. Why couldn't she finish that sentence?

"And?" he asked.

She would go back home and work as she always had, with no more interruptions or complications. No doubt, just like Ethan.

The frustration in her tone was obvious. "Would you like the tasting or should I cancel it?"

"I'll be there. One-thirty, right?"

She nodded and stood. "It's going to be at Fanfare restaurant in town, right on Main Street. Easy to find." She headed off toward the barn. Another shower sounded good, thirty minutes under hot water to clear her head and retune her attitude.

"I'll come by the barn to pick you up at one," Ethan called after her, making Mary stop in her tracks and whirl around to face him. "We can walk this time. No more horses."

"We?" she uttered hoarsely. "No, I don't need to be there. The staff will write down everything you like and don't like and report back to—"

"I want you there," he said, reclining on the bench, looking like the CEO of the world. "And at least until the end of the barbecue tomorrow, you work for me."

Without realizing it, the catering staff at Fanfare had romanticized an event that should have been nothing more than a business meeting. On the walk over, Mary had imagined that she and Ethan would stand at one of the prep stations in the restaurant's kitchen and sample a variety of dishes, writing down their thoughts on a piece of scratch paper in between bites, then they would thank the staff for their service and get out of there. Later, Mary would call the head chef and discuss what worked for the client and what didn't.

This was normally how it was done on the mainland, but clearly things were taken to an entirely different level on Mackinac Island when a hotshot millionaire was throwing a party for the island's upper crust.

On the restaurant's cozy deck overlooking the lake, a table had been dressed with exquisite white linens, funky blue plates, silver, wineglasses and frosted beer glasses.

"I feel like I should've worn a tie," Ethan said with a sardonic grin as he was seated at the table.

"Me, too," replied Mary.

"No. You look too good in that dress."

She smiled.

Taking in the elaborate scene before him, Ethan raised one dark brow at her. "Are you sure they're going to be able to pull off a beach barbecue?"

She tossed him a mock frown as the waitstaff poured

samples of wine and beer. "Are you questioning my abilities, Mr. Curtis?"

Lifting a mug, he gave her a silent toast. "I'd be a fool."

"Damn right." In spite of herself, she grinned at him as several dishes were set before them. "How about we taste and see?"

Amusement glittered in his eyes at the unintended double meaning in her words. "You make me crazy, you know that?"

"Right back at ya, Curtis."

Each item the staff laid before them was whimsical and over-the-moon delicious. Grilled whitefish and chips wrapped in paper, sweet-potato fries with a killer dipping sauce, salads, pork, chicken, desserts. And they sampled it all, along with fresh-squeezed lemonade, interesting wines and rich beer.

At long last, Ethan sat back in his chair and sighed. "I approve."

Mary laughed as she tried to get up from the table. "I thought you might."

After thanking the staff, they walked back to The Birches, thankful for the exercise as they were both stuffed to the gills. Several times, Ethan reached out to take Mary's hand, then stopped himself. They weren't a couple. Sure, there was an intense sexual attraction between them, unfinished business that he wanted to see to, taste again—damn, he couldn't get last night out of his head—but he was kidding himself if he thought they'd just been on a date, that they were starting a romantic relationship.

Once they were in the driveway, Ethan followed her to the barn and paused at the door. Mary's cheeks were flushed and she looked relaxed and satisfied with their day. She took off her sandals and stood there in her virginal white sundress, the same need he'd seen last night in her eyes—the same need that was no doubt echoed in his.

"I think I'm a little tipsy," she said, opening the door.

"There's nothing wrong with that."

She laughed. "It's three o'clock in the afternoon."

"Are you going to be operating any heavy farm machinery this afternoon?"

"No."

"Then you're fine."

"Thanks for walking me to my door, so to speak, but I'm good from here."

Cursing, he leaned against the door frame, feeling frustrated and dense. "Why the hell are we fighting this?"

She shrugged. "I don't think I am."

"Fine. Why am I fighting this?"

"Because you hate me?"

"No, I don't think that's true anymore." He reached out and took her hand. "In fact I don't think that was ever true. I think it's quite the opposite and that's why I'm fighting it." He took her other hand and pressed them behind her back, leaned in and kissed her gently, sensually on the mouth. "Come on," he uttered, leading her inside.

"No more games, Ethan," she said, her tone fragile for the first time since they'd met.

"No." He shook his head, led her up the stairs, but halfway there his need to kiss her, taste her, had him pulling her into his arms.

"The bed…" she uttered hoarsely.

Ethan nuzzled her neck, the curve of her ear, making her moan. "We'll get there."

Eleven

Somehow they stumbled up the stairs, clothes marking their way like Hansel and Gretel's breadcrumbs. Mary clung to Ethan like a rag doll, covering his mouth and neck with hungry kisses as he led them into the bedroom and onto the down comforter. She only knew her shirt and bra were off when her warm back met the cool, soft down and when Ethan lowered himself on top of her, the hair on his chest tickling her, and the delicious, hot weight of him making her heart jump with excitement.

Her skin felt as if it was on fire, itchy, needy, and she couldn't get him to touch her everywhere at once, so she had to force herself to relax as he lazily kissed her throat and breasts, nuzzling one nipple with his nose and cheek until Mary could hardly stand the torture and he finally gave in and suckled her deep into his mouth, tugging at the flesh with his teeth. She was in a dream—she had to be—but she didn't want to be. No matter how she and Ethan had begun, there was real, honest-to-goodness affection here. She was really falling hard for him, and she desperately wanted him to make love to her.

He found her mouth again, and as his hands took over, kneading the undersides of her breasts, cupping them, feeling their weight, slowly circling the firm peaks with his thumbs, Mary moaned, plunging her fingers into his thick hair.

His jeans and the small scrap of cotton at her hips were all that separated them, and Mary couldn't stand it. With deft fingers, she flicked the button and slid down his zipper, her hand delving inside to feel him, hold him, make him as insane with desire as she was.

Ethan sucked in a breath as her fingers wrapped the hard, solid length of him, and Mary smiled as he continued to kiss her. He was like silk, pulsating, hot, steel-hard silk, and she ached to have him inside her. As she stroked him, Ethan hooked his thumbs under the waistband of her underwear and slipped them down far enough that Mary could easily wriggle out of them. This was no sweet love scene; they wanted each other in a primitive way. They wanted to be connected, and Mary reveled in the fact that she felt like a horny teenager at the ripe old age of twenty-nine.

Ethan broke away for one second to pitch his pants to the floor, and when he returned, Mary pushed him back on the bed. She felt sexy and strong and wanted to climb on top of him and take what she wanted, be in control, and Ethan lay back and allowed her that, his hands instantly finding her hips.

She kneaded his chest with her hands, rolled his nipples between her fingers until his erection looked like a marble pillar, then she lifted up off him, pressed her hips forward and sank down until the curls between her legs met the coarse hair at his center.

Ethan uttered a curse, a deep throaty sound that went with the thrust he met her with. "Mary, I don't—"

"Want this?"

A deep, almost wounded chuckle escaped him. "Are you kidding? No, I don't have any protection."

"I do," she said breathlessly.

"You do?"

She pushed off him, her smooth legs brushing against his hair-roughened ones as she grabbed a foil packet from the bedside table drawer. "I'm not going to pretend I didn't want this to happen," she said, grinning down at him. "I came prepared."

Ethan reached for the packet, but Mary wanted to do it herself, wanted to feel the latex as it slid over him, wanted to place him inside her again. After feeling so out of control for so long, she needed this, and for once Ethan let her take what she needed, let her slide back down over him, let her place his hands on her breasts as she rode him, her hips swiveling and thrusting as she tried to feel him from every angle.

"Tell me," Ethan whispered, one hand trailing down her belly to the spot where they were joined, where wet heat made their movements quick and intensely pleasurable. "What do you want?"

Through gritted teeth, Mary cried out, "Yes, right there. Touch me there."

Ethan's fingers moved and played until Mary's head dropped back and her breasts rose and fell. She let him take over, one hand gripping her hips, rocking her back and forth, deeper and deeper, the other hand nestled between them, his middle finger flicking the tender button hidden inside until waves of pleasure so intense Mary could hardly breathe washed over her. Her hands slipped to his chest as he pumped furiously beneath her, guttural sounds erupting from his throat as he followed her over the edge.

Exhaustion flooded her and she collapsed on top of him, tears filling her eyes. She lay there, her heart thudding against his chest, and wondered what she'd been doing for the past two years besides working and remaining separate from the world. She'd never realized just how lonely she'd been, spending her time, energy and focus on the business. She'd completely cut herself off from living.

Ethan slid out from under her, and she gave him her back so they were spooning. It felt so good, so right to be held like this by him. How that was possible, after all they'd been through, she didn't know, but it was obvious to her that they might have a chance together.

Ethan trailed kisses down her back, down, down, raking his teeth against the sensitive spot right above her buttocks. Electric currents shot through Mary's weak limbs, and she uttered a playful, "What do you think you're doing?"

"I'm not done."

"Not done with what...oh."

He flipped her over and sat poised above her, staring down at her with eyes that glittered blue fire, his erection brushing against her leg, hard once again.

Laughing weakly, she grabbed the covers and hauled them up and over her head. "Can't. Tired."

"Mary," he began wickedly. "Do you actually think a few inches of cotton is going to stop me?"

With a little pleasurable scream, Mary saw Ethan appear at the bottom end of the covers, his gaze ravenous as he started at her ankles and crawled toward her, his mouth planting soft, wet kisses up her calves, knees and finally her inner thighs.

"You don't have to do a thing," he whispered, his mouth poised between her now widespread thighs.

Her fingers delving immediately into his hair, Mary lifted her hips tentatively. How could she resist? His head was down, the muscles in his shoulders flexing as he gripped her buttocks. His mouth was like heaven, his tongue…

"Ethan…"

He started slowly at first, just gentle laps at her sensitive sex, long, slow licks from hood to the opening of her body. But Mary's body responded quickly, writhing beneath him, twisting, her fingers leaving his hair to find herself. Ethan said something sexy and dirty as she opened the slick, hot folds at her core, then nuzzled and suckled at the taut bud that ached so badly. Following her rhythm, his pace quickened, moving with the thrust of her hips, until she arched her back and called out raw, insatiable moans over and over again, shuddering against his mouth.

Completely exhausted now, Mary curled over on her side and released a heavy, satisfied sigh, even smiling lazily when Ethan lay facing her on his side.

"I want to stay," he said.

"The bed's too small," she joked.

He draped one muscular thigh over her hips, pulling himself closer. "Is it?"

And they fell asleep that way.

The weather had been sketchy all morning, but miraculously by eleven o'clock the sun had pushed its way through the clouds and had started to warm the sand. Right alongside the staff, Mary helped set up tables, chairs, chaises and umbrellas, all in festive shades of blue-and-white stripes. The beach had been combed beautifully, leaving only the whitest, softest sand for their party, and when noon hit and the guests began to arrive, Mary breathed a sigh of relief. Despite the morning gloom and a night of amazing sex that had left her bone weary, she'd pulled it off.

Dressed in a simple though elegant navy-blue sundress and white hat, Mary walked from one station to another, making sure the drinks were flowing and the food was getting out in a timely manner. Barring one strange and obviously experimental plate of baked-bean custard that she immediately had the waiter send back to base camp, everything looked perfect.

Just as she was inspecting the barbecue grills and the delicious scents wafting from each, Ethan came up behind her and took her hand. She smiled instantly at his touch, and a warm sensation came over her heart as she recalled this morning, waking up together in a haze of touchy, feely, romantic sweetness, complete with breakfast and a killer make-out session at the door as they each complained about how late they were going to be but not really giving a damn.

"Twenty minutes into the party and I have two potential clients flying to Minneapolis next week for meetings," he said, brushing a kiss to her ear. "You're amazing."

He looked calm, relaxed and deadly handsome in white pants and black polo shirt, and Mary felt a strange sense of pride, as if they were actually together. "It's not me, it's the mojitos," she joked.

"No, it's you," he insisted, his blue eyes flashing with admiration. "Or maybe it's me around you."

"That's a nice thing to say," Mary said a little shyly, trying to ease her hand from his in case anyone was watching them. She didn't want to give anyone the wrong idea, especially Ethan. She had never been the kind of woman to have expectations, and no matter how much she wanted to curl into this man and whisper her feelings against his chest, she wasn't about to lay that kind of pressure on him. She may have come to a realization last night about what she had been missing, what she wanted now and how they'd both been stuck in a past that had ruled their actions. But Ethan might not have come to any realizations except that the two of them had just had great sex.

Whatever his beliefs, Ethan held firm to Mary's hand as they walked over to the bar, greeting guests along the way. It was odd. In all the years Mary had been one of NRR's partners, she'd never felt like an actual wife to a client, or wanted to be, until today. For brief moments she even caught herself imagining that she and Ethan were a couple as they circled the crowd.

"I should go and speak with the chef," she told Ethan after about twenty minutes of crowd watching. "We're running low on a few things."

Ethan nodded but didn't release her hand immediately. "Before you go, I have to ask you something."

"Okay."

"I feel like an ass—a romantic ass."

"A whole new thing for you?"

"You bet." Chuckling, he drove a hand through his hair. "Will you stay with me tonight?"

Pleasure circled her belly, and she grinned at him. "I seem to remember us agreeing to something…after the party ended."

He gave her a mock scowl. "No idea what you're talking about."

"Sure you do. Should I refresh your memory?"

"If you say one word about that conversation, I'll have to take drastic action."

Biting her lip to keep from laughing, she said, "After the party ended we were both supposed to—"

Before she could say another word, Ethan hauled her into his arms and kissed her hard and quick. "Don't make me take this to an obscene level in front of all these people," he warned against her mouth. "I'll ruin my reputation."

Mary laughed, a warm, rich sound that totally conveyed how happy he was making her in that moment. "Wasn't I supposed to take off just as soon as the last guest departed?"

"Oh, you asked for it," he said wickedly, taking her hand and slipping behind the bar where it was shady and devoid of party guests.

In seconds Mary had her arms around his neck as he kissed her with all the passion of the night before. When they finally came up for air, Ethan's eyes were glazed and hot and his voice was ragged with emotion. "Whatever we have going here, I want more of it."

All she could do was kiss him, passionately and without holding back.

He held her face in his hands. "Tell me you want that, too."

"I want that, but I'm a little scared."

"Of what?"

"All that's happened."

"That's over, Mary. Can't we decide to forget about it and leave it in the past?"

"I think we've both left too much in the past. Don't you think it's time to deal with it?"

His brow furrowed with frustration just as a loud trill erupted from Mary's pants pocket. With a quick look of apology, she grabbed her cell phone and flipped it open. "Hello."

"Mary, it's your grandmother."

"Grandmother, how are you?"

"Your grandfather has died."

Her heart sunk into her stomach. "What?"

"The funeral is Tuesday. You'll be here?"

"Yes, of course," she said quickly, uncomfortable with her grandmother's unemotional way of giving news. "How did it—"

"I will see you Tuesday," Grace continued brusquely. "St. Agnes, downtown. 10:00 a.m."

She hung up almost immediately after Mary said that she would see her at the church. Still in shock, Mary gripped the phone in her fist and stared at the sand.

"What's wrong?" Ethan asked gently.

"My grandfather died." Why was she feeling so blown away? She and Lars Harrington had never been close, but for some reason the news of his death reminded Mary of her mother's death, and of how short life really was.

"I'm sorry," Ethan said soberly. "How did it happen?"

"I have no idea."

He didn't push her for more. "When are you leaving?"

"Right away. Tonight."

He nodded. "I'm going with you."

"No," she said quickly, not sure why she didn't jump at the offer, but sensing in her gut that Ethan Curtis around her family right now might not be the greatest idea. "You have business to finish up here, people to see and deals to make. It's the reason why we came to Mackinac Island in the first place."

"All of that can wait a few days."

She eased away from him, from his embrace and the intimacy they'd shared only moments ago. "And lose momentum? No way. It was our plan, anyway, that I was going to leave today and you were going to stay. Let's stick with the plan, for now anyway."

Ethan wasn't a mysterious man; he said what he thought and didn't apologize for it. With an understanding but not altogether amused grin, he said, "You're almost as good at this as me."

"Good at what?"

"Pretending you don't give a damn."

They said nothing further as they walked back into the eye of the party.

The cemetery looked like an English garden, with buckets of daisies and vases of tulips and roses everywhere you looked. The woman next to Mary at the grave site had been nervous about what to say to Lars Harrington's granddaughter. She had bypassed the usual offers of sympathy and instead had gone on to explain that Sunday was the heaviest day for visitors to the cemetery, and that all the guilty relatives brought flowers. After a quick, tight-lipped smile to the woman, Mary had moved to the opposite side of the grave, to stand alongside her grandmother, aunt and cousins.

As the priest spoke, Mary gripped the stems of her lilacs—a flower her grandmother had always called "peasant flora" as they grew in just about anyone's backyard—recalling the day that she and her father had buried her mother. The weather had been far better than today, full sunshine and a heavy breeze, but the mood felt similar and, Mary noticed, some of the same crowd was there. But no one except Mary and Hugh had shed a tear that day, no one had left that cemetery broken the way they had.

Staring at the casket as it was lowered into the ground, Mary wondered if she'd actually healed from that whole ordeal: the illness and the loss. She'd always been so worried about fixing her father and helping him to get over his grief that she hadn't even looked at her own. No wonder she'd allowed herself to take that deal of Ethan's—she'd been a little out of her mind.

Ethan. Warmth spread through her and she wrapped her arms around herself. She missed him, missed sparring with him, lying in his arms, feeling alive. It had been a few days since she'd spoken to him, since he'd kissed her goodbye at the ferry and returned to the island.

Mary glanced up and spotted Tess and Olivia standing next to the woman who'd voiced the inappropriate cemetery comment. The two women looked quiet and sad, and even though she hadn't asked them to attend, Mary was thankful for their presence and support. And they weren't the only ones offering their support, Mary noticed as she shifted her gaze to the back of the crowd behind her partners.

Conservatively dressed in a black suit and bright-blue tie, Ethan Curtis stood apart from all the others, staring at her, his gaze solemn as Bible verses were read. At first, Mary felt a jump of excitement at the sight of him, then beside her, her grandmother opened her purse and noisily slipped out a tissue, which she used to dab her eyes. This probably wasn't good. Grace wouldn't want him here and might create a scene.

As soon as the service ended, Mary hustled over to him. He took her hand and kissed it. "I thought you might need…something. I wasn't sure exactly what, so I came instead."

"Thank you," she said, wanting to curl into his arms and let him comfort her. But she knew this wasn't the time or the place, and she needed to get him out of there before he was verbally attacked by her grandmother.

But unfortunately she wasn't quick enough.

"What is he doing here?"

It was as if a cold wind had blown in, encircling them like a tornado. Mary's grandmother walked up to them. She stared hard at Ethan, a sneer on her weary face.

"He came as a friend, Grandmother," Mary quickly tried to explain. "And—"

"He's no friend to this family," Grace snarled. "Your grandfather would be appalled."

"Grandmother, please—"

"You don't need to defend me, Mary," Ethan said calmly, then turned to Grace. "I was offering a little support to a friend, that's all."

Her eyes narrowed into nasty slits. "The blue-collar trash that took his company from him." She turned on Mary. "How could you allow this?"

"I didn't. I'm not. I—"

"Don't bother, Mary," Ethan said with a mild sigh before turning around and walking away.

"I'm surprised at you," Grace uttered to Mary when he was gone.

"And I wish I could say I'm surprised at you," Mary said tightly.

"You will not speak to me in that tone, young—"

"I understand that today is a difficult day, Grandmother," Mary said, feeling strong and in control with this woman for the first time in her life. "But I won't allow you to speak to my friends that way anymore. If you want a relationship with me, you'll need to restrain yourself in the future."

Leaving her grandmother standing there, mouth open, Mary went after Ethan. She caught up to him on top of the hill overlooking her grandfather's grave site. "I'm sorry. It's her grief talking."

"Then she's been grieving for a long time," he muttered.

"This is why I didn't want you to come here," she explained. "I knew she'd—"

"Stop trying to protect me, Mary. I don't need it."

"I'm not…" Even as she said the words, she knew they weren't true.

"Aren't you tired of it?"

"What do you mean?"

"Protecting everyone. Your father, your partners, your grandmother, me, yourself."

She stared at him unable to speak, her brain running a hundred miles an hour. Had he read her thoughts last night? How could he know that all of her life she'd been doing exactly this, hoping her interference would bring peace where there was chaos—and having no life of her own in the process. She could plan her work, her business years in advance, but could never see her personal future because she didn't think she deserved one.

"I have to go," Ethan said, mistaking her silence for indifference.

"No," she said sternly just as Olivia and Tess came toward them, waving.

"I'm so sorry, Mary," Olivia said sympathetically, placing an arm around her friend's shoulder. Then she noticed Ethan and gave him a curious smile. "Mr. Curtis. Hello. What are you doing here?"

"He took over my grandfather's company," Mary said quickly and without thinking. "But he was just leaving."

When Ethan's cold gaze found hers, she realized what she had said and how it had sounded. It was one thing to protect him, but to act ashamed of him... She wanted to explain, but with Tess and Olivia standing right there she knew it would have to wait.

Ethan nodded to both Tess and Olivia. "Ladies." Then turned and left.

Mary's heart sank.

"What happened here?" Tess asked.

Olivia grimaced. "Hope it wasn't something I said."

"No," Mary assured them, knowing it was about time to come clean with her partners. "I'm afraid it was something I said."

Twelve

"Yes, Mr. Valentine, I'll be there." Olivia rolled her eyes as she hung up the phone. "This is his third call in two days. The excessively rich can not only be bossy but paranoid, as well." She swiveled toward Mary and gave her a sheepish expression. "Sorry, Mary. I don't mean you."

It was quarter to five and they were all sitting in Olivia's office going over the appointments and events that were scheduled for the next two weeks. It was September and business was starting to really pick up.

As she sat beside Tess on the other side of Olivia's desk, Mary crossed and uncrossed her legs. "Hey, I'm not rich."

Tess looked up from her notes. "I thought your grandfather left you a small fortune."

"It still doesn't make me rich," Mary said on a laugh that sounded incredibly forced. "Comfortable, maybe— but I've found that rich is an attitude."

"I'll say," Olivia went on. "Just because this guy has a dozen or so women who'd do anything from shine his shoes to act as though they don't know where Darfur is just so he can feel like the smart one, doesn't mean he should expect the same from me." She snorted. "As if I would forget a meeting. The nerve."

"You'll make sure he gets a clue, Olivia, I have no doubt." Tess winked at Mary, who smiled in turn.

The three women had changed during the past several weeks—since the funeral and the three-hour dessert and coffee gab session they'd shared afterward. Exactly ten minutes after Ethan had walked away from her, Mary had broken down and confessed their relationship to Tess and Olivia.

The two hadn't been surprised, but they had asked, no pressure, if she'd wanted to talk about it. She did, and she had. Not that it had changed the situation any, but it had been moderately cathartic and had made Mary realize what she'd been missing in a friendship.

Both Tess and Olivia hadn't mentioned Ethan since, and she was beyond thankful for that because Ethan hadn't contacted her for two weeks except to send a check to NRR for services rendered. There hadn't been a note in the envelope, nothing that would make her think he missed her or had even thought about her at all. For her part, she'd called him to try and explain, but he'd refused to listen. Even so, she hadn't stopped thinking about him.

Tess closed her book with a sigh. "I think that's it. We're all going to be incredibly busy this month, so take every opportunity to relax."

"Agreed," said Olivia pulling out her Rolodex. "And I know just how to start the relaxation process."

Tess groaned. "I can't take another one of those seminars on How to Cool Your Cooperate Stress."

"Seriously," Mary agreed wholeheartedly. "I fell asleep at the last one and the group leader actually tousled my hair to get me to wake up. It was very freakish."

Shaking her head impatiently at both of them, Olivia explained, "I'm not talking about a seminar, I'm talking about Senõr Fred's—tonight." She wiggled her brows. "Spiciest salsa in town and dollar margaritas."

"Oh, I'm so in," Tess said without hesitation, standing up and heading out of the office. "Let me get my coat, finish up some paperwork and I'll meet you at reception in fifteen minutes."

"What about you, Mary?" Olivia asked. "I mean, can anyone really turn down a margarita?"

At that question, Mary wanted to laugh, but she didn't feel merry enough to make it happen. She could turn down a margarita, and pretty much anything alcoholic for the next nine months. She was back to where she'd started, with a pregnancy test hidden behind the rolls of toilet paper under the sink. And this time, she'd actually missed her period.

She scrubbed a hand over her face. How was she going to tell Ethan, or not tell him?

"I'd love to come," Mary said finally, feeling slightly

sick to her stomach at the thought of salsa and chips and happy hour chaos. "But I think I'll stick to soda."

Olivia smiled and shrugged. "Okay."

"But if you two end up completely hammered," Mary said, gathering up her notes and grinning. "Consider me your designated driver."

Dr. Eleanor Wisel was a kind, grandmother type of Ob/Gyn with cool hands and warm instruments and a penchant for delivering news with her eyes closed. Dramatic effect? Who knew, but it was exactly how she'd told Mary that yes, she was indeed pregnant.

With a prescription for prenatal vitamins stuffed in her purse and a small plastic bag of coupons, information and dates for future appointments hanging from her wrist, Mary walked out of the office building and across the parking lot toward her car. Her insides had stopped shaking long enough for her brain to start processing what all this could mean. She didn't have to worry about money or a future for this child—she had her business and the trust. She didn't have to worry about loving this baby, she already felt totally in love with him or her. But what she did have to worry about was the father. She had to tell him, of course, but things were so crazy right now, would it be better if she waited?

She opened her car door and was about to climb in when she heard her name being called across the parking lot. Her skin prickled and her heart raced, and she quickly tossed her free bag of goodies into her car and slammed the door. When she looked up again, he was there, looking incredibly handsome in jeans, a white button-down shirt and a gray brushed-wool blazer. She found herself fascinated with his features, wondering would her baby have his eyes or hers? His hair color or hers? His roguish smile or her quirky one?

"What are you doing here?" he asked in a tone he usually reserved for employees.

"Seeing a doctor."

Concern etched his features and he took a step closer to her. "Why? What's wrong?"

"Nothing." Why did he have to smell so good? All she wanted to do was fall forward, rest her forehead on his chest, tell him how much she missed him and that everything that happened the day of her grandfather's funeral was a stupid misunderstanding. "I'm perfectly healthy."

He looked relieved.

"And what are you doing here?" she asked, suddenly aware of the pregnancy packet laying on the back seat in full view.

"I had a meeting in the building next door, and I saw your car."

"Right," she said, patting the Mustang she'd have to get rid of now in favor of an SUV or something more child friendly.

"Well, it's been interesting." He looked ready to take off, but Mary was not about to let him leave without at least starting the groundwork for a decent future relationship.

"Ethan, I want to apologize for what happened at the funeral—"

He put up a hand to stop her. "No need."

"No, there is a need. What happened was a misunder-standing."

Beside them, a woman was getting into her car, tossing her purse and effects into the back of the car, just as Mary had done a few minutes earlier. But she was not just any woman, Mary realized, her stomach roiling sickly as she turned her head and tried to go unnoticed by the woman she had chatted with in the waiting room of Dr. Wisel's office.

"Oh, hey, there."

Too late.

Mary gave the woman a quick wave and a very tight-lipped smile as she silently begged her not to say anything more.

The woman waved, utter glee in her eyes at having heard good news today, as well. "See you later, and good luck with your baby."

Her heart in her shoes, Mary nodded as they woman got into her car and shut the door. "You, too."

She didn't want to look at him, afraid of what she'd see in his dark-blue gaze: horror, disgust, disappointment. It would be something she'd always remember, but she wasn't a coward, and she faced her child's father with a proud lift of her chin.

"Baby?" he repeated, his face registering utter shock.

"It looks that way. It's very early."

"But...how is that possible? I wore a—"

"I know."

"And the first time we had nothing at all and...well, nothing happened."

"I know."

He looked away, scrubbed a hand over his chin. "God, a baby. Your baby."

"Our baby," Mary couldn't stop herself from saying. She wasn't about to beg, but she loved the guy and she wanted him to want this child and her, too.

"Oh, Mary," he said with a softness she'd only heard when she was in his arms, when he kissed her. "Were you going to tell me?"

"Of course I was going to tell you," she assured him. "But you weren't taking my calls—"

"I would've taken this one."

"I had some things to think about first, some decisions to make—"

He went white as paper. "You're going to…to have it, right?"

Her heart leaped into her throat. How could he even think… "Yes."

He released a heavy sigh. "But you were going to wait to tell me?"

Around them people slammed doors and cars pulled in and out of their spaces. "Ethan, again, we haven't spoken in two weeks. I didn't know if we'd ever speak again the way you were ignoring my phone calls."

"I was pissed."

"I know."

"I had every right to be."

He did. "Okay."

"But that doesn't mean my feelings for you changed."

Mary felt her breath catch in her throat. What did that

mean? What feelings? Besides attraction and a strange friendship?

He continued, "That doesn't mean I didn't think about you every damn minute and want to be with you, around you, inside you."

"Ethan," she uttered, shaking her head.

"I have to know something, Mary."

"Okay."

"Are you ashamed of me, too?"

"What are you talking about?"

"What you did at the funeral—or what you didn't do. Your grandmother treated me like dirt and you stood there."

"You're right. I was an idiot. At first. But after you left, I told her off."

He didn't look as though he wanted that answer, he was still so angry—at her, and maybe at his life and past. "You couldn't get rid of me fast enough around Olivia and Tess."

Sighing, she leaned against the car. "That had nothing to do with shame, Ethan."

"What was it then?"

"I didn't want my partners to know about you."

He looked triumphant. "Exactly."

"No, not exactly. I didn't want them to know that I had allowed myself to be blackmailed by you, that I went to work for you afterward and then that I—" she swallowed "—fell in love with you in Michigan. If I'm ashamed of anyone, it's myself."

"For loving me?" he asked.

She studied him hard. "I'm coming clean here,

Ethan. I'm admitting my failings, how I've screwed up. I should have found a different way to help my father, or allowed him to find a way out himself. I know that all I've ever done is try to keep the peace, take care of everyone else but myself. Then I used it as an excuse to stay away from relationships with people." She looked heavenward. "But no more. I'm done with that. I have a child on the way, and I'm going to teach her by example to run headfirst into life and embrace it, and that the world's problems are not hers to solve." She looked at Ethan. "What are you going to teach her?"

Mary had hoped that her words, her own admission of past failures would jar him, make him see what a fool he'd been and how releasing the past was his only way to have a real future. But he wasn't ready for that, and she had to accept the fact that maybe he never would be.

"I have plenty to teach," he said proudly.

"The art of the deal?"

"There's nothing wrong with being ruthless in business matters—"

"Business matters?" She shook her head, disappointed. "You still don't understand what happened with us—or take any responsibility for it, do you?"

"If we're talking about the bargain—"

"Of course we are."

His chin set, his eyes blazing blue fire, he said, "I did what I had to do."

Mary laughed bitterly as she opened her car door and climbed in. "You know, with how brilliant you are, I'd have thought that by now you'd have come up with a far more creative answer. That one's getting a little tired, and frankly so am I," she said before closing the door in his face.

Ethan Curtis wasn't a big drinker, never packed up his troubles and headed to the nearest bar. Instead he preferred to solve his problems in a clear and rational way. Even in personal matters, this method worked well for him. Today, however, clear and rational just didn't exist.

He drove through the stone gates of the Days of Grace Trailer Park and past the office to the mobile home he couldn't seem to stay away from. The one-bedroom home seemed to stare back at him, wondering why he kept returning to a place that held such bad memories.

Ethan reclined his seat and shut his eyes, remembering the sound of his father cracking open another beer from his second six-pack, hearing the squeak of springs as the old man dropped down on the ratty couch before hurling beer caps at Ethan, along with a few choice words about how Ethan was the real reason his mother had left them.

Why the hell did he keep coming back here? Did he like torture? Did he feel he deserved it?

A loud knock on the window had Ethan awake and alert in seconds and he stared out the side window at the man who now owned the trailer. Still a little foggy with memory, Ethan pressed the button to his left, and the window dropped slowly.

The man had no baseball cap on this time and looked like a badass with his bald head, Iron Maiden T-shirt and sinister expression, but when he spoke there was no anger in his tone, only interest. "Is there a reason you like to park in front of my place or are you just a freak?"

"I used to live here."

The man's brows shot up. "Did you now?"

"With my mother and father—well, actually just my father."

"Yeah, I know about that." The man scratched his neck, said thoughtfully, "I got a boy myself. Teenager. Crazy at that age, but he's real smart. All As, every subject. Maybe he'll go to a good college and get a fancy car like yours."

"Maybe."

"That's why I moved here," the guy confessed. "For him, so he could go to the best public school in the city."

Ethan stared at the guy. He didn't have much, and he seemed to know the curse of a woman walking out on him or maybe never being around in the first place, and yet his biggest concern was his kid's future. Ethan hadn't had that kind of love and commitment from his own father, but he sure as hell wanted to be that kind of dad.

What the hell was he doing? Coming here, feeling sorry for himself when he had made a life that he should feel damn proud of. Mary had been right. He'd been lying to himself all along. The shame he felt for where he came from wasn't about the trailer—that was an easy excuse, and an easy place to throw the blame when he just didn't want to deal with the past. His shame came from a father who'd had no pride in himself and had blamed everyone else for his lot in life.

Kind of like Ethan.

He didn't need blue blood to feel worthy, and he didn't

need to be accepted by those people to feel real success. His real success was growing inside of Mary right now.

Ethan eyed the guy outside his window as he gave a quick wave to what was probably his teenage son on the porch. He'd never known the kind of love this man had for his kid, had no idea what it felt like, so to get it he'd forced a woman to create a child with him by threatening the one thing she loved.

"What a damn fool," he muttered.

"What was that?" the man asked, turning back.

"Just talking about myself, brother." Ethan took out his wallet. "Here." He handed the man a business card. "When your boy starts college, have him contact me."

The man read the card, then looked up impressed. "CEO?"

"Wouldn't have minded a leg up in the beginning," Ethan said. "We always have internships available."

"Appreciate it." The man pocketed the card, then gestured to the trailer. "You want to come in? We're just about to throw some steaks on the barbecue."

"Thanks." Ethan smiled. "But I think it's time I got out of here."

"Back where you belong?"

"That's right." He was only thinking about Mary and the baby when he said it.

Ethan drove away from the trailer park, knowing it was the last time he'd ever be back, realizing that if he wanted any future with the woman he loved and the child growing inside her, he had to leave the past where it was and look ahead to the future.

Thirteen

"I can't believe I'm going to be a grandpa."

Mary sat on the picnic blanket her father had laid out in the backyard beside the vegetable garden, a garden that was now going crazy with bushes of fragrant basil, vines of squash and pumpkin and rows of ripe cherry tomatoes.

"Well, it's true," she told him, taking a bite of her corned-beef sandwich.

He plunked down beside her, looking stronger than she'd seen him look in a year. His color was good, too, and when he spoke, his tone contained that rich, happy sound she remembered from her childhood. "Your mother would be so proud. I wish she could see…"

"I know. But she will, in her own way."

"I like that." He winked at her, then handed her a cookie. "I made these myself, chocolate chip."

She took a bite and sighed. "They're great. In fact, all of this food is wonderful. I may have to hire you to cater for the company."

He chuckled. "Sounds good. But let's wait until after I open my restaurant."

"You're opening a restaurant?"

"More like a roadside place. Sell my vegetables and offer some small meals, homemade ice cream, the cookies…" He grinned. "Who knows, it's still in the planning stages."

"Good for you."

He nodded, then shifting topics. "So, what are your plans? Are you going to stay in your apartment after the baby is born? It's pretty small."

"It is." She didn't know exactly what her plans were, only that she'd be okay and that this child would be loved beyond belief. "Oh, Grandmother called."

Hugh looked surprised. "Really? Even after the scene you told me about at the funeral?"

"She said she respects my choices—"

"She actually said that?"

Mary laughed. "I know. I was shocked, too. She even apologized and said my friends are my own business. Even after I told her who the father was. She wants me to move in with her, have the baby there."

"What did you tell her?"

"Thanks, but no thanks."

"Bet she wasn't too happy to hear that."

"No, but she said she understood and asked me to visit as much as I could."

Hugh munched on a carrot. "Boy, she's certainly changed her tune since her daughter married me."

"I guess so. She wants to be a part of my life and the baby's, and she said she was willing to let go of this feud with Ethan." Mary shrugged. "I'll believe it when I see it, but people have been known to change every once in a while, right? Even in small ways?"

"It's been known to happen," Hugh said, tossing aside his carrot and regarding her with serious eyes. "Did I say I'm not all that happy about the daddy myself?"

"You did." The sun was high in the sky, must be around one o'clock, she thought, reclining back on the blanket. "He made some mistakes, Pop. Some big ones, but then again so have I. So have you."

"Well, if sending that back to me was any indication of change, than perhaps you're right, lass."

Mary looked in the direction that her father was pointing. At the far end of the garden, where her mother had planted a circle of yellow roses, was the sculpture of mother and child that Hugh had risked so much in trying to get back.

"He gave that to you," she asked, stunned.

Hugh nodded. "Brought it by himself. We didn't say much to each other, but it was pretty decent of him."

Mary smiled to herself, knowing that for Ethan, coming to her father's house with that sculpture couldn't have been easy. He'd made a grand gesture.

When she looked up, her father was watching her. "You love him."

"Yes. I just hope that's enough. He's got some demons to exorcise, some new ideas to come to terms with and a life waiting for him. But I'm anxious to see what his next step will be."

Hugh lifted one grayish-blond brow. "And if he doesn't take a next step?"

"Then I'll be very sorry—" she lifted her chin, trying to ignore the ache in her heart "—but I'll survive."

It was Saturday morning around ten-thirty, and all three of the women of No Ring Required were working, sans receptionist. Business was crazy right now, and Mary, Olivia and Tess were all working overtime to accommodate their clients.

Tess stuck her head in Mary's office. She looked slightly anxious, unsure of how she wanted to say what she had come in there to say. "Mary, it's Mr. Curtis."

Her heart leaped into her throat. "Here?"

"No, he was on the phone."

"What line?" she asked, breathless.

"He's already hung up," Tess explained awkwardly. "But there's a message." She handed a slip of paper to Mary. "He asked if you'd meet him there."

"Asked?" Mary repeated.

Grinning, Tess nodded. "Good luck."

After Tess went back to her office, Mary stared at the address on the paper, her pulse pounding in her blood. After all they'd been through, she didn't want to go back to that place, especially now, but more than anything, she wanted to hear what Ethan had to say, so she stood up, grabbed her purse and headed out.

Ethan was actually nervous. Like a damn teenager asking out a girl he knew he was not even close to being good enough for. Thank God the baby shop wasn't packed with customers or he'd probably have to pay the owner to shut the place down for a while so he could really talk with Mary in private.

The bell over the door jingled, and he turned to see Mary walk in, looking so beautiful Ethan almost couldn't speak. Her blond hair fell in waves around her shoulders and she wore a cream linen pantsuit with sexy sandals and pale-pink toes.

He picked up a baby blanket from the railing of a nearby crib. "I think we should stay away from anything blue. Even if it is a boy."

With wary eyes she regarded him. "What am I doing here?"

"Sit." Grinning at the command that came so easily to him, he amended quickly, "Please."

She sat in the rocker next to him and waited.

"How are you?" he asked.

"Fine. Curious."

He nodded, knowing he needed to get to the point if he wanted to keep her attention. "Look, Mary, I get it now."

Her brows lifted. "Get what?"

"My hang-ups. All seven hundred of them. I get it. I forced you into a situation that was impossible, all for the sake of feeling like I was worth something. You have every right to be angry with me. But you have no right to be ashamed of yourself."

"I'm not."

"I'm glad."

She gave him a tight-lipped smile. "But thank you for saying that."

"Oh, honey," he said, dropping to his knees in front of her. "That's just the tip of the iceberg as far as confessions go."

Mary felt her pulse pick up speed as hope surged through her for the first time in weeks. Ethan's heart was open to her, completely. She could see it in his eyes, hear it in his voice.

He took her hand in his and kissed the palm. "I know after all I've done that asking you to love me again is asking a helluva a lot, but I'm asking anyway."

Her stomach flipped. She couldn't believe what he was saying. "You don't have to do this. If it's about the baby, you can be a part—"

"Mary, I love you. Finding out about the baby didn't change that fact, but it did force me to face what I've done, what I thought I needed and a past I just couldn't let go of."

Completely overwhelmed, Mary shook her head at him.

"What is it, sweetheart?" he asked, kissing her hand again so tenderly, so reverently it brought tears to her eyes.

"I just never thought we'd get here."

"But we did."

"I know and I'm so thankful."

"You wanted to know what gift I can give this child?" he said, reaching out to touch her belly.

Mary nodded, too emotional to speak.

"I can give the same gift our child's mother gave to me—love."

In that moment all Mary wanted to do was wrap her arms around Ethan and never let go. "I do love you, Ethan. So much."

He kissed her neck, her cheek, her eyelids. "I love you, too. Marry me?"

She laughed, insanely happy and so sure of her future. "Yes. Yes. Yes."

Ethan kissed her, a hungry, possessive kiss that she never wanted to end.

"Hi, there," came a feminine voice from behind them.

Still clinging to each other, Ethan and Mary glanced up and smiled sheepishly at the saleswoman.

"Are we shopping for ourselves or for someone else?" she asked.

Ethan reached in his pocket and took out the most beautiful yellow-diamond ring. He grinned at Mary as he slipped it on her finger. "What do you think, my soon-to-be Mrs. Curtis? Shall we do a little shopping?"

Mary kissed him squarely on the mouth and said happily, "I think it's about time."

* * * * *

THUNDERBOLT
OVER TEXAS
by
Barbara Dunlop

BARBARA DUNLOP

writes romantic stories while curled up in a log cabin in Canada's far north, where bears outnumber people and it snows six months of the year. Fortunately, she has a brawny husband and two teenage children to fetch firewood and clear the drive while she sips cocoa and muses about her new chapters. Barbara loves to hear from readers. You can contact her through her website at www.barbaradunlop.com.

For Angela of the Vikings.
Princess and Warrior

One

Most people loved a good wedding.

Cole Erickson hated them.

It wasn't that he had anything against joy and bliss, or anything in particular against happily-ever-after. It was the fact that white dresses, seven-tiered cakes and elegant bouquets of roses reminded him that he'd failed countless generations of Ericksons and had broken more than a few hearts along the way.

So, as the recessional sounded in the Blue Earth Valley Church, and as his brother, Kyle, and Kyle's new bride, Katie, glided back down the aisle, Cole's smile was strained. He tucked the empty ring box into the breast pocket of his tux, took the arm of the maid of honor and followed the happy couple through the anteroom and onto the porch.

Outside, they were greeted by an entire town of well-

wishers raining confetti and taking up the newly coined tradition of blowing bubbles at the bride and groom.

Somebody shoved a neon-orange bottle of bubble mix
into Cole's hand. Emily, the freckle-faced maid of honor,
laughed and released his arm, unscrewing the cap on her
bottle and joining in the bubble cascade.

Grandma Erickson shifted to stand next to Cole. She
waved away his offer of the bubble solution, but threw a
handful of confetti across the wooden steps.

"Extra two hundred for the cleanup," she said.

"Only happens once in a lifetime," Cole returned, even
though the soap and shredded paper looked more messy
than festive.

"I've been meaning to talk to you about that."

Cole could feel his grandmother's lecture coming a mile
away. "Grandma," he cautioned.

"Melanie was a nice girl."

"Melanie was a terrific girl," he agreed.

"You blew that one."

"I did." Grandma would get no argument from Cole.
He'd loved Melanie. Everyone had loved Melanie. There
wasn't a mean or selfish bone in her body, and any man on
the planet would be lucky to have her as a wife.

Problem was, Cole had plenty of mean and selfish bones
in his body. He couldn't be the husband Melanie or anyone else needed. He couldn't do the doting bridegroom,
couldn't kowtow to a woman's whims, change his habits,
his hair or his underwear style to suit another person.

In short, there was no way in the world he was getting
married now or anytime in the foreseeable future. Which
left him with one mother of a problem. A nine-hundred-
year-old problem.

"You're not getting any younger," said Grandma.

"I've been thinking," said Cole as Kyle and Katie climbed into a chauffeur-driven limousine for the ten-mile ride back to the ranch and the garden reception.

"About time." Grandma harrumphed.

"I was thinking the Thunderbolt of the North would make a perfect wedding gift for Kyle and Katie."

Even amid the cacophony of goodbye calls and well wishes, Cole recognized the stunned silence beside him. Heresy to suggest the family's antique brooch go to the second son, he knew. But Kyle was the logical choice.

Cole had already moved out of the main house. He'd set up in the old cabin by the creek so Kyle and Katie would have some privacy. Soon their children would take over the second floor, making Kyle the patriarch of the next Erickson dynasty. And the Thunderbolt of the North was definitely a dynastic kind of possession.

As the wedding guests moved en masse toward their vehicles, Grandma finally spoke. "You're suggesting I throw away nine hundred years of tradition."

"I'm suggesting you respect nine hundred years of tradition. Kyle and Katie will have kids."

"So will you."

"Not if I don't get married."

"Of course you'll get married."

"Grandma. I'm thirty-three. Melanie was probably my best shot. Give the brooch to Katie."

"*You* are the eldest."

"Olav the Third came up with that rule in 1075. A few things have changed since then."

"The important things haven't."

"Wake up and smell the bridal bouquets. We're well into the twenty-first century. The British royal family is even talking about pushing girls up in the line of succession."

"We're not the British royal family."

"Well, thank God for that. I'd hate to have the crown jewels on my conscience."

Grandma rolled her eyes at his irreverence. She started down the stairs, and Cole automatically offered his arm and matched his pace to hers.

She gripped his elbow with a blue-veined hand. "Just because you're too lazy to find a bride—"

"*Lazy?*"

She tipped her chin to stare up at him. "Yes, Cole Nathaniel Walker Erickson. Lazy."

Cole tried not to smile at the ridiculous accusation. "All the more reason not to trust me with the family treasure."

"All the more reason to use a cattle prod."

He pulled back. "Ouch. Grandma, I'm shocked."

"Shocked? Oh, that you will be. Several thousand volts if you don't get your hindquarters out there and find another bride." Then her expression softened and she reached up to pat his cheek. "You're my grandson, and I love you dearly, but somebody has to make you face up to your weaknesses."

"I'm a hopeless case, Grandma," he told her honestly.

"People can change."

Cole stopped next to his pickup and swung the passenger door open. He stared into her ageless, blue eyes. "Not me."

"Why not?"

He hesitated. But if he wanted her support, he knew he had to be honest. "I make them cry, Grandma."

"That's because you leave them."

"They leave me."

She shook her head, giving him a wry half smile. "You leave them emotionally. Then they leave you physically."

"I can't change that."

"Yes you can."

Cole took a deep breath. "Give Kyle the brooch. It's the right decision."

"Find another bride. That's the right decision. You'll thank me in the end."

"Marital bliss?"

"Marital bliss."

Cole couldn't help but grin at that one. "This from a woman who once threw her husband's clothes out a second-story window."

Grandma turned away quickly, but not before he caught a glimpse of her smile.

"You know perfectly well that story is a shameless exaggeration," she said.

His grin grew. "But you admit there were men's suits scattered all over the lawn."

"I admit no such thing, Cole Nathaniel." She sniffed. "Impudent."

"Always."

"You get that from your mother. May she rest in peace."

Cole helped Grandma into the cab of the truck. "The Thunderbolt would make a perfect wedding gift."

"It will," Grandma agreed, and he felt a glimmer of hope.

Then she adjusted the hem of her dress over her knees. "You just have to find yourself a bride."

So much for hope. "Not going to happen," he said.

"You need some help?"

Cole's brain froze for a split-second, then it sputtered back to life. "Grandma…"

She folded her hands in her lap and her smile turned complacent. "We're late for the reception."

"Don't you dare."

She turned to him and blinked. "Dare what?"

"Don't you try to match me up."

"With whom?"

"Grandma."

"Close the door, dear. We're running late."

Cole opened his mouth to speak, but then snapped it shut again.

His grandmother had inherited the stubbornness and tenacity of her ancestors. He knew all about that, because he'd inherited it, too.

He banged the door shut, cursing under his breath as he rounded the front grill. There was no point in arguing anymore today. But if she started a parade of Wichita Falls' fairest and finest through the ranch house, he was going bull riding in Canada.

Cultural Properties Curator Sydney Wainsbrook felt her stomach clench and her adrenaline level rise as Bradley Slander sauntered across the foyer of New York's Laurent Museum. A champagne flute dangled carelessly from his fingers and that scheming smile made his beady brown eyes look even smaller and more ratlike than usual.

"Better luck next time, Wainsbrook," he drawled, tipping his head back to take an inelegant swig of the '96 Cristal champagne. His Adam's apple bobbed and he smacked his lips with exaggerated self-satisfaction.

Yeah, he would feel self-satisfied. He had just outbid her on an antique, gold Korean windbell, earning a hefty commission and making it the possession of a private collector instead of a public museum.

It was the third time this year he'd squatted in the wings like a vulture while she did the legwork. The third time he scrabbled in at the last second to ruin her deal.

Sydney had nothing against competition. And she understood an owner's right to sell their property to the highest bidder. What galled her was the way Bradley slithered around her contacts, fed them inflated estimates to convince them to consider auction. Then he bid much lower than his estimate, disappointing the owner and keeping important heritage finds from the community forever.

"How *do* you sleep at night?" she asked.

Bradley leaned his shoulder against a marble pillar and crossed one ankle over the other. "Let's see. I spend an hour or so in my hot tub, sip a glass of Napoleon brandy, listen to a bit of classical jazz, then crawl into my California king and close my eyes. How about you?"

She pointedly shifted her gaze to the stone wall beside them. "I fantasize about you and that broad ax."

He smirked. "Happy to be in your fantasy, babe."

"Yeah? The broad ax wins. You lose."

"Might be worth it."

"Gag me."

His lips curved up into a wider smile. "Whatever turns your crank."

A shudder ran through Sydney at the unbidden visual. She took a quick drink of her own champagne, wishing it was a good, stiff single malt. It might have been a long dry spell, but she wouldn't entertain sexual thoughts about Bradley if he was the last man on earth.

Bradley chuckled. "So, tell me. What's next?"

She raised an eyebrow.

"On your list. What are we going after? I gotta tell you, Wainsbrook, you are my ticket to the big time."

"Should I just e-mail you my research notes? Save you some trouble?"

"Whatever's most convenient."

"What's most convenient is for you to stick your head in a very dark place for a very long time."

"Sydney, Sydney, Sydney." He clucked. "And here I tell all my friends you're a lady."

"It'll be a cold day in hell before I voluntarily give you any information."

He shrugged. "Suit yourself." Then he leaned in. "I have to admit. The chase kind of turns me on."

Fighting the urge to fulfill her broad-ax fantasy, Sydney clenched her jaw. What *was* she going to do now?

She was on probation at the Laurent Museum due to her lack of productivity this year. If Bradley scooped one more of her finds, she'd be out of a job altogether. Her boss had made that much clear enough after the auction this afternoon.

What she needed was some room to maneuver. She needed to get away from Bradley, maybe leave the country. Go to Mexico, or Peru, or…France. Oh! She quickly reversed the smile that started to form.

"See?" purred Bradley. "You like the game, too. You know you do."

Sydney struggled not to gag on that one.

He held up his empty glass in a mock salute. "Until next time."

"Next time," Sydney muttered, having no intention whatsoever of giving him a next time. She figured the odds of Bradley following her overseas were remote, which meant the Thunderbolt of the North was wide open.

She had three years' worth of research notes on the legendary antique brooch, including credible evidence it was once blessed by Pope Urban the Fifth.

Forged by the Viking King, Olav the Third, in 1075, the jewel-encrusted treasure had journeyed into battles and crossed seas. Some claimed it was used as collateral to found the Sisters of Beneficence convent at La Roche.

Most thought it was a legend, but Sydney knew it existed. In somebody's attic. In somebody's jewel case. In somebody's safe-deposit box. If even half the stories were true, the Thunderbolt had an uncanny knack for survival.

And if it had survived, she'd pick up its trail. If she picked up its trail, she'd find it. And when she found it, she'd make *sure* it stayed with the Laurent Museum—even if she had to hog-tie Bradley Slander to keep him out of the bidding.

Life was looking up for Cole. He'd spent the past three days at a livestock auction in Butte, Montana, with his eye on one beauty of a quarter horse. In the end, he'd outbid outfits from California and Nevada to bring Night-Dreams home to the Valley.

He might not be in a position to produce the next round of Erickson heirs, but he was sure in a position to produce top-quality cutting horses. That had to count for something.

Cole tossed his duffel bag on the cabin floor and kicked the door shut behind him. Of course it counted for something. It counted for a lot. And he had to get his grandmother's voice out of his head.

It had been months since the wedding. He wasn't a stud, and she could only make him feel guilty if he let her.

He pulled a battered percolator from a kitchen shelf and scooped some coffee into the basket. As soon as Katie was pregnant, he'd make his case for the Thunderbolt again. If Olav the Third could start a tradition, Cole the First could change it.

He filled the coffeepot with water and cranked the knob on his propane stove. The striker clicked in the silent kitchen. Then the blue flame burst to life.

A four-cylinder engine whined its way down his dirt driveway, and Cole abandoned the coffeepot to peer out the window. His family drove eight-cylinder pickups. In fact everybody in the valley drove pickups.

He leaned over the plaid couch and watched the little sports car bump to a halt beneath his oak tree.

He didn't recognize the car. But then a trim ankle and a shapely calf stretched out the driver's door and he no longer cared.

He moved onto the porch as a telltale hiss of steam shot out from under the hood and a spurt of water dribbled down the grill. The engine gurgled a couple of times, then sighed to silence.

Another shapely leg followed the first. And a sexy pair of cream heels planted themselves in the dust.

The slim woman rose to about five-foot-five. She wore a narrow, ivory-colored skirt and a matching jacket. Thick, auburn hair cascaded over her shoulders in shimmering waves. Her cheeks were flushed and her skin was flawless. She hadn't even been in the valley long enough to get dusty.

She smiled as she turned, flashing straight white teeth and propping her sunglasses in her hair. Cole sucked in an involuntary breath.

"Hello." She waved, stumbled on the uneven ground, then quickly righted herself as she started toward him.

He trotted down the three steps to offer his arm.

"Thank you," she breathed as her slim fingers tightened against his bare forearm.

A jolt of lightning flashed all the way to his shoulder and he quickly cleared his throat. "Car trouble?" he asked.

She turned to look at the vehicle, frowning. "I don't think so."

He raised a brow. "You don't?"

She blinked up at him with jewel-green eyes. "Why would I? It seemed fine on the way in."

He stared into those eyes, trying to decide if she was wearing colored contacts. No. He didn't think so. The eyes were all hers. As was that luscious hair and those full, dark lips.

"I think you've overheated," he said, breathing heavily. He knew he sure had.

She gazed up at him in silence and her manicured nails pressed against him for a split second. "You, uh, know about cars?"

He pulled himself up a fraction of an inch. "Some."

"That's good," she said, her gaze never leaving his, the tip of her tongue flicking over her bottom lip for the barest of moments. "I mostly use taxis."

"I take it you're not from around here?" Stupid question. If she lived anywhere near Blue Earth Valley, Cole would have spotted her before now.

"New York," she said.

"The city?"

She laughed lightly and Cole's heart rate notched up. "Yes. The city."

They reached the porch and a loud spattering hiss came through the open door. The coffee. "Damn."

"What?"

"Hang on." He took the stairs in two bounds, strode across the kitchen and grabbed the handle of the coffeepot, moving it back on the stove as he shut it down.

"You burned the coffee?" she asked from behind him.

"Afraid so." He wiped up the spilled coffee then rinsed and dried his hands. Then he held one out to her. "Cole Erickson."

Her smile grew to dazzling. "Sydney Wainsbrook."

She shook his hand and the jolt of electricity doubled.

"You want me to take a look at your car?" he asked, reluctantly letting her go.

"I'd rather you offered me a cup of that coffee."

"It's ruined," he warned.

She shrugged her slim shoulders. "I'm tough."

He took in her elegant frame and choked out a short laugh. "Right."

"Hey, I'm from New York."

"This is Texas."

"Try me."

Cole bit down on his lip. Nope. Not going there.

Her eyes sparkled with mischief and she shook her head. "Walked right into that one, didn't I?"

He quickly neutralized his expression. "Walked right into what?"

She brushed past him and retrieved two stoneware mugs from the open shelf. "Don't you worry about my delicate sensibilities." She held them both out. "Pour me some coffee."

"Yes, ma'am."

Sydney ran her fingertip around the rim of the ivory coffee cup. Even by New York standards, the brew was terrible. But she was drinking every last drop. Black.

She needed Cole to know she meant business, because he looked like the kind of guy who'd walk right over her if she so much as blinked.

She contemplated him from across the table. He was a big man, all muscle and sinew beneath a worn, plaid shirt. His sleeves were rolled up, revealing tight, corded forearms. He had thick hair, a square chin, a slightly bumped nose and expressive cobalt eyes that turned sensual and made her catch her breath.

He was going to be a challenge. But then, anything to do with the Thunderbolt of the North had to be a challenge. She'd have been disappointed if it had gone any other way.

"So what brings you to Blue Earth Valley, Sydney Wainsbrook?" he drawled into the silence.

She smiled, liking her audacious plan better by the second. She'd worried he might be obnoxious or objectionable, but he was a midnight fantasy come to life. Why some other woman hadn't snapped him up before now was a mystery to her.

"You do," she said.

"Me?"

She took a sip of her coffee. "Yes, you."

"Have we met?"

"Not until now."

He sat back, blue eyes narrowing. Then a flash of comprehension crossed his face and he held up his palms. "Whoa. Wait a minute."

"What?" Surely he couldn't have figured out her plan that quickly.

"Did my grandmother put you up to this?"

Sydney shook her head, relieved. "No, she didn't."

"You sure? Because—"

"I'm sure." The only person who had put Sydney up to this was Sydney. Well, Sydney and a thousand hours of research in museum basements across Europe.

She moved her cup to one side and leaned forward, her interest piqued. "But tell me why your grandmother might have sent me."

He tightened his jaw and sat back in purposeful silence.

Sydney wriggled a little in her seat. "Hoo-ha. I can tell this is going to be good."

He didn't answer, just stared her down.

"Dish," she insisted, refusing to be intimidated. She had a feeling people normally gave him a wide berth. And she had no intention of behaving like normal people. Surprise was one of her best weapons.

He rolled his eyes. "Fine. It's because she's an incorrigible matchmaker."

Sydney bit down on a laugh. "Your grandmother is setting you up?"

He grimaced. "That sounded pathetic, didn't it?"

"A little."

"She's a meddler. And…well…" He seemed to catch himself, and he quickly shook his head. "Nah. Not going there. You tell me what you're doing in Blue Earth Valley."

Sydney wrapped her hands around her coffee cup. Right. Stalling wasn't going to change a thing. She'd plunge right in and hope to catch him off guard. "I'm a curator from the Laurent Museum."

He didn't react. Didn't show any signs of panic. That was good.

"I've just finished three months' research in Europe."

He waited. Still no reaction.

"It supplemented three years of previous research. My thesis, actually."

"You wrote a thesis?"

"Yes, I did. On the Thunderbolt of the North."

Okay. That got a reaction from him. His eyes chilled to sea ice and his jaw clamped tight.

"I understand you're the current owner."

His palms came down hard on the table. "You understand wrong."

"Let me rephrase—"

"Good idea."

She leaned in again. "I know how it works."

"You know how *what* works?"

"The inheritance. I know it goes to your wife. And I'm here to offer to marry you."

Two

Everything inside Cole stilled.

He opened his mouth, then he snapped it shut again.

He stared at the perfectly gorgeous creature in front of him and tried to make sense out the situation. Was this a joke?

"Did Kyle put you up to this?" he asked.

"Who's Kyle?"

"My brother."

She shook her head and all that auburn hair fanned out around her perfectly made-up face. "It wasn't your brother, and it wasn't your grandmother."

"Then who?"

"Me."

He paused again. "You seriously expect me to believe you came all the way from New York—"

"Yes, I do." She reached into her clutch purse and pulled out a business card.

He read it. Sure enough, Laurent Museum. Okay, now he was just getting annoyed. The Thunderbolt wasn't a commodity to be bartered. It was a trust, a duty. "So was that breakdown nothing but a setup?"

"What breakdown?"

"Your car."

"My car is fine."

"Your car is fried."

"You know, I just proposed to you."

He stood up. "And you thought I'd say yes?"

"I'd hoped—"

"In what universe?" His voice rose, bouncing off the cabin walls. He was offended, offended on behalf of his grandmother, his ancestors and his heirs. "In what *universe* would I agree to marry a complete stranger and give away a family heirloom?"

She stood, too. "Oh, no. I didn't mean—"

"I have horses to shoe." He was done listening. She could fix her own car for all he cared, or call a taxi or hoof it up to the main road.

"Right now?" she asked.

"Right now." He scooped a battered Stetson from a hook on the wall and stuffed it on his head.

Sydney watched Cole march out of the small log cabin. Okay, that hadn't gone quite as well as she'd hoped. But then again, he hadn't really given her a chance to explain. She wasn't trying to *steal* the Thunderbolt. She merely wanted to display it for a few months.

She was pulling together a Viking show exceptional enough for front gallery space at the Laurent. With the Thunderbolt as the centerpiece, she would thwart Bradley

Slander and save her career. All she needed was the cooperation of one cowboy.

She moved to the cabin door and watched him head up a rise while she contemplated her next move.

The man had the broadest shoulders she'd ever seen. Solid as an oak tree, he had a confident stride and a butt that could stop traffic. She watched for a few more steps, then she forced her gaze away. His butt was irrelevant. The marriage would be in name only.

Her focus had to be on the brooch, not on the man. It wasn't as if she could put Cole on display in the front gallery. Although...

She squelched a grin and glanced at the rental car.

A breakdown, huh? Car trouble could be her ticket to more time with him. Swallowing the dregs of her coffee, she made up her mind. If that baby wasn't broken down now, it soon would be.

She waited until Cole disappeared over the hill. Then she popped the hood, yanked out some random wires and closed it up again, hoping she'd done some serious damage.

Dusting off her hands, she tucked her clutch purse under her arm and headed up the hill.

Three-inch heels were definitely not the best choice for the Erickson Ranch. Neither was a straight skirt and loose hair. By the time she closed in on Cole, she was disheveled and out of breath. She'd scratched her hand ducking through a barbed-wire fence, got a cactus stuck to the toe of her shoe and attracted a pair of horseflies that were now moving in for the kill.

Cole looked completely unfazed by the climb. He stood a hundred yards away, on the crest of the hill, with a coiled rope in one hand. He raised his thumb and index finger to his mouth and let out a shrill whistle that she was willing to bet would get the attention of every cab driver on Fifth Avenue.

The ground rumbled beneath her feet and she took an involuntary step backward. Then she forced herself to hold still and sucked in a bracing breath. If it was a stampede, it was a stampede.

The Thunderbolt had the power to launch her career to the stratosphere. And she'd studied too long and too hard to quit now. Better to be trampled to death trying to get her hands on it than give up and become a tour guide.

A herd of some twenty horses appeared on the ridge, their manes and tails flowing in a wave of black, brown and silver. In the face of their onslaught, Cole stood his ground. He lifted his battered cowboy hat and waved it in the air. The herd slowed, parted around him, then shuffled to a stop.

Okay. Now *that* was sexy.

And she wasn't dead.

The day was looking up.

Cole captured a big gray horse and led it through a gate. Sydney quickly followed. She was intimidated by the big animal, but she was more frightened of the two dozen of his friends they were leaving behind.

Cole tied up the horse then ran his hands soothingly along its neck. "Was there something about my *no* that was ambiguous?" he asked Sydney.

She found a log to perch on and gingerly plucked at the little round cactus on her shoe. Her skirt would probably be ruined, but that couldn't be helped. She played dumb. "You said no?"

He turned to stare at her for a moment. "Just in case you missed it the first time, no."

"You haven't heard me out."

"You're trying to steal my family heirloom. What's to

hear out?" With a firm pat on the horse's neck, he headed for a nearby shack.

She scrambled to her feet and followed. "I wasn't going to keep the brooch."

He opened the door. "Ah. Well, in that case…"

Her spirits rose. "Yes?"

"No." His answer was flat as he retrieved a wooden box and a battered metal stand.

Once again, he hadn't let her give enough information for a logical decision. "Are you always this unreasonable?"

"Yes."

"You are not."

He pulled the door shut. "Are you always this stubborn?"

"Will you at least listen to my offer?"

"No."

"Why not?"

"Have *you* ever listened to the wedding vows?"

"Of course."

He started back to the horse. "There's a little thing in there about loving and honoring and till death do us part. And there's generally a preacher standing in front of you, along with your family and friends when you make those promises."

Sydney hesitated. She hadn't actually thought through the details of the ceremony. She'd pictured something in a courthouse, a minimum number of words, mail-order wedding bands and a chaste kiss at the end.

"I could honor you," she offered.

He stopped and turned, leaning slightly forward to pin her with a midnight-blue stare. "Could you love me?"

Sydney stilled. What kind of a question was that?

His gaze bore into hers, searching deep, as if sifting through her hopes and fears.

She knew how to love. She'd loved her foster parents. She loved her mother. But those loves turned bittersweet when her parents died in the house fire and her aging foster parents passed away five years ago.

"Hey there, Cole," came a laughing feminine voice.

Sydney quickly pulled back, shaking off the unsettling memories.

Cole focused his attention over her shoulder.

"Hey, Katie." He nodded.

"You been holding out on us?" asked the voice.

Sydney turned to see a woman on horseback come to a stop in front of the little shed. She had shoulder-length brown hair tied back in a ponytail. A cowboy hat dangled between her shoulder blades, and her burgundy shirt and crisp blue jeans made her look as if she had ridden out of a Western movie.

Her saddle leather creaked as she dismounted.

"What?" asked Cole. "You wanted to shoe the horses?"

The woman smirked as she led her chestnut horse forward. Then her smile turned friendly and she stretched her hand out to Sydney. "Katie Erickson. Cole's sister-in-law."

Sydney reached out to shake the woman's surprisingly strong hand. "Sydney Wainsbrook."

"Nice to meet you," said Katie. She glanced speculatively at Cole for a split second before returning her attention to Sydney. "And what brings you to Blue Earth Valley?"

Sydney took in Cole's determined expression and decided she had little to lose. "I'm here to marry Cole."

He sputtered an inarticulate sound.

But Katie shrieked in delight and her horse startled. "So you *were* holding out on us."

"She's only after the Thunderbolt," said Cole, planting the metal stand with disgust.

But Katie's attention was all on Sydney. "How long have you known him? Where did you meet?" Her gaze strayed to Sydney's bare fingers. "Did he propose yet?"

"I proposed to him."

"She's after the Thunderbolt," Cole repeated. "She's a con artist."

"I'm a museum curator. I want to display the Thunderbolt. But I really am willing to marry him."

"She's—" Cole threw up his hands, turning to pace back to the horse. "Forget it."

Katie called after him. "Don't be so hasty, Cole. It sounds like a good offer. And you're not getting any younger, you know."

He muttered something unintelligible.

Katie laughed, turning back to Sydney. "From a museum, you say?"

"The Laurent."

"In New York?"

"Yes."

Katie's reaction to the proposition wasn't nearly as negative as Cole's. Maybe she would listen to reason. Maybe she would even have some influence over her brother-in-law.

"I was planning to display the Thunderbolt temporarily," said Sydney, keeping her voice loud enough to be sure Cole would hear. "It would only be a loan."

"How did you know it went to his wife?" asked Katie.

"Research."

"And how did you know he wasn't already married?"

"More research." Sydney raised her voice again. "I was thinking of something simple and temporary. At the courthouse."

"A marriage of convenience," Katie nodded.

"Right."

"And how would that be convenient for me?" Cole's hammer came down on a metal horseshoe and the rhythmic clanks echoed through the pasture.

"You could think of it as a public service," said Sydney.

"I'm not altruistic."

"You'd bring an important antiquity to the attention of the world."

"It's a private possession."

"It would only be a loan."

"Why don't you give up?"

While Sydney formulated a response, Katie spoke up. "Why don't you come for dinner instead?"

"Katie," Cole stressed, wiping the sweat from his brow.

"We can talk about it, Cole," said Katie. "No harm in talking about it."

Sydney felt a surge of hope. She definitely had an ally in Katie.

"You two can do whatever you want," said Cole, going back to hammering. "But I'm not coming to dinner."

"Of course you are," said Katie.

"Nope."

"I'll send Kyle after you."

"Good luck with that."

Katie put her hands on her hips and arched one eyebrow.

"You really need to do something about your wife," said Cole as he leaned on the rail next to the barbecue where his brother was grilling steaks.

Kyle closed the cast-iron lid and joined Cole. "It's not my fault you can't say no to her."

"Can *you* say no to her?"

"Why would I want to say no to her?"

"Not ever?"

"Not ever."

Cole folded his arms over his chest. "Don't you ever need to just put your foot down and lay out the logic?"

Kyle laughed. "You're joking, right?"

"How can a man live with somebody orchestrating his every move?"

"Are we talking about Katie or Sydney?"

"Katie's helping Sydney. And we're talking about women in general."

"And your fear of them."

"Don't be absurd."

"Then why are you freaking out over Sydney's idea?"

Cole peered at his brother, squinting in the dying light of the sunset. "Are you seriously suggesting I marry a stranger and give her the Thunderbolt?"

"She's from a museum, not some crime family. I'm only suggesting you hear her out."

Katie appeared in the doorway, a big wooden salad bowl clasped in her hands. "Hear who out?"

"Sydney," said Kyle.

"Oh, good," said Katie. "We're just in time."

Sydney appeared behind her with a basket of rolls, and Cole did an involuntary double take. She'd removed her jacket and her silk, butter-yellow blouse highlighted the halo of her rich, auburn hair. Her rounded breasts pressed against the thin fabric, and a small flash of her stomach peeked out between the hem of her blouse and the waistband of her skirt.

"Can you open the wine?" Katie asked Cole.

"Uh, sure," said Cole, with a mental shake, telling himself to quit acting like a teenager. He reached for the corkscrew.

"I was the high bid on Night-Dreams," he said to his

brother, not so subtly changing the direction of the conversation.

Kyle shot him a knowing grin but played along. "Planning to use Sylvester as a sire?"

Cole popped the cork on the bottle of merlot. "Come next spring, it's the start of a whole new bloodline."

After Sydney set the rolls down on the table, Cole automatically pulled out her chair. She accepted with a smile of thanks, and the scent of her perfume wafted under his nose.

"That reminds me," said Kyle from the other side of the table. "I need your signature on a contract with Everwood." He transferred the sizzling steaks from the grill to a wooden platter. "Gave me my price. He'll take all the beef we can supply."

Cole masked a spurt of frustration by focusing on the wine-pouring. He hated that Kyle had to run to him for every little signature. His brother was an incredibly talented cattleman, and the tradition that put the ranch solely in the name of the eldest son was archaic and unfair.

"Way to go," he said to Kyle, setting out the glasses. "You always were the brains of the outfit."

Kyle scoffed. "Yeah, right."

Cole pulled out his own chair and held up his glass in a toast to his brother's advantageous deal. "I'm dead serious about that."

"Are we going to talk shop all night?" asked Katie, sitting down.

Simultaneously, Cole said yes while Kyle said no. They both sat down.

Sydney leaned forward. "Maybe we could talk about my shop."

"I'm deeding you half the ranch," Cole said to Kyle, without so much as glancing in Sydney's direction.

Those words had the effect he was looking for. The air went flat-dead silent. The barbecue hissed once, and a sparrow chirped from the poplar trees.

"I talked to a tax lawyer in Dallas last week," Cole continued, reaching for a roll. "About our options."

"Cole," Kyle cautioned.

"I figure we can subdivide along Spruce Ridge, then follow the creek bed to the road."

Kyle planted the butt of his steak knife on the wooden table. "Stop."

"I'm going to do it," said Cole.

"Oh, no, you're not."

"You can't stop me."

"Boys," Katie interrupted.

"Oh, yes, I can," said Kyle. "I won't accept."

"It's not up to you." Cole took a breath. The guilt on this one had been burning inside him for a long time. He wasn't about to back off. "Sometimes a man has to put his foot down and make decisions that are in the best interest of his family."

"Was that a slam?" asked Kyle.

"No."

"It sounded like a slam."

Cole dropped the roll to his plate, regretting his choice of words. "I didn't mean that. I meant, a man needs his own land."

"Kyle?" Katie tried again. "Cole?"

"You saying all these years I haven't had my own land." That threw Cole. "Of course not."

"There you go."

"What about your kids?"

Kyle clenched his jaw but remained silent.

Cole hoped that meant his brother was running low on

arguments. "You need to build a legacy for your kids." He rushed on. "You need to leave them something. If you won't think of yourself, think about your children."

Sydney's hand touched Cole's thigh. His muscle immediately convulsed and he shot her a stunned look.

"Let's move on," said Kyle, a steely thread to his voice.

Cole looked back at his brother. "Let's agree to go to Dallas and talk to the lawyers."

Sydney's fingernails tightened, jolting Cole's nervous system.

What the hell was she doing?

"It's not just you anymore," Cole said to Kyle. "You have a family—"

Sydney pinched him. It actually hurt.

He swung his gaze back to her, but caught Katie's expression on the way.

He stopped.

He stared at his sister-in-law's white lips. "Katie?"

Kyle pulled back his chair as Katie started to tremble.

Katie stood and Kyle rose with her.

"What?" Cole jumped up. "What's wrong?"

Katie gave a little shake of her head and waved away their concern. "I'm fine."

"You're not fine," said Cole.

She placed her hand on Kyle's arm. "I'm really okay. I'm just going to get a glass of water."

Kyle put an arm around her shoulders and gave her a little squeeze. "You sure?" he whispered.

She nodded. "Really. The less fuss, the better. I'll be right back."

Kyle watched her disappear into the kitchen.

Cole raked a hand through his hair, trying to sift through the turn of events. "I'm sorry," he said. "What the heck…"

"Can I help?" Sydney asked Kyle.

Kyle closed his eyed and dropped back into his chair. He shook his head. "It's the talk of kids."

Cole slowly sat, opening his mouth to ask for an explanation, but Sydney's fingers closed on his thigh again.

He felt like a bull in a china shop. What was he missing here?

"She hoped to be pregnant by now," said Kyle.

Cole went cold.

Sydney tossed her napkin onto the table. "I am going to make sure she's okay."

Both men rose with her.

After Sydney disappeared, Kyle moved restlessly to the rail, taking a long, steady swig of his wine.

Cole followed, not sure of what to say. He and Kyle didn't exactly have heart-to-heart talks about their sex lives, never mind their sperm counts. Was this a medical problem? Did they need to see a doctor?

"Are you…" he began. "Uh, do you…"

"The doctor thinks it's stress," said Kyle. "But we don't know anything for sure, and Katie's worried she'll never have kids."

Cole could have kicked himself. "And I was a big help."

Kyle snorted out a dry chuckle as he gazed out over the Blue Hills. "Next time, watch my expression and grab a clue."

"Next time I'll pay attention when Sydney mangles my thigh." Cole regretted his bull-headed stupidity. "Is there anything I can do to help?"

"Get married and have some babies so Katie doesn't have this whole dynasty thing on her shoulders."

"That would be a trick."

"Hey, you've got a bona fide offer in my kitchen."

"We could have a bona fide con artist in your kitchen.

Besides, Sydney doesn't want babies, she wants the Thunderbolt. I'm pretty sure this is a platonic offer."

Kyle turned to face Cole. He braced his elbow on the rail and a speculative gleam rose in his eyes.

"What?" asked Cole, dragging the word out slowly, trepidation rising.

"You wouldn't *really* have to have babies with Sydney," said Kyle. "You'd just have to let Katie *think* you'll have babies with Sydney."

"That's insane." And even if it wasn't, Katie knew why Sydney was here. There's no way they'd ever convince her they were having babies together.

"No." Kyle shook his head. "It's brilliant. You pretend to fall in love with her, pretend to marry her for real. She gets the brooch and Katie relaxes enough to get pregnant."

"And I get a wife I don't know, who doesn't love me, won't sleep with me but takes my jewelry?"

Kyle took another swig of his wine. "I'm sure you're not the first guy that's happened to."

Cole snorted.

Kyle clapped him on the shoulder. "You get the satisfaction of knowing you put your foot down and made a decision that was best for your family."

"Somehow I don't think this is me putting my foot down."

"So you'll do it?"

"I never said that." How could Cole justify getting married on the off chance it would help Katie get pregnant? Then again, how could he justify not getting married if there was a chance it could help Katie get pregnant?

"We'd be lying to your wife," he pointed out to Kyle, looking for some loophole that didn't make him the bad guy.

"No, we wouldn't. We wouldn't have to say a thing. Katie's a hopeless romantic. Trust me, she's going to throw you and Sydney together no matter what you and I decide. All you'd have to do is hang around and look besotted."

"I don't do besotted."

"Just look at Sydney the way you were looking at her before dinner."

"I haven't—"

"That was more aroused than besotted, I'll admit. But it should work."

"You're out of your mind."

"She's a babe, Cole. It's not like it would be this huge hardship."

Alarm crept into Cole's system as Kyle's words started to make some kind of bizarre sense. He couldn't consider this. Then again, he couldn't *not* consider this.

"This is the dumbest plan I've ever heard," he said. "Take Katie on a vacation. She can relax on the beach. I'll pay."

"She'll worry about you."

"She doesn't have to worry about me."

"I know that, and you know that, but Katie…"

It was Cole's turn to gaze at the dark hillsides across the lake. "You know, this morning things were looking pretty good for me. I'd just bought a new mare. I was minding my own business, thinking about shoeing, thinking about building a new hay shed, maybe buying a combine…"

Kyle started to laugh.

"Then along comes Sydney Wainsbrook and suddenly she's taking over my life."

"Kyle?" Katie called from the kitchen.

"Yes, sweetheart?" he called back.

"Do you think it's too late for Sydney to drive to Wichita Falls all by herself?"

"Of course it's too late." Kyle waggled a victorious eyebrow at Cole. "It's way too late."

"She's going to stay over," Katie called.

"Sounds good."

"I haven't agreed to anything," Cole muttered to his brother.

"You have the easy part," said Kyle. "Just hang around and look besotted."

"I'm going home."

"Come back for breakfast."

"Nope."

"I'll send Katie after you."

"Good luck with that."

Three

Cole was steadfastly chowing down on hotcakes and coffee when a knock came on his cabin door.

"Come in," he called gruffly, ready to take on Kyle or Katie or both.

But it was Sydney who poked her head around the door. "Hey, Cole."

Cole cringed, cussing inside his head. *Low blow, Kyle.* "Good morning, Sydney."

She gestured inside. "May I?"

No, never. "Of course."

Her lips curved into that brilliant, sexy smile. "Thanks," she breathed, messing with both his equilibrium and his libido.

Katie had obviously lent her some clothes. Instead of her impractical suit, Sydney wore a tight pair of faded blue jeans, a short T-shirt, and her hair was pulled back in a perky ponytail. Her makeup was more subtle than yesterday but, if anything, it made her sexier.

"Coffee?" he asked, finding his voice and rising from his chair.

"Love some."

"It's a little better than yesterday." One cup of coffee. That was it. And no matter what, he wasn't letting her talk him into going back to the house for breakfast.

Kyle's plan might be crazy, but Cole knew he'd cave— even if there was only a slight chance it would help Katie get pregnant. Because Katie without babies was positively unthinkable. She'd be the greatest mother in the world.

"Yesterday's coffee was fine," said Sydney.

"You lie," said Cole.

She shrugged. "I've had worse."

"Don't know where." He put a fresh, steaming mug on the table in front of her.

"Sherman's on West Fifty-second. Ever been to New York?"

"Never have. You hungry?"

"Katie made eggs."

He nodded and sat back down. "How's she doing?"

Sydney wrapped her hands around the mug. "Sad, I think."

Cole nodded, trying not to feel like a heel.

"You know your brother's come up with a plan to fix this, right?" she asked.

Every muscle in Cole's body contracted. His brother had brought Sydney into the loop? Why, that low-down, sneaky...

He bought a few seconds by taking a swallow of his coffee. "What kind of a plan?"

"He said he'd explained it all to you last night."

Of course he did. "What did he tell you?"

"That my timing couldn't have been better. That you and I should get married and let Katie think we're expanding the Erickson dynasty."

It was a conspiracy. It was a bloody conspiracy. "You actually think Katie will fall for it?"

Sydney gazed knowingly at him from under her thick lashes. "You don't think she'll believe you're interested in me?"

"Fishing?"

Her smile turned self-conscious and she gave a shrug. "Maybe."

"Or cornering me, perhaps?"

Her smiled widened then. "Maybe that, too."

Cole sighed. "I meant no disrespect to you." He simply didn't want to marry a stranger. Was that such a horrible thing?

Sydney was assessing him with those gorgeous green eyes. "Okay, I'll go first. You're a good-looking, sexy guy. It's not a big stretch for Katie to think I might go for you."

Cole's chest tightened on the word *sexy.*

It was Sydney who wrote the book on sexy. The way she moved with such fluid grace. The way her husky voice caught on that trembling laugh.

He could still feel her touch on his arm, on his thigh. Okay, so the thigh one wasn't the most pleasant memory in the world. But it was still sexy. Which was pretty pathetic.

"Cole?"

"Hmm?"

"I think it's a good plan."

"Of course you do."

"If we're lucky, it'll help Katie. It'll definitely help the

Laurent—a respected public institution, I might point out. So where's the harm?"

"Don't you have places to go? Things to dig up?"

"That's archeologists. There's nothing higher on my priority list than the Thunderbolt."

Cole pushed aside his pancakes.

She wanted to take this seriously? Okay. They'd take it seriously for a minute. "What about your family? You'd lie to them about getting married?"

She waved a hand. "Not an issue."

"You're not close to them?" That surprised Cole. She was such a smart, perky, good-natured woman. What kind of a family wouldn't want to stay close to her?

A shadow crossed her face. "My foster parents died five years ago."

Cole's stomach clenched in sympathy. He knew what it was like to lose parents. "I'm sorry to hear that."

She shook her head. "It's okay."

"What about brothers and sisters?"

"None."

His sympathy rush escalated. Now he had a sexy, vulnerable little orphan Annie challenging him to do right by his sister-in-law.

He stood up and took his dishes to the sink.

She followed. "Cole?"

"Yeah." And there was that elusive scent again. He didn't dare turn around.

"Why are you hesitating? We can draft whatever legal documents you want to protect the Thunderbolt."

"It's not that." Well, actually, it was that. At least, that was part of it. He didn't know Sydney, and he'd be a fool to trust her.

But there was more to it than the legal risks. It was a

marriage, a marriage to a woman he didn't love, didn't even know. Maybe he was an old-fashioned guy, but he just couldn't bring himself to do it.

"The Laurent is a very reputable institution," she said.

"I believe you."

"Is it lying to Katie, then?"

Cole turned. And there was Sydney, mere inches away. A slight movement of his hand and he'd be touching her. A tip of his head and he'd be kissing her.

"It's lying to Katie," he said. "Lying to Grandma. Lying to God."

"We could have a civil service."

"Not a possibility."

She tipped her head, looking perplexed.

He moved in, just a little, pressing his point, hoping he could make her understand and give up on this ridiculous idea. "We're talking about my family here, and they know me very well. They know that if I loved someone—if I *truly* loved someone—I sure wouldn't say so in a civic office in front of a clerk and two impartial witnesses."

Sydney bit down on her bottom lip. Her cat-green eyes narrowed in concentration, but she didn't respond.

"You ready to walk down the aisle in a white dress, promise to love me and honor me, then kiss me and throw a bouquet?"

As he outlined the scenario, an unexpected vision bloomed in Cole's mind. Sydney in a white dress. Sydney in a veil. Sydney with a spray of delicate roses trembling in her hands. He could feel her skin, smell her perfume, taste the sweetness of her lush lips.

"We'd both know it was fake," she said.

Cole startled out of the vision and gave a short nod. "Yeah. Right. We'd both know it was fake."

"And that's what would matter. That's what would count." She squared her shoulders. "Knowing the benefits, I could do it."

Cole clenched his jaw. He'd hand the Thunderbolt over to her tomorrow if he could. But Olav the Third was specific, and Cole's grandfather's will was ironclad.

He examined the idea from every angle. From his, from Kyle's, from Katie's, from Sydney's.

She could do it? Of course she could. It wasn't as if it would be physically painful. And nobody would die. And nobody would ever be the wiser. Marriages failed all the time. After a decent interval, he and Sydney could simply divorce.

"Then so can I," said Cole, just as he'd known he would from the second his brother conceived the plan. His family needed him, and that was an unconditional trump card.

A brilliant smile lit Sydney's face. "Where do we start?"

"First thing we have to do," said Cole two hours later while Sydney watched him saddle a horse outside his cabin, "is convince Katie I'm falling for you."

Sydney eyed up the big animal from the safety of his porch, having second and third and fourth thoughts. Oh, not about marrying Cole; she was completely convinced that was the right thing to do. She was having second thoughts about getting on the back of an animal that could crush her with one stomp of its foot.

"Tell me again why that has to involve horses?" she said.

"Don't you watch the movies?" Cole pressed his knee into the horse's ribs and pulled snug on a leather strap. His strong, calloused hands worked with practiced ease, and she had a sudden vision of them against her pale skin.

He released a stirrup and secured a buckle. "People who are falling in love gallop their horses along the beach all the time."

Maybe so. But there was no way in this world Sydney was galloping any horse anywhere anytime soon. "Couldn't we just go to a movie?"

He rocked the saddle back and forth on the horse's back. "Where?"

"I don't know."

"It's a long way to Wichita Falls."

"What about a picnic? You, me, some ants, maybe a bottle of wine?"

"We want Katie to see us."

Good point. Cole and Sydney alone in a meadow didn't do anybody any good. Well, except maybe for the cowboy Viking fantasy she was working on. The one where Cole dragged her into his strong arms and kissed her until she swooned.

"Maybe you could double me on your horse?" That ought to give Katie something to think about.

"I wouldn't do that to my horse."

"Hey!"

He rolled his eyes. "Don't be so sensitive. I'm the heavy one, not you."

She scrambled for an alternative, any alternative. "I know. We could mess up our clothes and our hair and let Katie think we had sex."

He walked the smaller of the two horses over to the porch. "On our first date?"

"What? Are you a prude?"

"No, I'm not a prude. Come over here and get on."

She shook her head, moving backward until she came up against the cabin wall. "Then why not on a first date?"

"Because I'm supposed to be falling in love with you. Come on. Clarabelle won't hurt you."

He couldn't have sex if he was falling in love? "Don't tell me this is a good girl, bad girl thing."

His eyes darkened to cobalt and a shiver ran up her spine. "This is a horseback-riding thing."

"Because, if you've got some hang-up—"

"What? You'll refuse to marry me." His look turned challenging.

But then, Sydney was up for a challenge. There was nothing wrong with sex on a first date. Not that she'd ever done it. But she could have if she'd wanted to.

"I won't refuse to marry you," she answered, striking a pose. "But you'll have to tell me which kind of girl you want me to be."

His nostrils flared.

There. Now he was the one off balance. She took a few bold steps forward and her breasts came level with his eyes.

She made a show of reaching past his shoulder to pat the horse. It twitched at the contact—a warm muscle jumping against her fingers. She let her voice go husky. "Which kind do you want me to be, Cole?"

"Sydney."

"Hmm?"

"Don't do this."

"Don't do what?"

"Don't flirt with me."

She blinked in mock innocence. "I'm simply asking a question."

"No, you're not." He swung up on the porch, positioning himself behind her, speaking very close to her right ear, making her skin vibrate with his gravelly, sensual voice. "What you're asking for is trouble."

He was right. Tall, strong, sexy and right. And if that was trouble, bring it on.

But his voice went back to normal. "Hold on to the saddle horn," he instructed, placing his hand on the back of hers and moving it into place. "You're going to put your left foot in the stirrup and swing your leg over the saddle."

Sydney tensed. Flirting, she knew. Horses were something else entirely. "Listen, I've never, ever—"

"It's easy."

She fought his grip. "Cole."

"She's calm and gentle, and she'll follow right along behind me."

"I'm scared," Sydney admitted. What if the horse bucked? What if she fell? What if she was trampled?

"Tighten your grip." He pressed her hand against the hard leather of the horn. His palm was warm and sure, and for a moment she relaxed.

"I'm right behind you." He nudged her forward, urging her closer to the horse. "Foot in the stirrup now."

She took a deep breath and did it.

"Up and over." He placed a broad palm under her butt and all but lifted her into position.

It was a quick thrill, but a thrill all the same. And now she was straddling a shifting horse, staring down at a rough-and-ready cowboy with a knowing glint in his blue eyes.

She could feel the heat coming off her cheeks and tiny quivers jumping in her thigh muscles.

"For the record," he said, back to husky and sexy.

"Yeah?"

"You should feel free to be good *and* bad."

It was a long mile from Cole's cabin near the creek up to Katie and Kyle's house on the hill. They took it at a slow walk, and Clarabelle followed the black horse along a faint trail through a wildflower meadow. Sydney's thigh muscles grew tight, but otherwise the ride went without incident.

"Katie said you used to live up here," she called to Cole as the two-story house rose up in front of them.

He twisted in the saddle to look back. "I moved out when Kyle got married."

"Was it just the two of you?"

He nodded, then did something to drop his horse back so they were side by side. "My parents died when I was twenty. Kyle was eighteen."

"I'm sorry."

"It was tough. But at least we had Grandma."

"The matchmaking grandmother."

Cole smiled. Then his eyes dimmed. "She's going to be really excited about you."

Sydney felt a twinge of guilt. Grandmas didn't seem like the kind of people you should lie to.

"Will it be okay?" she asked.

He seemed to ponder the question. "Well, she'll definitely book the church. Probably start baking the cake."

He brought the horses to a halt but didn't dismount. "You know, if we want to pull this off, we'd better make sure we have our stories straight."

Trying to lighten the mood, she tossed her hair over her shoulders. "How about you fell head over heels and I'm marrying you out of pity?"

"That'll work."

"Cole, I was only—"

"It *will* work."

Katie appeared at the back door, giving an exuberant wave. "Sydney. You're still here?"

Sydney smiled at Katie. "Cole offered to teach me how

to ride," she called back, deciding it was better to stick to the truth as far as they could.

Katie skipped toward them. "That's fantastic."

Sydney shifted in her saddle. "It's pretty hard on the butt. I don't know how you guys do it."

"Callouses," said Cole as he dismounted. Then he grinned at her. "You'll be developing some soon."

Was he flirting?

He looked as though he was flirting.

And she'd sure felt a shiver at the reference to her butt.

He walked a few paces and tied his horse. Then he came back for her. "You want some help down?"

"Sure," she said. It wasn't as if she had a hope of getting off by herself. Plus, her skin was already tingling in anticipation of his hands.

"Kick out both feet," he instructed. "We don't want you getting hung up."

She kicked free of the stirrups.

Katie grabbed the bridle and held the horse steady.

"Lean forward and bring the other leg over his back," said Cole.

She did.

Cole wrapped his hands around her waist and slowly lowered her to the ground.

It wasn't nearly as exciting as mounting the horse, but she got to inhale his scent, and for a second there his body was pressed full length against her back. She shivered deep down inside.

He didn't immediately step away.

"She's catching on pretty well," he said to Katie. Then he leaned around and brushed a lock of hair from Sydney's cheek. "She'll be running barrels in no time." He gave her shoulders a little squeeze before shifting away.

Sydney blinked at him in amazement. She'd never met anyone so caring and attentive. It was almost as if... She stopped herself. He was playacting. Wow. He was very good at it.

Katie let go of the horse's bridle and reached for Sydney's hand. "So you *are* staying for a while?"

"Okay with you?" Cole asked.

"Of course it is." Katie gave Sydney's hand a quick squeeze. "You're welcome to stay with us as long as you like."

Cole led Clarabelle to the post and tied her alongside his black horse while Katie insisted they come in.

The visit didn't last long before pillars of black clouds moved down the valley. Soon, fat raindrops plunked onto the warm earth and battered against the windows.

Kyle arrived, taking refuge from the storm, shaking his hat and wiping raindrops off his face.

Katie greeted him with a hug and a kiss, and Cole moved up close to Sydney's ear. "Okay," he whispered, glancing surreptitiously at his brother and sister-in-law. "This is perfect."

"What? You mean me?" Was she hitting just the right note here?

"No. I mean the rain."

Oh. Sydney glanced out the window. Perfect wasn't exactly the word she'd use to describe the growing torrent. "Is there a forest fire or something?"

"No. But the horses are all wet now. And so is the tack. It's going to be a miserable ride back to my place." Cole sounded unnaturally excited by the prospect.

Sydney grimaced. "Well, it doesn't get much more perfect than that, does it?" Her inner thighs chafed at the thought of getting back on a dry saddle, never mind a wet one.

He patted one of her shoulders. "You need to think strategically."

"Okay." She nodded slowly, trying to figure out how the rain fit into their plans. Would it flood the road? Maroon them together?

"When Kyle and Katie break it up back there," said Cole, "I'll suggest we ride home. Kyle will offer to ride Clarabelle, but you insist on doing it yourself."

Sydney watched the raindrops battering the window pane. "And why would I do that?" Other than a latent masochistic streak.

"You want to be with me, of course. You're dying to spend time with me, because I'm so sexy and irresistible."

Sydney cocked her head to one side. "How could I possibly forget?"

"I don't know. Thing is, if you're willing to ride a wet horse through a rainstorm, Katie will know you're in deep."

It made sense, in a wet, squishy, ugly kind of way. Sydney steeled herself. So be it. She was prepared to take one for the Thunderbolt.

"So Kyle knows about the plan?" she asked.

Cole shook his head. "I just came up with it."

"What if he doesn't offer?"

"Don't be ridiculous."

She gave him a questioning look.

"If he didn't offer, we'd have to kick him out of Texas. Now, no matter what he says, you ride that horse."

"This is secretly revenge, isn't it?"

Cole tapped the tip of her nose with his index finger. "Nah. When it's revenge, you'll know it."

Cole's plan worked like a charm.

Soon Sydney stood dripping wet and saddle sore in the middle of his cabin. And, though he was just as soaked as her, he had gallantly lit a fire then gone back outside to take care of the horses.

She'd briefly considered offering to help. But she was exhausted. Instead, she shook the droplets from her hands, finger-combed her hair and glanced around the little room.

She had to admit, the cabin was charming and homey in the rain. It was built of peeled logs that had mellowed to a golden yellow. The floor was hardwood, scattered with rugs, and the walls were decorated with antique pictures and hurricane lamps. The pieces weren't valuable, but she suspected Cole's ancestors had purchased them and handed them down over many generations.

She ran her finger along the stone fireplace mantel as she moved closer to the heat. It was only September, but there was a definite chill in the air. A plaid armchair with a folded knit blanket looked inviting. Too bad she'd soak the upholstery.

Cole returned, banging the door shut behind him.

"You should go get dry," he said as he pulled off his dripping Stetson and hung it on a peg. "There are a couple of robes on the back of the bathroom door. I'll make us a hot drink."

"I should do something to help." Not that she didn't appreciate this gallant he-man stuff. But she was beginning to feel like a dead weight.

He shook off the sleeves of his denim shirt. "Don't worry about it."

But she did worry about it. He'd agreed to marry her, and she didn't want him to change his mind because he thought she was high maintenance. "Am I keeping you from work?"

He jerked his thumb toward the kitchen window. "In *that?* Are you going to be a nagging wife?"

Sydney couldn't help but smile. "Sorry."

"Get dried off. I can't marry you if you've got pneumonia."

She gave up. She left Cole to the teakettle and closeted herself in the tiny bathroom, stripping off her wet clothes. There was barely room to turn around in there. She banged her butt against the pedestal sink and nearly fell into the claw-foot tub. But she managed to strip down, find some towels and rub her skin dry.

She chose a three-quarter-length, plaid flannel robe with buttons all the way up the front. The shoulders drooped halfway to her elbows, and she had to roll up the sleeves, but it was warm and comfortable. She hung her wet clothes over the shower curtain.

They reminded her that she needed to get back to Wichita Falls and check out of her hotel room. She couldn't keep wearing Katie's clothes, and she should really return the rental car.

She cringed, remembering the wires she'd yanked out of the motor. Should she confess the sabotage to Cole, or just wait until it was discovered and pay the damages? Hard to say. Ultimately, she'd rather give up money than mess up her chances with Cole.

She rubbed her hair dry and found a comb. Makeup, she'd have to do without.

When she wandered back into the living room, Cole's gaze slid down her body, lingering on her bare feet. He cleared his throat. "You want some socks?"

She glanced down at the billowing flannel. The tails hung past her knees. "You might have hit on the one way to make this outfit less attractive."

"You look fine."

"I look like a refugee from *Little House on the Prairie*."

Cole chuckled low. "Who cares? I'm a sure thing, remember?"

"That's an excellent point. I've never had a man see me at my worst and not had to care about it." She sat down in the big armchair and eased her saddle-sore legs under her. This was restful, in a bizarre sort of way.

All those years she'd spent fussing and primping and worrying. Cole could see her in a gunny sack and it wouldn't make a bit of difference. Come to think of it, this was pretty close to a gunny sack.

"This is your worst?" asked Cole.

She smoothed back her wet hair and nodded. "Pretty close."

"At least there'll be no surprises in our marriage." He headed into his bedroom.

Sydney leaned back into the soft cushions. He was forcing her to think past the wedding. What would they do? She had to take the Thunderbolt to New York. But what if Katie didn't get pregnant right away?

Would they keep up the charade? And if they did, would Sydney stay *here?*

She scanned the cabin again. It was a quaint little place. Maybe too quaint.

The kettle let out a shrill whistle. She waited a couple seconds, but Cole didn't appear. Finally she flipped off the blanket, groaned and straightened, then hustled toward the kitchen, nearly colliding with him as he appeared out of the bedroom.

He was shirtless. His feet were bare. And the button at the top of his clean jeans was undone, revealing a flash of skin below his washboard abs.

"Sorry." She put up her hand to forestall the collision and it came flat against his chest.

His fingers closed over her elbow to steady her and his thighs brushed up against hers.

"You okay?" he asked

She nodded, her heart skipping double-time. This was one good-looking cowboy. He looked great in his clothes, but out of them... Hoo, boy.

He reached over and shut off the burner.

Then his hand came up to cover hers, pressing it into his chest. His skin was warm and smooth. She could feel his heart thudding against his rib cage.

Her fingers made out the ridge of a horizontal scar. It was an uneven gash, three inches long, and she wondered what had happened.

From the little she'd seen of his life, she knew it was rough and physical. But what had caused this? And what other secrets were there on the body she'd admired for two days?

Before she could voice a question, their gazes met. His eyes turned a deep, ocean blue, and she inhaled his scent, marveling at how familiar it had become.

He slowly reached out to stroke her hair. Sensations washed over her like warm rain, and she longed to lean into him and absorb the full warmth of his strength. She held his gaze instead, finding flecks of gray among the storm-tossed blue. His look was turbulent, challenging.

He dipped his head ever so slightly. Then he stopped and his eyelids came down in a long blink.

"Is it just me?" he asked, refocusing. "Or is this a really stupid idea?"

She couldn't stop the slow, sultry smile that grew on her face. "It is a really stupid idea..."

His lips parted. "But..."

"Have we ever let that stop us before?"

Four

Cole was going to kiss this woman.

Stupid decisions were his stock-in-trade around her, and he saw no reason to give that up now.

"You're gorgeous," he said in all honesty, brushing the pad of his thumb across her cheek.

"So are you," she responded.

He grinned at that, sliding spread fingers through the thickness of her hair.

To his surprise, she rocked forward and placed a hot, moist kiss on his chest.

He sucked in a tight breath, and she kissed him again, her soft lips searing into his skin. It took a second to realize she was tracing the scar on his breastbone. She was kissing away his pain, soothing what was once a gaping wound, calming a memory he'd sworn he'd have to fight forever.

His hands convulsed and he tilted her head, searching her eyes for the reason behind her caring touch. What he saw was smoky jade and simmering passion.

Lightning exploded in the sky above them. Rain crashed down on the shake roof and clattered against the window-panes. The oak trees creaked and the willows rustled as the wind whipped the world into a frenzy.

That same storm swirled to life inside him. He couldn't wait another second to taste her lips. He dipped to capture them, touching, tasting, savoring. They were as lush as he'd imagined, but sweeter, more giving, the perfect shape and size and pressure.

He kissed her again, this time pulling her soft body against his, opening wide, praying she'd follow suit. His skin was on fire and his chest tightened with a deep longing.

She parted her lips and a small moan escaped. The sound tugged at him, surrounded him, buried itself deep inside him as she wrapped her arms around his neck and hung on tight.

He inhaled her scent, wishing the moment could go on and on. He wanted to close his eyes, block out the world, lose himself in her, pretend nothing existed outside their cocoon.

But that was impossible.

The world did exist. The world of Kyle and Katie and the Thunderbolt. He slowly pulled back.

Her face was flushed and her eyes were glazed.

He suspected he looked exactly the same way.

She rubbed his chest and eased off with a deep breath. "Guess it's good to get that out of the way," she said.

"Our first kiss?"

She nodded, her gaze fixed somewhere below his neck. "Yeah. Could have been awkward in front of Katie."

"I'll say." He stepped back, raking a hand through his damp hair. "Now at least I'll know what to expect."

"Me, too."

"So it wasn't such a stupid idea after all."

"I think it was quite brilliant."

"Yes." He nodded. "Brilliant." He took a tight breath. "I'm, uh…" He gestured vaguely toward his bedroom door then escaped quickly and grabbed a clean shirt, stuffing his arms into the sleeves.

Brilliant was just the word. *Brilliant.* Now he wouldn't be able to look at her without getting aroused.

When he returned to the living room she was curled up in the armchair again with a pen and paper in her hands.

"We should talk logistics," she said.

Cole's steps faltered.

Maybe her mood could shift one-eighty in the blink of an eye, but he needed a few minutes to recover. He made a show of securing his buttons and tucking the shirt into his waistband, before he dropped down onto the couch and met her eyes.

"What have you got so far?" he asked, struggling to get back on an even keel, trying to ignore that fact that she was wearing his clothing.

She tucked her auburn hair behind one ear. It was beautiful even when it was wet.

"How fast do you think we can pull this off?" she asked.

"Why? You in a hurry?"

She glanced up in surprise. "Yes. I've got a whole display to coordinate. Dozens of pieces."

"I don't think Katie's going to buy love at first sight."

"I didn't mean this afternoon. It'll take a couple weeks to prepare the gallery."

"A whole two weeks?"

"Probably a little more."

Cole tamped down his annoyance at her business-like approach. They'd shared one kiss. Nothing had changed. There was still nothing more to their relationship than a commercial transaction.

"What's wrong?" she asked.

"Nothing." He neutralized his expression.

"You sure?"

"What could be wrong?"

She nodded. "Okay. Where's the Thunderbolt now?"

"In a lawyer's safe in Wichita Falls."

"Can we get it?"

"Not until after the wedding."

Sydney nodded again. "I'm going to need to make a few calls."

"Kyle has a land line at the house. So does Grandma." You couldn't pick up a cell signal in the Valley.

"You don't have a phone?"

Cole shrugged. "I only moved in after Kyle and Katie got married. Haven't updated much."

"No problem." Sydney flipped the page. "Okay. So what's our next move with Katie?"

"You might not want to takes notes on that."

"Why?"

He raised a brow.

"Oh. Right. We don't want to leave an evidence trail."

"Rain's stopping," Cole noted. "How about I drive you back to her place and you can wax poetic about me for a while?"

A slow smile grew on Sydney's face and Cole relaxed for the first time since the kiss.

"Let me see…" She began counting off on her fingers. "You are a good-looking guy. Smart, funny and oh—"

She snapped her fingers and laughed. "I can tell her you're sexy."

Cole wasn't sure how to take that. Was Sydney saying she thought he was sexy, or that she was willing to lie about it? He couldn't ask. It would sound stupid. And there was no logical reason for him to care.

Still, he couldn't help but wonder if she meant it.

When Katie found out Sydney was still checked into the hotel in Wichita Falls, she offered to drive her in to pick up her suitcase. The rental car was down for the count, and it was looking as though they'd need a tow truck to retrieve it. Exorbitantly expensive, but the drive alone with Katie seemed like a perfect opportunity to go all moony-eyed over Cole.

Not that it was such a huge stretch. That man could kiss like there was no tomorrow. She still got a little flushed thinking about it. In fact, she was hoping for an excuse to do it again. Soon.

The next morning, Katie's pickup truck bumped over the ruts of the ranch's access road.

"That's Grandma's house at the top of the hill," she said. "Kyle and Cole's dad grew up there. Kyle and Cole, too, for a while. But after the boys were born, their dad built the house where we live now."

"Cole mentioned his parents had died."

Katie nodded, gearing down to negotiate a series of potholes. "Light plane crash."

"Oh, no." A pain flashed through Sydney's chest, her mind going back to the horrible day when she'd learned her own parents had been killed in a house fire.

"Cole was in the plane," Katie continued. "He was the only one who lived."

"Was he all right?"

"Cuts, bruises, broken ribs. He was really lucky."

"But he lost his parents." And he had at least one scar to remind him. She was glad now she hadn't asked him about it.

Katie nodded again, keeping her gaze fixed on the road. "He's a good man, Sydney."

"I know he is."

"He's been through a lot."

"Yes, he has." Sydney understood better than most the horrible pain of losing your parents.

Katie cleared her throat. "I can understand…"

Sydney turned to try to gauge the odd tone of Katie's voice.

"I can understand that you might be tempted to, uh, romance the brooch from under—"

"Katie!"

"I'm not judging you. I have a sense of how important it is."

"I would *never*—"

"Like I said, I'm not judging. Women make choices all the time." Katie glanced at Sydney, a mixture of pain and awkwardness in her eyes. "I just don't want to see him hurt again."

Sydney frantically shook her head. "I've been completely honest and up-front with Cole."

"I saw how he looked at you."

"And I like him, too, Katie." Sydney's stomach clenched with guilt.

"He's falling for you."

"Maybe. I don't know." Sydney had to remind herself that she was being honest with Cole. She wasn't conning him, and she wouldn't hurt him.

"I don't know where this is going," she told Katie honestly. "But I won't lie to him about my feelings. I promise you."

"He's a good man," Katie said in a quiet voice.

"He's a very good man," Sydney agreed. "And he's lucky to have you."

Katie cracked a small smile.

Sydney reached out and touched her shoulder. "I'm serious, Katie. You are a terrific sister-in-law. Cole knows full well that I want the Thunderbolt. If anything happens between us, we'll both go into it with our eyes wide open."

Katie wiped her cheek with the back of her hand, giving Sydney a watery smile. "So, you think there might be a chance for the two of you?"

Sydney took a deep breath, turning back to the windshield as she chose her words. "I think Cole and I are going to have a very interesting relationship."

Sydney's answers must have satisfied Katie, because at the end of the day, Katie suggested stopping at her grandmother's for dinner. She said Saturday night was traditionally for family, and a perfect opportunity for Sydney to meet Grandma.

Cole had warned Sydney that his grandma was an incorrigible matchmaker, and that she'd go for broke the minute she laid eyes on Sydney. So Sydney was prepared for anything.

What she got was a sharp, funny, sweet-natured, little woman in a floppy hat and bright gardening gloves with a dream of a period house. Circa 1940, it had an octagonal entry hall, with an archway that led to a living room, while another doorway led to what looked like the master bedroom.

The wallpaper was yellowed and russet tiles were faded with age. But the wood trim shone with a dark patina and the leaded windows were definitely original.

"Your home is beautiful," Sydney said to Grandma, peering into the living room. The couch and armchair were burgundy, looped brocade, dotted with doilies that Sydney would bet Cole's grandmother had crocheted herself.

Grandma glanced around. "Never thought of it as beautiful before."

"It's *gorgeous*," said Sydney, smiling at the incongruous wide-screen television and the personal computer perched on an antique, rolltop desk. Oh, how she'd love to check her e-mail.

"Sydney's here to visit for a few days," said Katie. "She's interested in the Thunderbolt of the North."

Sydney stole a quick glance at Katie, trying to decide if she was giving Grandma a subtle warning about her possible motives.

"Have to marry Cole to get the Thunderbolt," said Grandma as she led the way through the living room.

"So I understand," said Sydney.

They passed into a second octagonal hallway in the middle of the house, and then through a doorway to the kitchen at the back.

"Good news is that he's available," said Grandma.

"You know, he told me that himself."

Grandma looked back and cocked her head. "Did he, now?"

Sydney nodded.

The older woman smiled. She took a blue enamel kettle out of a painted cupboard and filled it with water from the deep, old-fashioned sink. "From New York, you say?"

"Yes."

"Like it here in Texas?"

"So far I'm having a wonderful time."

"That's good." Grandma nodded her head. "Cole's mother passed away, you know."

"Katie told me about that."

"His dad, too. My Neil."

"I'm very sorry."

"Well, I'm still here. And I've always figured that meant I've still got a job to do with one wayward grandson."

Sydney grinned, assuming she was in for the full court press. "You mean Cole or Kyle?"

"Cole, of course." Grandma paused. "You want to help me?" Then a split second later she gestured to a bowl of freshly picked blueberries so that the question could be interpreted either way.

"I'd love to help." Sydney was ready to give her all on both fronts.

"Good!" Grandma winked. "You can wash the berries. Katie, you get down a mixing bowl."

Katie opened a high cupboard and retrieved a large stoneware bowl. "Grandma's scones are renowned in this part of Texas."

"Recipe is a family secret," said Grandma. "Handed down from generation to generation."

"Can't wait to try them," said Sydney, pushing up the sleeves of her shirt.

"Grandma?" Katie ventured. "Why don't you explain to Sydney why the Thunderbolt goes to the wives?"

"I'll do that," said Grandma with a nod.

Katie turned to waggle an eyebrow at Sydney. "I love this story."

"Near as I can figure," said Grandma, scooping into a tin flour canister, "it started around the middle of the fourteenth century."

Sydney was instantly riveted. There was nothing she

liked better than family lore. As far as she was concerned, stories were as important as antiquities.

"The family went through a streak of good-for-nothing eldest sons," Grandma continued. "Worry was, if the young scoundrels got control of the Thunderbolt, they'd sell it for wenches and ale."

Sydney ran some water over the blueberries.

"Old Hendrik wanted to make sure they earned their money the Viking way," said Grandma, her practiced hands cutting a block of butter into the flour mixture. "By raiding and pillaging."

Sydney longed for a pen. She'd have to ask permission, of course, but she'd love to write this down for the museum.

"So, that's why Cole can't get the Thunderbolt until his wedding?" Sydney worked the stubby green stems off the berries.

"Can't have Cole going after ale and wenches," said Grandma with a wink and a sparkling smile.

"Do you have a lot of stories?" asked Sydney.

"Some," said Grandma.

"I'd love to hear them."

"And I love to talk. We'll get along just fine."

Grandma opened a drawer beneath the counter and pulled out a wooden rolling pin. "Berries ready?"

Sydney quickly turned her attention to the bowl, picking out the last of the stems, draining the water. Then she rolled the blueberries onto a clean towel.

"So, what do you say?" asked Grandma. "You willing to give my grandson a go?"

The front door slammed. "Grandma?" called Cole.

Grandma winked at Sydney again as she rolled out a round of dough. "That man needs a strong, intelligent woman," she stage-whispered.

Cole sauntered into the kitchen. "There you are." He gave his grandma a hug. He nodded to Katie. Then he clasped Sydney around the shoulders and gave her an affectionate squeeze. Good compromise.

"How was the trip?" he asked.

"Bought a Stetson and some blue jeans," said Sydney, finding it ridiculously easy to act excited about Cole's presence.

"Can't wait to see them." He dropped his arm from her shoulders and turned back to his grandma. "Need anything from the garden?"

"Potatoes and carrots," she answered.

"Want to help?" he asked Sydney.

"Sure."

Cole strode for the kitchen door, opening it and motioning for her to go first.

As she crossed the back deck to the stairs, she took in the spectacular panorama. She could see the roof of Cole's cabin, the winding creek, the blue-green lake and Katie and Kyle's house on a distant hill. Evergreens on the mountain ridges spiked up to a crackling turquoise sky.

"Be careful. They're steep," Cole warned from behind.

Sydney put her hand on the painted rail as she started down the long staircase that led to a lawn and a huge vegetable garden.

"How did it go?" Cole kept his voice low.

"Your grandma's definitely on board," said Sydney. "But Katie thought I was trying to romance the brooch out from under you."

Cole moved up beside her as they hit the bottom. "How do you know that?"

"She didn't pull any punches. She flat-out accused me of pretending to fall for you in order to get the Thunderbolt."

Cole shook his head, placing a hand on the small of Sydney's back and guiding her to the far side of the garden. "That Katie's more than just a pretty face."

"I'll say." His warm hand felt good against her back. It felt sure and strong. This chivalrous streak might be annoying in another man, but somehow it suited Cole. It wasn't put on and it wasn't a put-down. He was genuine. Genuine was nice.

"What did you tell her?"

"I swore up and down that I was being completely honest with you."

Cole grinned. "Good one. You're more than just a pretty face, too."

She stopped at the edge of the garden, telling herself he was just being polite. "Thank you. I may have a brain, but I'm not a gardener. What do we do?"

"I'm thinking something silly and romantic."

"What?"

"I can guarantee you they're watching us from the window." He picked a plump tomato from a vine and tossed it meaningfully in the air, catching it with one hand and advancing toward her with an evil grin.

She took a step back. "That doesn't look very romantic, Cole."

"I'm teasing you. Guys in love do that all the time."

"You stay back."

He kept advancing. "It's plump and ripe and very juicy."

She took another step backward and stumbled on a clump of grass. "Cole."

He lunged, and she shrieked, covering her eyes, expecting a face full of tomato juice. But he snaked an arm around her waist, pulling her up tight against his back, holding the tomato a safe distance away.

Guys in love. Cole did guys in love very, very well.

He kissed her neck. The heat of his lips and the puff of his breath made her knees go weak. She grabbed at his arm to support herself.

"Nice move," he whispered, kissing her again.

Oh, no. Her hormones surged to life. Her head dipped back to give him better access. The mountains blurred and the sound of cicadas magnified in the long grass.

"Sydney," he breathed, and she turned to meet his lips.

The world instantly shrank to the two of them. She'd been thinking about this all day, missing this all day, every second she was in Wichita Falls, every second she'd been away from Cole.

She couldn't understand it, but nor could she deny it that his kisses seemed the center of the universe. The world pulsated out from the moisture of his lips, the touch of his hands. He lowered them slowly to the soft, fragrant grass, released the tomato and wrapped his arms fully around her.

She closed her eyes. The afternoon sun heated her skin, soaked into her hair. Cole was a delicious weight on top of her, and his lips were working magic. She needed to stay here, just another second, just another minute.

Somebody cleared their throat.

Sydney's eyes flew open and a pair of worn boots came into focus. She squinted up to where Kyle's Stetson blocked the sun.

"Much as I admire your dedication to the cause," he drawled, "I think you two might be overacting."

Cole eased his weight off her.

"Sorry," said Sydney, adjusting her shirt. Where exactly had Cole's hands roamed? What had Kyle seen?

Cole rolled to his feet and held out a hand for Sydney. "Just trying to do our part," he said to Kyle.

Kyle fought a grin. "Next time get a room."

"What would be the point in that?" asked Cole.

Kyle glanced at Sydney and snorted before turning away.

Cole pulled her into a standing position and patted her on the back. "Way to go, partner."

She smoothed her hair. "No problem." No problem at all. If that was Cole faking it, some lucky woman was going to live in paradise someday.

Cole scooped his hat from the ground. "Potatoes and carrots."

"You think that was overkill?" she asked.

"Nah. It was romantic."

"So you figure we're getting it right."

He walked into the garden and crouched down. "Aside from you making Katie suspicious, I think it's going according to plan."

Sydney turned to watch Kyle stride up the staircase. "You know, you three blow me away."

"What do you mean?" Cole dug into the black dirt.

"Katie's protecting you from me. Kyle's protecting his wife from stress. And you're compromising your principles to help them both."

"Something wrong in that?"

"Something nice in that. I'm just trying to save my job." She liked what that said about Cole. She wasn't completely sure she liked what that said about her.

Cole rose to his feet, dusting one hand off on the thigh of his jeans as he made his way out of the garden. "Your job is in jeopardy?"

She nodded. "Yeah," she admitted. "I'm on probation. There's this guy…"

Then she stopped herself and shook her head. She wasn't letting thoughts of Bradley mar the day. "Truth is,

I haven't been delivering the way the museum needs. If the Thunderbolt hadn't worked out, I'd have been out of a job."

"Hold these." He filled her hands with long, crisp carrots. "So, do I get extra points for helping you *and* with Katie?"

"Absolutely." She tried to think of something nice she could do for Cole. "You want to come to New York and see the display?"

He shrugged, heading into another section of the garden. "Maybe. If we're still faking it."

Sydney watched Cole unearth a handful of potatoes and tried to imagine him in her Sixth Avenue apartment. He was too big for New York, too raw, too wild. He belonged on horseback in the rain, or half naked in his cabin kitchen.

She shivered at that particular memory. This urge to kiss him was turning into an obsession. And the obsession was moving way past kissing.

Cole was untamable and exciting and exotic. He was sexy as all get-out, and challenged her on every level. Aside from the Thunderbolt, aside from the charade, she wanted him in every way a woman could possibly want a man.

"You'll never get anyone to marry you without a decent house," said Grandma, plunking a well-thumbed catalog down on the low table in front of him.

Cole snapped to attention, pulling his arm from the back of the porch swing where he'd been toying with Sydney's hair. "Huh?"

"I've been after you for months to pick out plans. And with Sydney here, well, it seems like the perfect opportunity to get a female opinion."

"As opposed to yours and Katie's?" Cole wasn't picking out house plans. He had other things to spend his money on, and he had a perfectly good cabin down by the creek.

"Great idea," said Katie, pulling her patio chair closer. Her eyes shone with anticipation as she flipped open the book.

"Cape Cod or Colonial?" asked Kyle, placing his hands on his wife's shoulders.

Cole glared at his brother. "I do not need a new house."

"You're joking, right?" said Katie.

She shifted her attention to Sydney. "Tell him no self-respecting woman would live in that cabin."

Sydney tensed, and Cole automatically reached out to squeeze her hand. "You're putting Sydney on the spot, Katie."

Grandma sidled up next to Sydney. "I'm sure she doesn't mind. We just want to take advantage of your cosmopolitan taste, dear."

Sydney kept her mouth shut tight, and Cole shot Kyle a meaningful glare. Unfortunately his brother's only response was a mocking grin.

"I need a new hay barn," said Cole. "An addition on the tack shed, and an upgrade to the combines. We all agreed in the spring."

"No. *You* agreed in the spring," said Katie primly. "The rest of us thought you needed a new house."

Cole reached out and shut the book. He'd agreed to a marriage of convenience. He'd agreed to pretend it was real. But he wasn't building any damn house just to keep Katie from being stressed.

"The cabin's fine," he said, moderating his voice. "Even if I was to get married—" he turned to Sydney "—that cabin would be okay in the short term. Right?"

She swallowed. "Uh—"

Katie jerked the catalog out from under Cole's hand.

"Now you're the one putting Sydney on the spot. If the cabin's so fine, we'll move into it. You take the house."

"Don't be ridiculous."

"Why is it ridiculous when I say it?"

"There are two of you. And you're a woman."

"Now you're sounding sexist."

Cole turned to his brother. "You'd actually let your wife live in the cabin."

"Nope," said Kyle. "But it sounds like you're willing to let yours."

Cole opened his mouth, but he couldn't immediately come up with the right argument. Damn Kyle. This was *not* his opportunity to push the new house agenda.

"And what about the children?" asked Katie. "There's absolutely no room in the cabin for children."

All eyes swung to Sydney. "Maybe an addition?" she offered.

Katie laughed. "Yeah, right. Cape Cod or Colonial?"

Grandma patted her hand. "Don't be shy, Sydney. We value your input."

Sydney hesitated, but she was being stared down by the entire family. "I've, uh, always liked a nice Cape Cod."

"Page thirty-nine," said Grandma.

"Well, you were a big help," Cole said to Sydney as they walked down the ranch road in the moonlight. After her initial protest, she'd plunged into the planning session with gusto.

"I tried to keep quiet."

"And that didn't seem to work out for you?"

"I'm supposed to be falling for you, so I tried to make myself sound like actual wife material. I answered all your Grandma's questions. We swapped recipes—"

"You know recipes?"

Sydney shot him a look. "I made them up. Point is, if I'd balked at planning my future house, it would have looked suspicious."

"Now they're going to want me to build the damn thing."

"So what? The cabin is falling apart."

"What am I going to do with a two-story, octagonal great room?"

"I didn't vote for the octagonal great room. That was Katie."

"Well you voted for the dormer windows."

"They're pretty."

"And a turret?"

"Adds detail."

"And what am I going to do with a hot tub?"

Sydney was silent for a moment. "Uh, bathe?"

"Very funny. I don't need jets and bubblers rumbling under my butt to get clean."

"Ever tried one?"

"No."

She grinned and bumped her shoulder against his arm. "Don't know what you're missing, cowboy."

"Why? Have you?"

"It just so happens I *own* a hot tub."

A visual bloomed in Cole's brain—of Sydney, glistening skin and swirling water.

"Cole?"

He cleared his throat. "Yeah?"

"You ever stop to think there might be some deep-seated, psychological reason you shortchange yourself?"

"No." He didn't shortchange himself, and he didn't have deep-seated reasons for anything. He herded cows. He raised horses. He kept the ranch running. What you saw was what you got.

"You're living in a cabin where you wouldn't let any other member of your family live."

That wasn't true. He turned from the ranch road down his short driveway and the roar of the creek grew louder. "I'd let Kyle live there."

"And you've never been married."

"Lucky for you." If he was married she wouldn't be getting this opportunity with the Thunderbolt.

"See, I have a hard time believing women aren't interested in you. If you'd wanted—"

"Plenty of women are interested in me." He felt ego-bound to point that out. Well, maybe not plenty. But some. Enough. He wasn't exactly a monk out here.

"Then why haven't you settled down?"

"It's not by choice."

"Bet it is."

"Not my choice."

"The women said no?"

He refused to answer, wondering how he and Sydney always ended up having such personal conversations. He was a private man. He liked it that way.

"Come on, Cole," Sydney prompted.

"Why aren't *you* married?" He tried to turn the tables.

Her answer surprised him. "Nobody ever proposed."

"Did you even want them to?" he asked.

"You mean, have I ever been in love?"

"Yeah."

"I don't think so."

"You don't know?" That surprised Cole.

She shook her head. "What about you?"

"I guess not."

She grinned and bumped him again. "But *you're* not sure?"

He cocked his head, considering her. "You know, it's hard, isn't it? To know for sure."

"Is that why you never asked anyone."

"Nah. Never got that far. Truth is, they all left me once they got to know me."

She tipped her head back and gave him a hint of that sexy laugh. "No way. You left them."

He had to squelch an urge to wrap his arm around her. She was just the right height, just the right size, just the right shape for his arms.

Instead he shook his head. "I'm a bit of a selfish jerk deep down inside."

"No. You're the opposite. Just like I said. You're the one sacrificing to take care of everyone around you."

They came to the porch and he preceded her up the three steps. "Do you happen to have a degree in psychology?"

"I have a degree in art history."

"Good." He pushed open the door and stood to one side. "You can decorate the turret and leave my brain alone."

She grinned as she walked past him. "Your brain is beginning to fascinate me."

"I don't want a new house, because I don't need a new house. This is a working ranch, not a Dallas subdivision. Next thing they'll be putting in a pool."

"I've hit on something here, haven't I?"

"You haven't hit on anything." His voice came out unexpectedly sharp as he flipped the kitchen lamp.

Her eyes went wide. "I'm sorry."

Cole swore under his breath. He shook his head and moved toward her. "No. I'm the one who's sorry." He was falling back on defense mechanisms now.

"It's none of my business," she said.

"Of course it's not. But we're playing this silly game."
He took a breath. "Ah, Sydney. We should have known it
would get complicated."

She gave him a nod and a hesitant smile, and he found
himself easing closer. He inhaled deeply, filling his senses.

Her lips were burgundy in the lamplight. Her emerald
eyes were fringed by thick lashes. Her skin was ivory-
smooth, flushed from the walk. And the memory of it was
indelibly pressed into the nerves of his fingertips.

Unable to stop himself, he smoothed a lock of hair from
her forehead.

"Complicated," he whispered one more time.

Her lips parted, softly, invitingly. He should have known
the second he got her alone, he'd give in to the cravings.
He cupped her cheeks, pulling her closer. His lips closed
over hers and relief roared through his body.

He'd been watching her all day, wanting her all day. She
was under his skin and into his brain in a way that he
couldn't control.

He kissed her harder, stepping toward her, pressing her
back against the door. A bronc had blasted off inside him,
and there was nothing he could do but hang on for the ride.

He tipped his head to find a better angle, and she came
alive under his hands, all movement and sound and scent.

This was good. This was right. This was more than he'd
ever found in any other woman. He stopped thinking about
the Thunderbolt. He stopped thinking about Katie. He
stopped thinking about plots and plans and deceptions.

There was only Sydney, her taste and her touch.

"Cole," she breathed, her fingertips tightening on his
shoulders.

"I know." He kissed her eyelids.

"This *is* complicated."

"This is inevitable."

She paused for a second. "Maybe."

"Absolutely." He slipped his hand under her shirt, skimming across the small of her back. Her skin was sinfully warm, sinfully soft. She was a treasure he hadn't earned and didn't deserve.

"We can stop," he whispered reassuringly, kissing his way along the crook of her neck. "You say when."

"Not yet," she whispered back.

"Thank God," he sighed.

Her hand inched its way slowly up between them and, one by one, she popped the buttons on his shirt. When the last one gave way, she burrowed inside the fabric.

He kissed the top of her head and rocked her in his arms. He wanted to carry her to his bed, press himself against her—kiss her, talk to her, make love with her, simply breathe the same air. Whatever she wanted, whenever she wanted it.

She kissed his chest, her hot tongue flicking out to sear his skin.

He struggled for air as passion commandeered his senses. "We're pushing it," he warned.

She kissed him again. "Let's push it further."

He pulled back and gazed down at her. Her lips were swollen, her eyes were slumberous and her hair was tousled out like a halo.

"You want to make love?" he asked.

"Yeah."

"You sure?"

She smoothed her palms up the front of his chest. "You're right. It's inevitable."

Five

Sydney held her breath, wondering if Cole might actually refuse.

"I want you *so* bad," he said instead.

Her breath whooshed out. "You had me worried there for a second, cowboy."

He shook his head, smoothing back her hair. "Don't you worry. Don't you ever worry."

Something settled deep inside her and her worries vanished.

Cole had to be the most honest and honorable man she'd ever met. Yeah, he was getting in her way over the Thunderbolt. But he was doing it out of respect for his family.

Unlike the men she'd dated in New York, unlike some of her colleagues and contacts at the museum, everything she'd seen, everything he'd done, told her Cole was a man to be trusted.

She'd missed trust.

She'd missed honor.

She wanted him and he wanted her. It didn't get much more honest than that.

She focused on the feel of his rough palm against her scalp. His eyes burned smoky-blue, and she felt like the most desirable woman in the world. Her lashes grew heavy and she tilted her head into the sensation of Cole.

His palm cupped her face and he kissed her eyes. Her body felt as if it were drifting on air, soaring up to the ceiling. The dying fire gave off a faint, distinct tang. The creek roared over boulders outside the window, and Cole left trails of shooting sparks wherever he touched.

She tasted his salty skin, then she squeezed his hard body tighter and tighter until she was safe and surrounded by his warmth. He lifted her into his arms as if she weighed nothing. Nobody had ever carried her before. He started to walk, and she was sorry the bedroom was so close.

"Hold me for a minute," she said when they got there.

His arms flexed. "No problem."

She sighed against his chest. "You think you could stop time? Right here? Right now?"

"I wish I could."

"Try really, really hard."

His chuckle rumbled through her. "I can go slow."

"Easy for you, maybe."

"Nope. Not easy at all."

"But you'd do it for me?"

"I'll do anything for you. Just say the word."

Let me into your world, she wanted to say. Not just your bed, but your heart and your soul.

But that was impossible. They had here and now, and that was all. She forced a light note into her voice.

"Get naked."

"Okay. But that might speed things up a little."

"Or I could get naked."

"That would be worse." His voice sounded strangled.

She struggled to push his shirt from his shoulders. "Let's play with fire."

He slowly lowered her feet to the floor. "Sydney, I've been playing with fire since the first second I laid eyes on you."

She took a shaky step back and reached for the hem of her T-shirt. He stared down at her with such longing and reverence that a shudder ran straight through her body. She peeled the shirt over her head, gauging his reaction, loving his reaction.

His nostrils flared and his gaze latched onto her lacy bra. Without a word, he shucked his own shirt.

She stared unabashedly at the play of muscles across his chest. "You think we want this so bad, because we know we shouldn't?"

"Yeah." He nodded. "It probably has nothing to do with the way you look, taste, smell or feel."

"That's it."

"That's what?"

"The way you smell."

"It's bad?"

She shook her head, gliding toward him, burying her face in his chest again. "It's good. So good."

He reached between their bodies and flicked the button on her jeans. "You, too."

She smiled and went on her toes, kissing his mouth as he lowered her zipper. "Let's not tell anyone," she said.

"That we made love?"

She shook her head. "The smell secret."

"You got it."

He rolled off her pants then got rid of his own. Then he gently pressed her back on the bed, covering her with kisses, whispering words of reverence and encouragement, sending her heart rate soaring and her hormones into overdrive.

His fingertips skimmed her stomach, circling her navel with a featherlight touch that made her breath come in a gasp and her muscles contract. Before she could adjust to the sensation, he bent over her breast, taking one nipple into his mouth, swirling and circling the crest with his tongue.

She moaned, and her hands went to his hair. Sensations rocketed through her body as his teeth raked her tender flesh and his hand began a downward spiral.

This wasn't going to be slow. It was going to be lightning fast if she didn't do something.

"Cole," she gasped.

"You're delicious," he answered, fingers dipping lower, increasing the onslaught of sensation.

"Slow…down…" she begged.

She felt his smile. "No way." He crossed the downy curls and pressed into her in one swift motion.

Her hips came up off the bed, and her hands convulsed against his head. "Cole," she wailed.

"Go with it," he said.

"But…"

He moved to look into her eyes, his fingers pulsing in a way that made her world shift to the exquisite touch on her tender, moist flesh. She flexed her hips. He kissed her mouth.

"There's more to come," he rumbled against her. "I promise."

She closed her eyes. She was past the point of resisting. Past the point of coherent thought. She was going where he led her, and there was no way to stop it.

Her world roared, then went silent.

They were skin to skin, soul to soul as he eased inside her. True to his word, he took it slow, watching her closely, gauging her desires. Their breathing synchronized as the corner clock ticked away minutes.

A warm rush of sensation crested up from her toes. He smiled and deepened his kiss, increasing his rhythm until her world imploded, the clock's ticks slowed to a crawl and paradise stretched on and on.

She wrapped her arms around his neck, guilt nipping at her conscience. Nobody had ever done that before. No one had ever set aside their own needs to take her to paradise.

As the power of speech returned, she searched his deep eyes, worried that he'd made some stupid, gentlemanly decision against making love. "We're not…uh…stopping, are we?"

He shook his head and brushed a lock of hair from her cheek, shifting so that his big body covered hers. "Oh, sweetheart. We're just getting started."

He kissed her mouth. His thumb returned to her breast and, against all odds, her desire instantly rallied.

She ran her hands down his back, sliding them onto his taut buttocks and pressing his erection against her stomach, shivering with anticipation. She kissed his harder, swirling her tongue against his.

He opened wide, and she could feel the tension rising in his muscles.

She moaned and wriggled beneath him, shifting her thighs in a clear invitation.

He gasped. "Hey. This is supposed to be the slow part."

"Fast is fun," she assured him, shifting again, even more meaningfully this time.

He grabbed her hip with a broad hand and held her still,

pulling back to look into her eyes. "If I go now, I'm going to break a land-speed record."

"Now," she said. "I don't care. Now." Slow had been a stupid idea anyway. Nothing between her and Cole was ever going to be slow.

He flexed his hips and was instantly inside her.

She groaned, nearly melting around his heat.

He buried his hands in her hair, thumbs stroking her temples. His breath came in gasps next to her ear.

She could feel the tension cresting in his steel, hard muscles. Her body tightened and strained and pulsated.

She reached for the comfortor, fisting her hands into the fabric as their rhythm increased.

He repeated her name, over and over again. Then his hands found hers, covered hers, their fingers entwining as the world exploded into black and time ceased to exist.

Cole kissed her damp brow. "You okay?"

She sighed, sinking into his incredibly soft bed. "I don't think okay is exactly the right word."

"You hurt?"

"No. It's fantastic. Fantastic is the right word."

He chuckled low in her ear, easing most of his weight off her. "You give me heart failure all the time, you know that?"

"You're pushing things too fast," said Kyle as he tapped the remainder of the glass from a broken window in the toolshed.

Cole set a new pane on the ground, leaning it against the wall of the shed before he retrieved a hammer from the toolbox.

Kyle didn't know the half of how fast they'd pushed things. Cole had never done that before—made love after only two days.

"I think we're doing fine," he said, strapping on a leather belt and dumping a handful of nails into the pouch.

Kyle whacked at a stubborn corner of glass and it tinkled into jagged pieces. "First you're necking on the lawn, then you bring her home after midnight."

A grin split Cole's face. "Will you listen to yourself? You sound like her father."

"I'm just saying, Katie's not going to buy it if you don't slow it down."

Cole moved up to the shed wall and dug his claw hammer into the window frame. One by one, the finishing nails popped out. "It's a compromise. Sydney's on a deadline with the Thunderbolt."

"You're worried about her deadline? This from a guy who was willing to throw her off the property two days ago?"

"I'm getting to know her now. And I didn't realize her job was on the line."

Kyle stopped, fixing his attention on Cole. "She told you her job was on the line?"

"Yeah."

Kyle glared at him impatiently.

"What?"

"Cole. What are you doing?"

Had Kyle guessed what had happened last night? Was it that obvious?

"I'm pretending to fall for Sydney," he said with exaggerated patience, trying to gauge his brother's expression.

"You sure about that?"

"I'm positive about that. What are you suggesting?"

Kyle whacked the glass again. "I'm suggesting you watch yourself."

Cole nearly choked on that one. "Hang on. This was *your* idea, little brother."

"Yeah." Kyle tugged his leather work gloves from his back pocket. "And I may have been wrong about that."

"Wrong? Hello? What did I miss?"

"She could be playing you," said Kyle, settling his fingers in the grooves.

"Playing me how? She's been up front and honest about everything." Unlike him and Kyle who were pulling one over on Katie.

"Has she?"

"Yes!"

Kyle brushed shards of glass from the sill. "Think about it, Cole. She's getting exactly what she came for."

"Uh, yeah. That was the deal."

"The deal was Katie would think Sydney fell for you. But now *you* think Sydney's falling for you."

"No, I don't," Cole snapped.

"Yes, you do. And what the hell are the odds of that?"

Cole hadn't honestly thought about the odds last night. But then, he didn't think Sydney was falling for him, either. Not really. It was more a chemical thing. A very powerful chemical thing.

Not that he could tell Kyle he'd slept with Sydney. How suspicious would that look?

"It's under control," he said to Kyle.

"You telling me you're not falling for her?"

"We're faking it for Katie."

"You and I shared a room for fifteen years, Cole. Quite frankly, you're not that good an actor."

"So, what are you suggesting? I call it off? Kick her out?"

"I'm just suggesting you watch your back. Don't trust her too far too soon."

"Fine."

"I'm serious."

"I said fine."

"Just think about the possibilities."

Cole dug in on the upper frame. "What part of *fine* didn't you understand?"

He would think about the possibilities. He was thinking about the possibilities. Because he didn't know Sydney.

Yeah, he felt as though he knew her. But she had an agenda, and that agenda included getting him to the altar.

What he'd interpreted as sweet, sexy vulnerability, could have been cold, calculated manipulation. Maybe she was hot for him, or maybe she was playing to his ego.

As bad as it sucked, Kyle had a point. What *were* the odds of a woman like Sydney wanting to sleep with a man like Cole after only two days?

Katie had offered Sydney the use of Kyle's office phone to contact the museum. Sydney's heart thumped in her chest as she dialed Gwen Parks's number. Saying it out loud was going to make it real.

"Gwen, here," came her friend's voice over the phone line.

"Hey, Gwen. It's Sydney."

"Hey, Sydney." There was a smile in Gwen's voice. "How's the hunt going?"

Sydney took a deep breath. "Well. I found it."

There was silence on the other end of the line. "Define 'it.'"

"The Thunderbolt of the North."

Gwen squealed and Sydney jerked the phone away from her ear.

"You actually found it? Where are you? Where is it? What happened?"

"I'm in Texas."

Another silence.

"Who'd have thought," said Sydney.

"Did you bring it over from Europe?"

"It's been here the whole time."

"Oh, wow. When are you coming back?"

Sydney lowered her voice. "Not right away. It's complicated. Can I get you started on the show?"

"Without you?"

"Yeah."

"Of course. But you *do* have the Thunderbolt, right?"

"It's in a lawyer's office in Wichita Falls. But don't tell a soul. Bradley Slander is still gunning for me, and I don't want him getting wind of this until it's a done deal."

"If it's not a done deal, why am I setting up the show?"

Sydney twisted the phone cord around her hand. "It is. Sort of. Well... I have to marry the owner."

Another silence.

"It's a complicated inheritance thing."

"You're going to *marry* into the Thunderbolt family?"

"It's a marriage of convenience."

"Don't you think that's above and beyond?"

"It's the only way. I'm pretending to fall..." Sydney hesitated over the details. "Anyway, we'll divorce as soon as the show's over."

"I don't know, Sydney."

"Trust me on this. I've got it under control. My notes on the other antiquities are in my computer, along with the contact names. I'm going to reserve the front gallery."

"You're making me nervous."

"I can do this."

"You sure?"

"Yes."

She had to do this. She had no choice but to do this. It didn't matter how complicated her feelings got for Cole.

Nor did it matter how much she was starting to love this crazy Texas ranch.

She was here to do a job. Once she got back to New York it would all fall into perspective. She'd be hailed a hero, and her professional reputation would be saved.

"Okay."

"Great. Talk to you in a few days." Sydney let out a sigh of relief and hung up the phone.

It was going to happen. It was truly going to happen.

Then she glanced up, and there was Katie, white-faced in the doorway.

Damn. She opened her mouth, but Katie turned on her heel.

"Katie!" Sydney scrambled around the desk, sprinting to the door. "Katie, it's not what—"

"Don't!" Katie gritted her teeth, her hands balling into fists as she stomped down the hallway. "You lied to me. You lied, straight-faced, and I let you into my family."

"Cole knows."

"Yeah, right."

"He *knows*."

Katie shook her head, her voice quavering. "No, he doesn't. But he's going to. Right now."

She stormed out the door and Sydney took off after her.

The plan was ruined. Sydney had screwed up everything. She should have talked quieter. She should have closed the door.

Cole was going to kill her, and so was Kyle, and now Katie would be more stressed than ever.

"Katie, listen," she gasped, rushing through the open doorway and struggling to catch up. She tried running, but her pace in heels was no match for Katie in her boots. Katie easily outdistanced her to the toolshed.

"She's a con artist and a liar and thief," yelled Katie as Sydney rapidly approached the three.

Kyle dropped a tool onto the ground and wrapped his arms around his wife. "What the hell?"

"She overheard me," Sydney called as she made her way through cacti and range grass.

"She's pretending to fall in love with Cole." Katie's voice broke. "I heard her. She's only after the Thunderbolt."

Cole stuffed a hammer into his tool belt and moved toward Katie, laying a hand on her shoulder. "It's okay, Katie. I know that already."

"How could you know that?" she sniffed. "She's lying to you. She's lying to all of us." She shot Sydney a look of venom.

"I am so sorry," said Sydney, her voice shaking, a sick feeling swirling in the pit of her stomach.

"I'll just bet you are," Katie snapped.

"Sweetheart." Kyle spoke against her hair in a soft voice. "This is all my fault."

Katie tipped her chin to look up at him. "How is it your fault?"

Sydney wished the ground would open up and swallow her whole. Katie was such a wonderful human being. She didn't deserve this heartache. She deserved Kyle's love every minute of every day, plus a whole troop of little Ericksons running around her house.

"*I* did something really stupid," said Cole.

"It was *me*," said Sydney. She didn't want to break up this happy family. They loved each other. They meant the world to each other.

"Will you two stop?" asked Kyle.

"Katie," said Cole. "After the baby thing—"

Katie turned a shade paler.

"—I thought your stress level would drop if I got married and had babies."

"We weren't really going to have babies," Sydney put in. "We were just going to let you think we'd have babies. It seemed like the perfect plan. I'd get the Thunderbolt. You'd probably get pregnant. By the time we got divorced, you'd be okay again."

Katie turned to Kyle. "You went along with this?"

"I—"

"We talked him into it," said Cole. "*I* talked him into it. Thing is, Katie. I'm going to make it come true."

The breath rushed from Sydney's lungs and she blinked at Cole's rugged profile. Because of last night? Because of what they'd shared?

Was it possible? Did Cole think there was something growing between them?

Her chest expanded with a warm glow. She had no idea how they'd work it out, but the thought of Cole wanting to try settled around her like a soft blanket.

"As soon as I divorce Sydney," Cole continued, and Sydney's heart went flat, "I'm going to find another wife. A real wife. I'm going to take on some of the responsibility of this damn dynasty."

Cole's words died away to silence and Sydney took an involuntary step back.

Of course he'd find a real wife. What on earth was she thinking? Cole couldn't do New York, and Sydney wasn't staying in Texas. Her career and her life were about to take a quantum leap. The sky would be the limit after the Thunderbolt show.

Katie stared at her, and Sydney forced out a shaky laugh. "See? It'll all work out."

"Cole," said Kyle. "You don't have—"

"My mind's made up." Cole rubbed Katie's shoulder. "I just hope I can find a wife who'll hold a candle to you."

Katie wiped her cheeks with the back of her hand. "I'm sorry," she whispered to Sydney.

Sydney moved closer. "You have absolutely nothing to be sorry about." Katie had come to a perfectly logical conclusion.

She nodded her agreement. "Okay. But we probably shouldn't tell Grandma it's a sham."

Cole looked at Kyle, and Kyle looked at Cole.

"You're right," said Cole. "We still have a wedding to plan."

Sydney parked herself on an old workbench to watch Cole finish the window repair. It had seemed like a good idea to give Katie and Kyle some time alone. She wanted to ask Cole about his marriage promise, but she didn't want him to think she cared.

If she didn't care, would she ask or stay quiet? Hard to know. Probably ask. After all, it was all academic to her.

She made up her mind. "Cole?"

"Yeah?"

"Were you serious? Or were you just trying to make Katie happy?"

"Serious about what?"

"Finding a real wife." She hated the pain that flashed through her chest when she said those words. It was almost as though she was jealous. Which made no sense. She was never going to see Cole again after the museum show. That had always been the plan.

Just because she'd slept with him, she didn't need to get all moony-eyed about it. She'd slept with men before. Men she'd liked and trusted. But she'd never gone around the bend over it. She'd never started imagining forever. Never even been jealous of the women they *might* date in the future.

Cole nodded as he hammered tiny nails around the wood that held the new glass. "I am putting too much pressure on Kyle and Katie. It's time I held up my end of the family."

"Do you think planning to marry some unknown wife is such a good idea?"

He stopped hammering and gave her a long look. "Yes, I do."

"It doesn't strike you as just a little bit self-sacrificing?"

He went back to hammering. "Not really. We Texans take loyalty and honor very seriously."

Sydney shifted on the bench. "Ouch."

Cole shrugged. "Not a criticism."

"Yeah, right." Obviously her values were a question mark in his mind. She might be fine for a night in bed, but she sure didn't meet his standards for a wife.

Good girl, bad girl again. At least this time she knew which one she was.

"We can probably move the marriage plans up," he said.

Sydney nodded. "That's good." The sooner she got away from him, the better.

"If Grandma suspects anything," he continued, "it'll be that you're pregnant and we need a quickie wedding."

"But you've only known me a few days."

He pounded in a final nail and dropped the hammer into his belt. "I travel a lot. She'll assume we've met before."

"Of course." Sydney nodded. Because a bad girl is always good for a one-night stand when a guy's on the road. She gritted her teeth and forced herself to focus on business. "I've asked a colleague to start preparing for the show."

Cole gave a nod.

"Is there any way I could take a look at the Thunderbolt before the wedding?"

"I guess so. What for?"

"It'll help me conceptualize a display for it. It would really help if I could take a couple of pictures to send to the museum." Business, business. All business. She could do this.

Cole stood back to scrutinize the job. "I'll drive you in as soon as I can get away."

Six

One thing about having Katie in on the marriage plan, it meant Sydney didn't have to see nearly as much of Cole. While she waited for the trip to Wichita Falls, she made museum arrangements by long distance and spent some time visiting Grandma.

Sydney was growing to like the eccentric old woman. Grandma was smart, opinionated and had one zinger of a sense of humor. She also told stories about the Thunderbolt and about her early years in Texas that fascinated Sydney.

Like the time the pack string stepped in a wasps' nest. The first horse through was stung once and did a little crow hop off the trail. His burden of flour and utensils stayed put. The second horse through was a bomb-proof mare. She barely flinched when three wasps stung her rump.

Unfortunately, the third horse through took the brunt of the attack. He was a reliable four-year-old entrusted with the month's supply of whiskey. The horse leapt off the ground, all four feet in the air. His frantic bucking loosened the pack saddle, sending the whiskey swinging under his belly.

The unnatural load spooked him even more, and he ran hell bent for leather into the creek. Though the cowboys raced to his rescue, the precious cargo was washed over the falls.

The cook was so frightened at the prospect of showing up at the cattle drive without a fresh whiskey supply that he rode two days and two nights to restock.

When Cole finally announced he had time to take Sydney to the city, she eagerly hopped into his pickup. She couldn't wait to see the Thunderbolt, even if it meant a two-hour drive alone with him.

"Haven't seen much of you," he commented as they pulled onto the main road.

"Haven't seen much of you, either," she returned, gauging his tone, wondering how to read him and annoyed that she felt the need to try.

He shrugged. "Had work to do."

"Me, too." She did have a life. It wasn't as if she'd been pining away, wondering if he regretted their lovemaking, or if he'd found any likely Susie Homemakers to take her place.

"Have I done something to annoy you?" he asked.

Did he mean other than announce to his family that he was finding a "real" wife just as soon as he dumped her?

"I'm not annoyed," she said.

"So this is the level you've picked for our relationship?"

The level *she'd* picked? "You wanted something more?"

He shrugged, flipping on his right signal and leaving the gravel road behind in favor of the four-lane interstate. "You must admit, it all turned on a dime there after Katie got in the loop."

"Ah." Sydney nodded, wishing she could control the jealousy cresting in her veins. "So you did want more sex."

He twisted his head to look at her. "Excuse me?"

"Sorry about that. I guess I did turn off the tap all of a sudden."

His eyes narrowed, and he glanced to the highway and back to her again. "Was there a particular reason you backed off?"

She shrugged. No reason that was remotely logical, just a horrible, kicked-in-the-gut feeling when he'd rejected her. "We didn't need to pretend anymore," she said.

"You mean, the Thunderbolt was in the bag."

"Yeah. Right. Something like that." She turned her head to look out the window.

"I see."

"Okay."

"Fine." He pressed on the accelerator and turned up the radio.

Neither of them spoke until they hit Wichita Falls.

At a traffic light in the heart of downtown, Cole turned on the left turn signal and waited for a space in traffic. "This is it."

Despite his brooding presence, Sydney's stomach leaped in anticipation. "Which one?"

He pointed to a tall, gray office tower as he angled into a parking spot in front.

Sydney scanned the building. This was it. The treasure of a lifetime was waiting inside for her. Despite her anger with Cole, she felt like a kid on Christmas morning.

They entered the building and took an elevator to the tenth floor. The brass sign on the oversize office doors read Neely And Smythe, Attorneys-At-Law.

"Auspicious," said Sydney.

"It's been the family firm for four generations."

"And the Thunderbolt's been here the whole time?"

"Most of it."

"I'm getting goose bumps."

As he opened the door, Cole gave her his first smile in three days.

It felt good. Way too good. Pathetically good.

She preceded him into the reception area, and a smiling brunette woman greeted them warmly. She sat behind a marble counter in a room decorated with leather furniture and fine art.

"Mr. Neely can see you right away," she said to Cole.

Cole moved to open another doorway that took them to a private hall.

A balding man met them at the far end of the hallway. He shook hands with Cole then turned to Sydney. "Joseph Neely." He offered his hand to her. "I understand you're here to see the Thunderbolt."

"I am," she agreed. "Sydney Wainsbrook."

"I enjoy an excuse to look at it myself," he said, turning his key in the lock and pushing the door inward.

"It's pretty exciting," she admitted.

"I'll leave you two alone then." Joseph Neely gestured to the interior of the office.

Sydney went in first, blinking to adjust her vision to the dimmer light.

Cole came in behind her and pointed to a round, mahogany meeting table.

She followed his signal and everything inside her turned still. Laid majestically out on a purple, velvet cloth, was the Thunderbolt of the North. The brooch of kings. The stuff of legends.

Sydney sucked in a breath. It was large, boldly crafted,

magnificent in every way. The polished-gold lightning bolt was scattered almost randomly with rubies, emeralds and diamonds. It was big. It was audacious. It was everything she'd ever hoped for.

She circled it, running her fingers across the soft cloth, letting them get close, but not touching the treasure. "You are one lucky man," she said in a reverent, husky voice.

His voice was equally hushed. "Sometimes I think so."

"This is the thrill of a lifetime."

"You can touch it, you know."

She rubbed her fingertips together, sensitizing them. Then she leaned in ever so slowly, resting her hips against the edge of the table.

After a long minute she dared to touch the bottom point of the brooch.

She immediately snatched her hand back, a chill creeping into her veins. She felt it again, and her world came to a screeching halt.

"Cole?" she ventured slowly, stomach clenching.

"Yeah?" He'd moved closer, but his voice seemed to come from a long way off.

She tested the bottom diamond one more time and her heart went flat, dead cold.

"This is a fake."

"Don't be absurd," said Cole, studying Sydney's shocked expression.

"It's a fake," she repeated more passionately.

"Right," Cole drawled, glancing down at the brooch. Somebody had bypassed the alarm and broken into the lawyer's safe to reproduce the Thunderbolt without anyone noticing. That was likely.

"When was it last appraised?"

Cole tried to figure out where she was going with this.

"When?" she demanded.

"It's been closely guarded for hundreds of years." The odds of it being a fake were ridiculously slim.

Had Kyle been right about her? Was this some kind of an elaborate con?

"What are you up to?" he demanded.

"I'm *up to* giving you my professional opinion."

"Uh, huh." He struggled to figure out her angle. How she could turn this little ruse to her advantage?

She pointed to the brooch. "See those diamonds? The little ones on the points?"

He glanced down. "Sure."

"They're cut."

"So what?"

"So, nobody faceted diamonds until the fourteenth century. They didn't have the tools. The process hadn't been invented. I don't know who made this brooch, but it sure wasn't the ancient Vikings."

Cole's gaze shot back to the Thunderbolt. He'd seen it dozens of times. It looked the same. It always looked the same.

But she was sounding alarmingly credible, and he couldn't for the life of him figure out how lying about its authenticity would help her get her hands on it. His stomach sank. He had to allow for the possibility that she was telling the truth.

Her voice went up an octave. "Cole, you're not reacting."

He lifted it, holding the glittering gold to the light, speaking to himself. "Who would fake it?"

"We need more information," said Sydney, squinting at the jewel. "I have a friend who's a conservator. She could pinpoint the date more closely, give us somewhere to start."

Ah. Okay. There it was. He could see the scam now.

"You have a friend," he mocked, palming the brooch.

"Gwen Parks. She's worked at the Laurent for—"

"And your *friend* is going to come out and value my brooch?"

Sydney's eyes narrowed. "She's not going to value it—"

Cole let out a chopped laugh. "Let me guess." He took a pace forward. "It'll be worthless. You'll offer to take it off my hands. And the next thing I know it'll be on display in New York."

Sydney's expression lengthened in apparent horror. "Cole, I'd never—"

"Never *what?*" He stepped closer to her again. "Never try anything and everything to get your hands on the Thunderbolt? Never lie? Never cheat? Never marry me or sleep with me?"

She clenched her hands into small fists. "I really don't give a damn what you think of me right now. But the brooch is a fake. Get my expert. Get your own expert. Take it to the Louvre. But if you don't find out *when* it was faked, you're never going to find out *why* it was faked, you are never, *ever* going to have a hope in hell of getting the real one back."

Cole stared at her in silence. Was she serious? She looked serious.

He opened his palm and inspected the brooch.

"Think about it, Cole," she stressed. "Run it through your suspicious, little mind. How could I possibly get away with it? How, in the world, could I think for one minute that I could get away *pretending* the Thunderbolt was a fake?"

Cole closed his hand again, letting the points of the brooch dig into his palm.

She was right. But who would fake it? Who *could* fake it? And who could do it so well that nobody had ever noticed?

There were no pictures of it in circulation. It would have to be somebody who had access to it for more than—

A light bulb exploded in his brain. He stomped his way to the office door, flinging it open.

"Joseph!" he bellowed.

The lawyer appeared almost immediately, bustling his way down the corridor. "Mr. Erickson?" His voice betrayed his obvious concern.

Cole stepped back into the office and closed the door for privacy. "We need an appraiser. Now."

"A conservator," said Sydney.

Both men turned to look at her.

"A museum conservator," she repeated. "One who specializes in gems and jewelry."

"Is something wrong?" asked Joseph Neely.

"The brooch has been faked," said Cole, watching the man closely. Somebody at the firm could easily be the culprit.

Neely was silent for a long moment. He didn't look guilty, but his lawyer brain was obviously clicking through the implications. When he finally spoke, his voice was a rasp. "I don't see how it could have—"

"We need to find out when and how and why," said Cole, accepting that Sydney was telling the truth.

This was a catastrophe.

His chest tightened at the thought of his grandmother's distress. He had to help her. He had to protect her.

No matter what happened, she could never find out.

In Neely's office eight hours later, the words on the newly penned conservator's report blurred in front of Cole's tired eyes. Joseph had offered the use of the facilities as long as they needed them. It was probably half generosity, half concern for the firm's liability. Cole didn't particularly care which one. He just wanted some answers.

After gauging the level of expertise at the local museum, he'd given in and flown Sydney's colleague Gwen Parks down from New York. The two women had talked technical for a couple of hours, quickly losing Cole. But it didn't matter. The only thing important to him was the final verdict.

Gwen had just confirmed that the brooch was indeed a reproduction, and that it was made sometime between nineteen fifty and nineteen seventy-five. It didn't tell them who, and it didn't tell them why, but it did tell them that they had at least a small hope of finding the real one.

"I can put out some feelers," Gwen was saying to Sydney while Joseph put the brooch back in its box to be returned to the safe.

Cole dimly wondered why he bothered. Sure the jewels themselves were valuable, but they were also replaceable. A fifty-year-old ruby, emerald and diamond reproduction was hardly something to lock up in titanium.

He clenched his fist, crumpling it around the report.

"If anybody's ever sold it, or offered it for sale…" Gwen continued, leaning against Joseph's wide mahogany desk "…somebody out there will know something."

Gwen might be dressed in blue jeans and a Mets T-shirt, but the woman had convinced Cole she knew her stuff.

"You got a way into the black market?" asked Sydney.

Gwen nodded her pixie blond head.

Both women were silent for a moment. Sydney didn't ask any questions, and Gwen didn't offer an explanation.

Sydney turned her attention to Cole. "I think we should go talk to Grandma now."

Cole jerked his head up. "What?"

"Gwen's going to try her contacts, but we need to get information from Grandma. The sooner, the better."

"We're not telling Grandma." That point was nonnegotiable.

Sydney brought her hands to her hips. "Of course we are."

Cole dropped the report on the desk. "Do you have any idea how much this will upset her?"

Sydney took a couple of paces toward him, gesturing with an open palm. "Of course it'll upset her. But never finding the Thunderbolt will upset her a whole lot more."

Cole clenched his jaw. "We'll find it without her."

"She had it during the years it was copied. She's our best lead."

"No."

"Cole. Be reasonable. She can tell us where it was, during what time periods."

"The lawyer's records will tell us that."

"All they can tell us is when it was or was not in their safe. Grandma can tell us if it was ever missing, if anybody borrowed it—"

"My answer is no."

Sydney moved directly in front of him and crossed her arms over her chest. "What makes this your decision?"

A pulse leaped to life in Cole's temple. He straightened to his full height, matching her posture. "You will *not* go behind my back and talk to my grandmother."

"The police might. A crime has been committed here, Cole."

"We'll take care of it privately." There was no way in the world Cole was losing control of the investigation, having it dumped into the lap of some overworked police precinct.

"Cole," came Gwen's voice.

Sydney and Cole both turned. Gwen straightened away from the desk, tucking her blond hair behind her ears and moving her small frame into the thick of the conversation.

"Sydney's right. No matter who you talk to, who you ask for help, public, private or otherwise, the first thing they're going to want to do is talk to your grandma. And if they don't, you should fire them for incompetence."

Sydney spoke up again. "She's our only lead."

It didn't matter. "She's seventy years old."

"She's tough as nails."

"The stress could kill her."

Sydney stared at him levelly with those penetrating green eyes. "It's not going to kill her."

They were intelligent eyes, Cole acknowledged. Clear-thinking, logical eyes. He'd never doubted she was smart. Never doubted she was capable. And this was definitely her field of expertise.

Damn.

If he wanted to keep the police out of it, he needed to keep Sydney and Gwen in, which meant he needed to take their advice.

He hated it, but there it was.

"Okay," he said. "Fine. We'll talk to Grandma."

"Tonight?" asked Sydney.

"Tomorrow," said Cole. He wasn't waking Grandma out of a sound sleep to give her bad news.

Gwen plucked her purse from the desktop. "In that case, I'd better get back to New York."

Cole quickly crossed the room and held out his hand. "Thank you very, very much for coming on such short notice." He was a lot more grateful to Gwen than he'd probably let on.

"Thanks for chartering the plane," said Gwen with a shake.

"Whatever you need," said Cole. "You just call me. Anything. Anytime."

Gwen nodded. "For now, I'll just be making phone calls. But I'll keep you guys posted." She glanced at her watch. "It'll be morning in London by the time I get home."

"You think the brooch is overseas?" asked Cole, his stomach hollowing out all over again. They were looking for a needle in a haystack.

"I'm going to check every possibility," said Gwen.

Sydney moved between them to give Gwen a hug. "Thank you," she whispered.

"Happy to help," said Gwen, glancing sideways at Cole and giving him a final once-over. "Talk to you tomorrow."

As Gwen left the office, Sydney sucked in a deep breath, blinking her exhaustion-filled eyes. But instead of complaining, she touched Cole's shoulder. His muscle instantly contracted beneath his jacket.

"We'll break it to her gently," she said.

Cole felt the weight of forty generations pressing down on him. "I don't see how we'll manage that."

Grandma greeted Sydney with a hug in the octagonal entryway. "Well? Did he do it? Did he pop the question?"

"Grandma," Cole warned.

"I hope he had a ring."

"He didn't have a ring," said Sydney.

Grandma glanced from one to the other. "But Katie said it was love at first sight. I'd hoped that was the point of this special trip."

"We are getting married," said Cole, although Sydney couldn't imagine why he bothered keeping up the charade. Katie knew their secret, and the Thunderbolt might never be found. A quickie wedding sure didn't matter anymore.

She hadn't let the full impact of that sink in yet. The odds of finding the Thunderbolt in time for the show one month away were almost nonexistent. She'd have to call it off. She'd lose her job, and her reputation would be ruined. She'd be lucky to get a position as a tour guide.

"I knew it," said Grandma, clasping her hands together. "I could tell by the way you looked at her."

"Grandma."

"Come in, come in." She backed into the living room. "I'll make tea. Tell me everything. What's the date? Where's the ceremony? Sydney, dear, you'll have to give me a guest list."

"We don't need tea. And there is no date."

"Of course we need tea. There are arrangements to make, plans to finalize. Thank goodness we already picked out the house." She took a deep breath and her grin widened.

Sydney felt sick. This should have been a happy occasion. It should have been a celebration.

"Can we please sit down?" asked Cole in a grave tone.

"Of course." Grandma gestured toward the burgundy couch. "You sit down. I'll be right back."

"Grandma." Cole's tone was sharp.

Sydney squeezed his arm, but he shook her off.

"What?" asked Grandma, blinking.

Sydney shifted between them and took Grandma's hand, trying to diffuse the building tension.

"Grandma," she said, looking into her blue eyes. She tried to let her tone give away the mood of the upcoming conversation. "We need to talk to you about something."

Grandma glanced at Cole then back to Sydney. A sly grin grew on her face. "Will it be a…quick…wedding?"

"You're not helping." Cole ground the words out from behind Sydney.

"We have some…unsettling news," said Sydney.

Grandma glanced from one to the other again. The expectant glimmer in her eyes dimmed slightly. "Oh?"

Sydney eased Grandma onto the couch. Cole crouched down in front of them and took a breath. "There's no easy way to say this," he began.

"Is someone sick?" asked Grandma, looking worried.

"No. Everybody's fine. Grandma. It's the Thunderbolt."

She stilled. After a silent heartbeat, her eyes went wide and her lips paled a shade.

"We stopped at Joseph's office," Cole continued. "The real Thunderbolt is missing. The one that's in the safe is a fake."

Grandma's hand went to her chest and her cheeks turned white as paper.

Cole jumped up. "Grandma?"

Sydney stood, too, mentally cursing herself for not taking Cole's advice. The shock really was too much for Grandma.

"Grandma?" Cole repeated.

But she still didn't answer.

"Let's lay her down," said Sydney, tossing a pillow to the far end of the couch. "Grandma? We should elevate your feet."

Cole stood back while Sydney gently repositioned her.

"I'm calling Dr. Diers," he said.

"Good idea," Sydney agreed, mentally berating herself. Why had she thought Grandma could take this? The woman's heritage had been stolen. They should have looked for it themselves, exhausted all other possibilities. But, no, Sydney had gone for speed, and she might have harmed a wonderful woman in the process.

Grandma gripped Sydney's hand, trembling slightly. "I don't need a doctor."

"Don't try to talk," Sydney whispered.

The old woman's eyes fluttered closed. Her wrinkled skin looked frail and transparent. Her gray hair was thin, and there were age spots dotted over her forehead.

Cole hung up the phone. "Dr. Diers is on his way. How is she?"

Grandma's breathing was shallow but steady.

"I don't need a doctor," she rasped.

Cole moved forward. "Well, you're getting one anyway."

"Waste of time," said Grandma.

He crouched down and Sydney shifted out of the way. "Grandma," he said in a gentle voice, taking her hand. "We're going to find it."

Her eyes opened and she stared at him in silence for a long moment. "I know you will." And then tears formed in the corners of her eyes.

"She's resting comfortably," said Dr. Diers, quietly closing the door to Grandma's bedroom. "She's obviously had a shock."

"We gave her some bad news," said Cole, turning from the big picture window. "Probably should have kept our mouths shut."

His shoulders were tense and Sydney knew he blamed himself. But it was her fault. Trying to salvage her career on the back of an old woman was unforgivable.

"I've given her a light sedative," said Dr. Diers. "She's going to be fine. She'd like to see you."

Cole nodded and made a move toward the bedroom.

"Sydney," said the doctor.

"Yes?" asked Sydney.

"Your grandma asked to see Sydney."

Sydney straightened in surprise and Cole blinked.

"Why does she want to see Sydney?"

The doctor gave a slight shrug. "Maybe she'd rather talk to a woman?"

"I can go get Katie," he said.

"She did ask for Sydney."

"I'll go in," Sydney agreed.

Cole took a jerking step toward her.

"I promise," said Sydney, holding up her palm. "I'll just listen to what she has to say."

"I can't let you upset her," said Cole. "We've made enough mistakes already."

"I'm not going to upset her."

Cole's mouth was taut and his knuckles were white; guilt was obviously eating him up.

"We had no choice," said Sydney, trying to reassure him.

"Oh, yes, we did."

True enough. She wasn't about to take on that debate. "I'll go find out what she wants, then we can talk, okay?"

Before he could tell her no, she cut through the entrance foyer to the bedroom door, turning the cut-glass knob as quietly as possible, just in case Grandma had fallen asleep.

Grandma's eyes were open, but the sparkle was gone from their blue depths. The harsh, noonday sun streamed in through the paned window, making her look small and frail beneath the patchwork quilt.

"Sydney," she whispered, reaching for a hankie.

Sydney clicked the door shut and came to her side. "Can I get you anything? A drink of water? An aspirin?"

"I've done something terrible, Sydney," said Grandma, dabbing the hankie beneath her nose.

"Grandma?" Sydney crouched down by the bed. "What's wrong?"

"Everything's wrong."

"Tell me."

Grandma grasped Sydney's hand, searching her eyes. She drew a breath. "I have no right to ask."

"Go ahead and ask."

"What I did. What I'm going to say. Please don't tell my family."

"Of course I won't."

Grandma drew a breath, and there was a catch in her voice as her glance slid away from Sydney's. "It was me."

"What was you?"

"I faked the Thunderbolt."

A jolt of shock ricocheted through Sydney's body. "What? When? How?" Then she quickly shut her mouth, biting back more staccato questions.

She forced herself to moderate her voice. "Do you know where the real one is?"

Grandma shook her head miserably. "No."

"I don't understand," said Sydney, straining not to sound judgmental. Why on earth would Grandma fake her own heirloom? Did she need money?

"It was a long time ago."

Sydney nodded, waiting for this to start making sense.

"I was young, only twenty." Grandma's voice faded and a faraway look came into her eyes.

Sydney carefully lowered herself to the carpet, trying not to interrupt the flow of the story. She rested her back against the small bedside table, placing her hand on Grandma's.

"It was Harold's and my second anniversary, and I was pregnant with Neil. And there was this woman…"

Sydney's heart sank.

"She had a baby. A son." Grandma's voice broke. "He was six months old…"

"I'm sorry."

Grandma shook her head. "She said things. She knew things." She looked into Sydney's eyes. "I could tell it was all true."

Sydney groaned in heartfelt sympathy. What a hurtful secret. What a terrible thing for Grandma to experience. "I am *so* sorry."

"Things weren't like they are now," Grandma continued, "the neighbors would have gossiped, Neil would have been ostracized, sales from the ranch might have dropped."

"Did you talk to him?" asked Sydney. It was Harold's responsibility to make it right.

Grandma shook her head.

"Why not?"

"We'd been through so much. We'd come so far."

Sydney didn't understand.

"I was lonely that first year, and I blamed Harold, and we weren't…" The silence stretched.

"It wasn't your fault," said Sydney. Infidelity was not justifiable, no matter what was going on in a relationship.

Grandma gave a watery smile. "The Thunderbolt was all my doing." She stabbed a finger against her chest. "Me. I was young and inexperienced. Then I was afraid of what people might say. Bottom line, I wanted my husband and our life *more* than I wanted a piece of jewelry."

A cold chill snaked up Sydney's spine. "What are you saying?"

Grandma impatiently swiped at a tear with the back of her hand. "I gave it away."

Oh, no.

"She demanded the Thunderbolt and I gave it to her."

Sydney's entire body cringed.

"She said Rupert was the first-born Erickson, and so he was entitled. She promised she'd leave us alone forever."

"She blackmailed you?"

Grandma nodded, her voice quavering. "And I was a willing victim. To save my marriage, I betrayed my family."

Sydney closed her eyes. "Did it work?"

Grandma gave a short laugh. "It worked. It worked for thirty years. Except..."

Sydney dropped her head forward onto her chest. There was nothing she could say, nothing anybody could say. The Thunderbolt was gone.

In her mind she saw a flash of her mother's blond hair, the twinkle of her silver locket—the heirloom that had been snatched away from Sydney. She didn't know for sure, but she thought it was the day before the fire. She was five years old, and it was the last day her mother had held her. The last day she'd seen the silver locket, or anything else her family had ever owned.

"Can you get it back?" Grandma asked in a small voice. "Because if you could get it back..."

Sydney opened her eyes and nodded. "Yes," she promised, although she had no idea how she was going to keep it. Then a vow came from the deepest recesses of her being. "No matter who has it. No matter where it is."

Hope rose in Grandma's eyes, and a little color came back to her cheeks. "I made a mistake."

"No, you made a decision."

"How can I explain—" Grandma's voice broke. "The boys..."

"Cole and Kyle don't have to know." Sydney shook her head. "Your secret is safe with me."

Seven

"**K**atie?" Cole held the phone to his ear as he watched the dust billow out behind the doctor's deep-treaded SUV tires.

"Hey, Cole," his sister-in-law answered cheerfully around the whistling of a teakettle. "What's going on? Where was Sydney last night?"

"Can you come down to Grandma's right away?"

"Why?" The whistling subsided.

Cole shifted away from the closed bedroom door, dropping his voice to make sure he wasn't overheard. "Because we need you."

A beat went by before Katie spoke. "What's wrong?"

"Is Kyle there?"

"Cole, what's wrong?"

"It's not…" he began. Not what? Not bad? Not major? Not terrible?

The reality was, it was all of those things and more. He straightened the black-and-white picture of his grandfather that hung above the mantel. "Listen, I'd really rather tell you guys in person—"

The tension rose in Katie's voice. "To hell with that."

Cole gripped the carved wood fireplace mantel. "You sure Kyle's not there?"

"He's in the barn. Give!"

"Fine. Okay." Where to start? He couldn't just blurt out that the brooch was missing. "Sydney and I stayed over in Wichita Falls."

The concern in Katie's voice vanished, replaced by interest. "You did? But I thought…"

"Not for that."

"No? Because, you know, she's really a—"

"Can you just come down to Grandma's?"

"Is Sydney still with you?"

"Yes."

Katie paused and he could almost hear her smiling. "Sure. We'll be right there."

"Good." Cole squeezed his eyes shut, trying to alleviate the pounding between his temples.

The door to Grandma's bedroom squeaked open and he punched the off button on the phone.

He turned to face Sydney. "She okay?"

Sydney nodded, blinking glassy, reddened eyes, rubbing her upper arms as if the air-conditioning was too cold for her. "She's fine."

"You okay?" he asked, peering more closely. Was she upset about her career? That would be understandable.

"I'm perfect." She waved away his concern, as if it was a gnat buzzing around her head.

Okay. No sympathy. Fine. "What did Grandma say?"

"She said the brooch was at the ranch for several months in 1978."

"Does she know who faked it?"

"My best suggestion is you talk to the local people who were around back then. Maybe——"

"So, she doesn't know."

Sydney took a sharp breath, as if he was annoying her again. "Maybe you could find out who saw it, if anyone seemed to have a particular interest in it..."

Cole told himself to ignore her mood. She had to be disappointed in the turn of events. Her career was on the line, and he couldn't blame her for thinking about herself.

He nodded. Interviewing the neighbors seemed like as good a place as any to start.

Sydney turned to gaze out the front window, tugging the elastic out of her hair and finger-combing it to redo the ponytail. "While you talk to the local people, I'm going to California——"

"California?" Where the hell had that come from?

She nodded, still gazing at the snowcapped mountain peaks on the far side of the valley. "Gwen is, uh, sending a list of likely antique dealers. There's a concentration of them in California, and I can check——"

"Uh-uh. No way." Cole shook his head. He acknowledged that she was a valuable asset to the search, but he wasn't letting her take over completely. It was his family, his property. She simply had a passing commercial interest.

Sydney turned to face him. "What do you mean no way?"

"I'm going to California."

"You don't know a thing about antiques."

"If you go, I go."

"But somebody has to stay here."

"Kyle can interview the neighbors."

Sydney jerked back. "Kyle?"

"He and Katie are on their way here."

"Now?"

"Yes. Now."

Her eyes narrowed. "You told them?"

"No. But I'm about to."

"But…"

"But what?"

Sydney bit down on her lower lip, the wheels of her brain obviously churning a million miles an hour. "I just think the fewer people who know…"

"Kyle's my brother."

She got a funny look in her eyes.

Was she worried?

Afraid?

Scheming?

Would he ever be able to trust this woman again? She couldn't have predicted the brooch had been faked. But Kyle had pegged her as an opportunist. Was she trying to make this latest turn of events work for her?

"I think this'll work better if you stay here," she said, her gaze darting away from his.

"Not going to happen, Sydney."

"But—"

"Kyle can do the home front. I go with you."

"I, uh, work better alone."

He took two steps toward her. "Tough. Get used to me. Because I'm your new partner."

Cole just had to come to California.

He had to be underfoot. He couldn't have stayed home and interviewed the neighbors like a good little cowboy.

Sydney wriggled beneath the desk in her hotel room

at the Sands in Oceanside, searching for the power outlet for her rented laptop. Why did they always have the electrical plug stashed behind furniture? Did they cater to contortionists?

It took all her strength to inch the desk away from the wall. Then she yanked out the lamp cord, plugged in her converter and shimmied her way back up to the chair.

She pushed her hair off her face and shot an uneasy glance at the connecting door as she flashed up the power. The front desk had given them adjoining rooms, but she hadn't opened the door, and Cole hadn't knocked.

Right now, all she wanted was to get Gwen's e-mails downloaded. Neither Cole nor Gwen knew Grandma's secret, and handing Gwen's leads to Cole in careful sequence was the only way Sydney could get the job done.

They *were* here canvassing at antiques stores, just as she'd told him. But Oceanside was also the city where Harold's illicit lover, Irene Cowan, had once lived.

As soon as Sydney ditched Cole, she was heading two blocks down to city hall to take a look at the historical property records. The new tax rolls were online, but Irene Cowan wasn't a current property owner. So if a trail existed in property records, it was going to start on microfiche.

While the blue bar edged its way along the bottom of her computer screen, a knock sounded on the adjoining door. Sydney stood up, silently urging the e-mail download to hurry.

Cole knocked again.

The word "complete" came up, and Sydney snapped the lid on her laptop before crossing the room.

Cole stood in the doorway in a crisp, white shirt, a burgundy tie and a beautifully cut charcoal suit with polished, black shoes. He was freshly shaved and his hair was neatly combed. If the clerks in the antique stores were female, Sydney was pretty sure they had a shot at getting information from them.

"I thought we'd get more cooperation if we looked like big buyers," he said.

Big buyers nothing, the staff would be too busy flirting with Cole to care whether or not they'd make a sale.

Sydney glanced down at her black jeans and the cropped, lacy top that was streaked with dust from her foray under the desk. She was definitely outclassed.

She opened the closet and took an ivory suit in one hand and a little black dress in the other. "Professional or flirtatious?" she asked.

His gaze moved back and forth. "What usually works best for you?"

"Professional," she said. Then she paused. "No. I'm lying." She hung the suit back up and closed the closet. "Flirtatious wins hands down." She rounded the privacy wall to the powder room.

Cole laughed behind her. "I know it would work on me."

"Yeah? Well, you're easy."

"So is most of the male population of this country."

"There's a list of antique stores on the desk," she called, bailing on this conversation before it went bad.

She wiggled out of her jeans and peeled off her blouse, turfing the white bra that would show at her shoulders. "I thought we'd start on Zircon Drive," she called.

"Does Gwen think one of these dealers has seen the Thunderbolt?" he asked in return.

"Nothing specific so far." Sydney ran a brush through her hair and dug into her makeup bag.

"So, what exactly are we doing here?"

"We take the picture of the fake around to the employees and see if they recognize it."

"And if they don't?"

His voice was closer, and Sydney quickly glanced around for the dress. Not that she was afraid he'd come in. He was way too much of a gentleman for that. It was more that his voice and her naked body were a potent combination.

She slipped the dress over her head, the silky fabric teasing her breasts on the way down.

"Sydney?"

"Then we move on to the next store," she said in a voice that was more than a little husky.

Cole was silent for a moment. "You really think this is going to work?"

"I don't know," she answered honestly.

"You almost ready?"

"Just putting on my shoes." She brushed her hair one more time and popped a pair of diamond studs into her ears before heading out to meet him.

His gaze strayed up and down her clingy outfit. His expression gave away nothing, but her skin prickled as if he actually touched her.

"We should go," she said, forcing her thoughts to the search instead of her hormones.

Cole stared at her a minute longer. Then he cleared his throat. "Right. Zircon Drive." He abruptly turned and headed for the door.

"This is ridiculous," said Cole as they exited from the fourth Oceanside antique store. Despite Sydney's cleavage and Cole's sexy baritone, none of the staff admitted having seen or heard of the Thunderbolt.

"We've barely started," Sydney countered, knowing that no matter what they wore or what they promised, their odds of finding information were almost nil. She was feeling guiltier by the hour for keeping him in the dark about the real search.

"We could blow off a year like this," he said.

"You and I are only one part of the investigation," she argued. "Gwen is checking Europe, and Kyle is interviewing your neighbors."

"While you and I are wasting time."

Sydney skirted around a group of teenage boys who strutted three-wide on the sidewalk in the opposite direction. She hop-stepped in her high heels to catch up to Cole. "Give it a chance."

"We need more manpower," he said as the oncoming crowd parted around him. "I'm hiring a P.I. firm. Somebody national, with lots of investigators."

She ducked in behind him, following in his wake as she fought a spurt of panic. A dozen private eyes? Sticking their noses into the investigation? They'd make it impossible to keep Grandma's secret.

"Let's wait and see instead," she suggested.

"Wait and see what?"

The crowds thinned and she moved back to his side. "Wait and see what Gwen comes up with."

He peered down his nose at her, obviously unconvinced.

"Before we do anything rash," she elaborated. "Okay?"

"Hiring a P.I. firm is *rash?*"

"I think we need to focus our effort."

He turned his palms up, fingers spread wide in a gesture of incredulity. His voice rose as they angled toward the curb. "There's nothing to focus *on.*"

"You're so impatient."

Cole glared his frustration while he unlocked the passenger door. "Impatient? Excuse me, but the Thunderbolt is worth half a million dollars."

Sydney folded herself into the passenger seat, adjusting her dress on the hot leather as Cole clicked the door shut.

She hadn't quantified it from the money angle yet. But the real Thunderbolt represented one of the first documented uses of diamonds as ornamentation in Europe, and the jewels themselves were dozens of carats. It was impossible to put a price on that.

Cole dropped into the driver's side and slammed the door. He cranked the engine and turned the air-conditioning up to full. "For half a million dollars, I think I can be forgiven for a little impatience."

"Fine. You're forgiven."

"And we hire a firm."

"No. Not now. Not yet."

Sydney's cell phone rang.

She could feel Cole working up a counter argument as she hunted through her purse. She hoped it was Gwen with something, *anything*. They needed a bogus lead or a false rumor to distract Cole.

She pushed the talk button. "Yes?"

"Well, well, well," Bradley Slander drawled through the grainy speaker. "You've been holding out on me, babe."

Sydney stilled, cursing under her breath, eliciting a look of surprise from Cole.

"I'm not your babe, Slander." Her voice grated into the mouthpiece as she turned toward the passenger door in a vain attempt to keep the conversation private.

"The Thunderbolt of the North?" Bradley continued. "That's big even for us."

She flicked her hair back from her sweaty forehead.

"There *is* no us." How had he found out so fast? Who did he bribe?

"Oh, there's an us, Sydney," said Bradley. "We're inextricably connected, both cosmically and financially."

"Get over yourself."

"Where are you?"

She glanced back at Cole. He was watching her intently, his hand poised on the stick shift.

"None of your business," she said.

"Gwen's bush league, Sydney," said Bradley.

"Gwen is brilliant."

"What's she found for you so far?"

Sydney clamped her jaw. She wasn't giving Bradley a thing. Not a damn thing.

"Thought so," said Bradley with a self-satisfied chuckle. "Team up with me. I know everybody who's anybody from here to Istanbul."

"Do the words 'cold day in hell' mean anything to you?"

His voice dropped to that reptilian level. "Together, babe, you and I can—"

She straightened, no longer caring if Cole or anyone else was listening. "Get this through your thick skull, Bradley. I will *not* work with you."

"Sure you will," he purred.

"No."

"You know it's just a matter of time."

"Not now. Not ever—"

Cole snagged the phone from between her fingers.

"I think you heard the lady," he said to Bradley.

Her jaw went slack in amazement.

"Really?" asked Cole mildly, his gaze drifting to Sydney. "Well, I doubt very much you know who you're messing with, either."

Then he took the phone from his ear and snapped it shut. He plopped it back into her palm. "Who *was* that?"

"Bradley Slander," she answered, staring at the compact phone, trying to decide whether he was being gentlemanly or controlling. In the end, she decided he was just being Cole. Which was…nice.

She had to admit, she'd experienced a momentary thrill when she pictured Bradley's expression. But now she was thinking about the possible ramifications. Bradley was unpredictable, and they'd just waved a red flag in his face.

"Old boyfriend?" asked Cole, still watching her closely.

She shuddered at the very thought. "Antiquity snake. Now *there's* a guy with contacts in the black market."

"But you're not willing to work with him?"

"I'd rather be dragged naked through an anthill."

Cole quirked a half smile. "Thanks for the visual."

She fought a grin, the tension finally dissipating. She was letting herself get paranoid here. Nothing terrible was going to happen. Bradley was far way, and he didn't have a clue about Grandma's secret.

"So what did he want?" asked Cole.

"He's after the Thunderbolt."

Cole's hand tightened on the shift. "Why? It's mine."

"Possession is nine-tenths of the law."

"That would make him a thief."

"I know." Sydney closed her eyes for a brief second. If Irene Cowan had sold it or given it away, especially if it was overseas, the ownership issue was going to get complicated.

"We need to find it before he does," she said. "Keeps our life simple."

Cole's stare raked over her for a silent moment. "There's something you're not telling me."

She tried not to flinch. She couldn't let him see her fear. "There are plenty of things I'm not telling you," she said, going on the offensive. "But I *am* doing everything in my power to find your brooch. I won't lie to you, if the brooch is already on the black market, Bradley's a threat."

"How big of a threat?"

"He's after it. But we've got Gwen. And Gwen is good."

Cole's expression turned speculative. "What about you, Sydney?"

"What about me?"

"Are you good?"

"At finding antiquities? I'm very good."

He nodded toward the antique store they'd just left. "So why does this feel like amateur hour?"

She struggled to keep from squirming under his gaze. "Because we haven't gotten started yet."

"Then let's get started."

Sydney nodded. "Right." She'd get the real search under way the very minute she ditched Cole.

He put the car into first gear and checked his side mirror. "Let's start with what Bradley is to you."

"A thorn in my ass."

Cole grinned, and another layer of tension dissipated.

"Ever slept with him?" asked Cole conversationally as he pulled into traffic.

"No!" She folded her arms across her chest. "And, by the way, that's none of your business."

"Sure it's my business."

"Why? Because we—" She stopped herself short.

"Because I want to know how deep this guy's vendetta goes."

Sydney puzzled over that one. "Would it be better if I'd slept with him, or worse?"

"A scorned lover makes a powerful enemy." He stopped at a red light.

She hesitated, then asked softly, "Are you my enemy, Cole?"

He turned his head. "Have I been scorned?"

She immediately realized her mistake. Reminding him of their lovemaking was a stupid idea. She cringed. "Sorry."

"For what?"

"Bringing it up."

The light changed and he pulled ahead. "What? You thought I'd forget?"

"This conversation is a bad idea."

He flipped on his signal and took a right turn. They accelerated past a sandy beach lined with palm trees and colorful umbrellas.

"Sydney," he said, keeping his attention fixed on the straight road. "Since you were there." He shifted to third. "And I was there." He pulled it into fourth. "And since we both have pretty damn good memories." He climbed on the brake pedal and swerved around a minivan exiting a parking stall. "I don't think it matters much whether we have this conversation or not."

She gripped the door handle. He made a good point. She remembered everything in vivid detail. Everything.

"We had sex," he said bluntly. "And that's that."

She pictured him mentally brushing his hands together. He was done with the subject and done with her.

Her stupid chest contracted. "Okay."

He was silent for a split second. "No hard feelings?"

"No hard feelings." None at all.

Eight

It took Sydney the entire next morning to convince Cole they needed to split up. But she finally sent him to some antique dealers across town, freeing her up to walk to city hall.

Hunched over a microfiche reader in the bowels of the building's basement, she discovered Irene Cowan had paid taxes on a little house at Risotto Beach for ten years running. But Irene's trail disappeared in the early eighties. She could have started renting, or she might have moved away.

Sydney moved on to utility records. But she found nothing new. Then, two hours later, just when she was sure she'd hit a dead end, it occurred to her to check marriage licenses.

She moved to the State offices upstairs. There, finally, she had another lead. Irene Cowan had become Irene Robertson. She and her husband had paid taxes in Oceanside for a further fifteen years. Then they'd died in a car accident in the mid-nineties.

But they'd raised one son, Rupert Cowan. And according to the Oceanside *Gazette,* he'd graduated from Edison High School and won a small scholarship to Southwestern State Fashion Design College. The Southwestern State alumni newsletter revealed that he'd received his degree then taken a job in New York.

Then Google picked up a local fashion show from last year in Miami. Rupert Cowan's company, Zap, had been a contributing designer.

It was a break. A huge break.

Rupert could be in Miami.

Sydney needed to get there just as soon as possible. She began formulating a plan. She'd approach him the way she approached any other potential seller. Not on the phone, not with a letter, but in person. She needed to see his expression, gauge his mood, his interests, his weaknesses.

This was the most important antiquity purchase she'd ever make. She was doing it step by careful step.

Her heels clicked on the floor of the cavernous, marble foyer while she dialed Gwen's number.

"Hello?" Gwen answered.

"I need you to send us to Miami."

"Sydney?"

"Yeah. It's me."

"What's in Miami?"

"I can't explain, but you need to give us some kind of a lead for Miami."

"Whoa. A false lead?"

"Yes."

"What's going on?"

"You know I wouldn't ask if it wasn't important."

"You've got something. What've you got?"

"I've got a name," Sydney admitted.

"Who? Where? How?"

"I can't tell you that. It would give away a confidence."

"You have someone else working on this?"

"It's, ah, complicated."

"I'm reasonably intelligent."

"I know." But Sydney couldn't tell Gwen. She couldn't tell anybody Rupert's name. She'd given her word to Grandma.

"So, what exactly is it that I'm doing here?"

"You're sending us to Miami."

Gwen's tone hardened. "That's not what I meant."

Sydney sighed, not sure how to answer.

"So, what? I'm window decoration?"

"Right now. Yeah."

Gwen's voice rose, her exasperation coming through loud and clear. "You mean I can stop *calling in favors* from Edinburgh to Rome?"

"Yes."

"Sydney!"

"I didn't know until this very minute. I swear, I just found out—"

"Fine."

Sydney felt like crud. "I'm sorry."

Gwen's voice was flat. "Call me if you need help."

"I will. And, Gwen?"

"Yeah?"

"I'll tell you what I can later. But this is important."

"I hear you."

"I'll call you from Miami."

"I'll be asleep." Gwen disconnected.

Sydney snapped the phone shut and pushed open the glass door.

Out on the wide, concrete staircase, she swore under her

breath. Gwen was a good friend, and a consummate professional. Maybe it would be safe to tell her…

Sydney trotted down the steps, rubbing her thumb over the keypad of her phone, trying to decide how much she could afford to tell Gwen. As she ran through the facts, Grandma's stricken expression flashed through her mind. Sydney heard her own heartfelt vow, and remembered her determination to do right by the woman.

Good friend or no good friend, she knew she'd take the secret to her grave.

"I gotta ask myself…" came a familiar, mocking voice.

Sydney blinked the world back into focus and stared directly into the face of Bradley Slander.

"…what does the Oceanside City Hall have to do with our little search?"

A cold wave of fear momentarily paralyzed her.

"This is the best one yet, Sydney." He chuckled. "Come on, tell ol' Bradley what you've got."

"Nothing." She gripped her phone, cursing herself as she increased her pace in an effort to get him away from the building.

She frantically cataloged her movements over the past few hours. Had she covered her tracks? Would the clerks remember her? Had she written anything down? Tossed evidence in the wastebasket?

How could she have been so careless as to let Bradley sneak up on her? He could have overheard her phone call to Gwen. He might already know about Miami.

"We can go fifty-fifty," he said, pacing along beside her.

"Get lost."

"Now, that's just rude."

Sydney stopped on the sidewalk and turned to stare at him, a horrible thought crossing her mind. What if he'd talked to Cole's grandmother? What if he'd gone to the ranch, lied about who he was and pumped the family for information.

"If you're so damn good, why do you need me anyway?" she asked, fishing to see how much he knew.

He moved in closer. "Because we're a *team*, Wainsbrook. It wouldn't be near as much fun without you."

"You mean, you don't want the entire profit?"

His beady eyes narrowed. "Yeah, right. You don't think for one minute I'm going to find it."

"Frankly," said Sydney, with what she hoped was an unconcerned toss of her hair, "I don't think either of us is going to find it."

"They why are you wasting your time?"

"It's my time to waste."

"What've you got?"

"I've got a missing brooch." She waited, hoping his ego would force him to give out his own information.

"We know the age of the fake," he said.

"Of course we do." She waited again.

"We know it's the Erickson family."

Sydney nodded, concentrating on keeping her expression neutral. Had he talked to Grandma? Had he been to Texas?

"You talked to them?" asked Bradley.

"I've got Cole Erickson with me now," she admitted. Maybe if she focused on Cole, Bradley wouldn't realize Grandma was of any significance.

If Bradley was surprised that she volunteered Cole's name, he didn't show it. He probably chalked it up to his superior interrogation techniques, thinking he had her right where he wanted her.

"He the guy on the phone?" Bradley asked.

"Yeah." Sydney gave a long sigh, trying to appear tired

and vulnerable. "He hasn't given me anything. You want to give him a try?"

This time, Bradley did eye her with suspicion.

She hoped she hadn't overplayed her hand.

Then he grinned, reaching out to touch the bottom of her chin. "Not."

Relief shuddered through Sydney. By sheer force of will, she didn't brush his hand away. Instead she raised her eyebrows in a question.

"Don't want to make him nervous." Bradley chuckled. "I think he's got the hots for you. Not a good idea to bring him face-to-face with his competition."

She nearly choked on that one.

Bradley moved in closer, dropping his voice to an intimate level. "Why don't *you* talk to him? I can come up with a few questions for you, and you can tell me what he says, hmm?"

Sure didn't take much for the man to think they'd joined forces. "Okay." Sydney agreed with a nod. If Bradley focused on interrogation questions for Cole, he might just stay out of city hall wastepaper baskets.

Bradley snaked an arm around her waist and she forced herself to remain still.

"Don't be afraid to get persuasive," he whispered, his hot breath irritating her skin.

What? She was supposed to break Cole's legs?

"You know what I mean." Bradley rubbed his knuckles up and down her arm. "Flirt a little. Give a little."

Sydney tightened her jaw and swallowed hard against her scathing retort. "Right," she said instead.

"That's my girl." He gave her a kiss on the cheek.

Cole watched with disbelief as an overpolished, ridiculously urbane-looking man kissed Sydney right there on the sidewalk. He gripped the steering wheel and everything inside him clenched to stone. He reached for the door handle, intent on ripping the jerk's head off, but a horn sounded behind him.

He looked up to see the light had turned green. Then he glanced back at Sydney. She was smiling at the man, their posture intimate and telling. Cole's nostrils flared and he stuffed the transmission into First.

No wonder she'd been so anxious to get rid of him this morning. She had something going on the side, and he was in the way. Whether this guy was a lover or a secret contact, her interests obviously weren't those of the Erickson family.

Cole wasn't about to sit still for that. Miss New York's plotting days were over. He was taking over as of right now. He was calling up the best PI firm in the country and putting them on retainer until the job was complete. Sydney could get the hell out of his way.

He pulled into the hotel underground and parked the car. Then he grabbed an express elevator and stomped his way down the hallway. He'd call Kyle, see if his brother had come up with any leads from the neighbors. Then he'd call Joseph Neely and get some PI firm recommendations.

Kyle didn't have any new information, so Cole moved on to Neely. Five minutes later he was armed with a list of the top-ten firms.

"Cole?" Sydney's voice wafted through the connecting doorway.

He picked up the phone, planning to start with the L.A. firm.

Her footsteps sounded on the carpet behind him. "You find any... What are you doing?"

He turned to look at her lying, cheating, beautiful face. "Better question is, what are *you* doing?"

She glanced from him to the phone and back again. "I'm looking for the Thunderbolt."

"Find it?"

"Uh…no."

"Find anything new today?"

She shook her head.

"Nothing at all? Nothing interesting?"

"Cole?"

That was it. She'd blown her last chance.

"I'm calling P.I. firms," he said, punching in the last few numbers.

She took a step forward, but something in his expression made her hesitate. Smart woman.

"Why?" she asked.

"Amber and Associates," came the voice on the telephone.

"I'm interested in hiring a private investigator," said Cole. "I need to find some missing jewelry."

Sydney moved around the bed, stopping directly in front of him. "Don't."

He ignored her.

She shot a telltale glance at the disconnect button.

He covered the mouthpiece. "Don't even think about it."

"I'll put you through to Dean Skye," said the receptionist.

"Thank you," said Cole, warning Sydney with his eyes.

"Hang up," she insisted.

"No."

"Why are you doing this?"

"So I can find the Thunderbolt."

"We *are* finding the Thunderbolt."

Cole scoffed out a sound of disbelief.

"Cole!"

"Dean Skye speaking."

"Mr. Skye," said Cole, ignoring Sydney. "I have a situation involving—"

Sydney's hand shot out.

Cole grabbed her wrist. But he was too late. The line went dead.

He squeezed. "What the—"

She winced and he immediately let her go.

"What the hell do you *think you're doing?*" he bellowed, slamming down the receiver.

"You can't do this."

"Yes. As a matter of fact, I *can*. It's my brooch. It's my problem. You don't even need to be here."

"But—"

"You're dead weight, Sydney. Go home."

She blinked. "I don't understand. What happened?"

He'd seen her in the arms of another man. That's what happened.

And he knew in that instant that he couldn't trust her. He also knew she was under his skin. He'd spent one single night in her arms, but there was no denying the acid spray of jealousy that burned through his body.

He was making decisions on emotion here. He had to send her away before he did something really stupid and compromised his family.

"Cole?"

"I know your little secret." He spat the words out.

All the color drained from her face. Her green eyes went wide, and her arms went slack by her side. "How…"

Well, if there was any doubt at all left over, *that* reaction sure confirmed that he'd seen what he'd thought he'd seen.

Cole sneered. "I saw you kissing him. Hugging him—"

"Who?"

"The guy on the sidewalk."

"Just now?"

What the hell kind of a question was that? "Yes, just now. How many guys did you kiss today?"

"You mean Bradley?"

"I don't know his name."

The color was coming back to her face. Now she looked more confused than scared. "You called in a P.I. firm because you saw Bradley Slander kiss me?"

"I called in a P.I. firm because you spent the afternoon with *Bradley* instead of doing your job."

"I was with him for two minutes."

Cole snorted. "That must have been disappointing. And, by the way, if that was Bradley Slander, he sure hasn't been scorned yet."

"You think I was having *sex with him?*" Her question ended in an incredulous shout. Then silence took over the room and she stared at him with impressive indignation.

Okay, if her reaction was anything to go by at this point…

"You kissed him goodbye," said Cole.

She paced across the room. "*He* kissed *me*. On the cheek. In public."

"You didn't exactly slap his face."

"I didn't exactly kiss him back, either. He's smart, and he's unpredictable. I just wanted him to go away."

"I saw what I saw," Cole insisted, but his voice was losing conviction.

"You saw him kiss me on the cheek, because that was all he did."

"You didn't have to smile."

"I was gritting my teeth."

Cole swallowed, allowing that he might not have connected the dots in precisely the right formation.

"Cole, I spent the afternoon researching the Thunderbolt. And I'd slit my wrists before I'd sleep with that man."

Something relaxed inside Cole. Bad sign, he knew. But there was nothing he could do about it.

Her eyes burned an emerald fire as she moved closer. "And I'm insulted that you jumped to that conclusion. Just because I slept with you—"

"I'm sorry."

"—doesn't make me—"

"I'm sorry."

She took a breath. "You're a cad, you know that?"

He nodded. "I'm a cad."

She poked him in the chest with her index finger. "You ought to be ashamed of yourself."

He nodded again. "I am."

She poked him, and this time he captured her hand.

She looked up into his eyes and her voice softened. "I'm a very reliable person. I could get references."

"I don't need references," he whispered.

She searched his expression. "Then what do you need?"

What did he need? He needed to be sure that emotion wasn't overriding reason when it came to her. He needed to know she was on his side. He needed to know she didn't have an ulterior motive.

She sighed into the silence. "Once, just *once,* do you think you could give me the benefit of the doubt?"

"Yeah," he answered. "I will."

"Good."

He inhaled the scent of her hair and something primal rose up inside him. She might not have been interested in Slander, but Slander was sure as hell interested in her. Cole felt an overpowering need to stamp out the other man's taint.

He needed to hold her, to kiss her, to remind himself that *he* was the one she'd made love with. It might be an over-reaction, but the blood of pillaging Vikings pounded through his veins. Ericksons took what they wanted, and Cole wanted Sydney.

He wanted her bad.

He bent his head, bringing his lips down onto hers. He forced himself to keep his arms by his sides. She could step away if she wanted. He wasn't holding her, but he wasn't holding back, either. He was going to kiss her until she told him to stop.

But she didn't step away, and passion crested within him. His hands went to her hair. How he'd missed its satiny texture. He cradled her head, taking a small step forward, his body coming up against hers, her heat flaring against his skin.

"I missed you," he whispered, the words almost painful. "I missed you so much."

Had it only been a week since they'd made love? It seemed like an eternity.

"I missed you, too," she sighed, her soft body snuggling into the hollows of his own. "I know you're marrying someone else…"

"And I know this is just business for you…"

Their kiss deepened. He wished he could absorb her, keep her, bind her so tight she'd never touch another man. Never look at another man.

He plucked at the buttons of her blouse, needing to feel her satin skin once more.

Her blouse fell open and his fingertips skimmed their way over her stomach.

He covered one lacy cup, filling his hand with the weight of her breast. Her nipple poked into his palm and he wanted to rip off her clothes then and there. She wasn't going near another man. Ever. *Ever!*

He didn't care that it was only business. His hand convulsed around her breast, and the other went to her buttocks, dragging her tight against his body, leaving no question about the strength of his desire.

"Cole," she moaned, her body going lax.

He wrapped an arm around her waist, supporting her slight weight.

"What you do…" she groaned.

"What *you* do," he muttered back.

She wound her arms around his neck, holding him tight, her lips searing his skin.

"Cole, please," she gasped.

"Anything," he said. "Anything."

"We have to go."

"Huh?"

She stopped kissing, released him, her breath coming in short gasps. "We have to go to Miami."

Cole felt as though he'd been bucked off and hit the dirt sideways. "What?"

"I found out… Gwen called… We need to go to Miami."

He stared down at her open blouse, her lacy bra, the creamy breasts that mounded up like ambrosia. *"Now?"*

"Now. Bradley's here. We can't waste any time."

Cole pulled back, irrational anger bubbling up at the mere mention of Bradley's name. "Is that what you call this? A *waste of time?"*

She closed her eyes and let out an exasperated sigh. "Don't."

Fine. Forget it. They'd drop everything and fly across the country to play hurry up and wait. "Sure, we'll go to Miami."

"You think I *want* to stop?"

"Just say it—you're stopping, aren't you."

She tightened her jaw, bringing her hands up to her hips. "Cole Nathaniel—"

He froze at the intimate sound of his middle name.

"—I want you more than I've ever wanted any man in my life. And if I had my way—"

"You want me?"

"Yes."

"But we're leaving?"

"Yes! Bradley's going to stake out the hotel."

"But, you definitely want me." Suddenly life didn't seem so bleak. Miami was only four hours away. They could be there before morning. Nothing to do before the antique stores opened up…

She shook her head. "Yes, I want you. Should I make up a sign or something?"

"And you'll still want me in Miami?" He'd take it in writing if she'd give it to him.

"Not if you don't shut up."

Cole grinned. "Shutting up now."

"Good. Grab your bag."

"Should I call a cab?"

"No. Let's duck out the back way and catch one a few blocks down."

He gave her a squeeze. "It's sexy when you go all secret agent on me."

She shot him a look of impatience. "Want meter is going down."

"Shutting up again."

"Good thinking."

Nine

The minute the door swung shut on their Miami hotel suite, Cole pulled Sydney into his arms. Passion burst to life inside her, and she fumbled with the buttons at his collar, loosening his tie while he shucked his jacket.

She moaned her satisfaction, burrowing her face into his neck, inhaling deeply. She didn't know what it was about his scent, but if they could bottle it, they'd make a fortune. She flicked her tongue out to taste his skin, then she suckled a tender spot near his collarbone.

"You make me crazy," he rasped, running his hands through her hair.

She started on the buttons of his shirt. "You just make me want you."

"How is it I do that?"

"Breathing," she answered.

He returned her kisses, reaching for her blouse, popping

the buttons and peeling it off her shoulders. He stood back and gazed once more at her lacy bra. "I like it when you breathe, too."

She unsnapped the hooks and dropped the wisp of fabric to the floor. His eyes darkened, and her body began to hum in earnest.

"Oh, man." He slowly pulled her in, pressing them skin to skin, holding her tight and setting off tiny explosions in her brain. His hands worked magic. His kisses grew harder, sweeter, ranging further and further.

She tangled her hands in his hair, loving the touch, loving the texture. "Stop time again," she begged.

He feathered his fingertips down her spine. "I'll do my best." He tasted her earlobe. He kissed her neck. He delved sweetly into her mouth, and she thought she never wanted him to stop.

How had she imagined she could live without this?

They'd wasted six whole days, avoiding each other when they could have been in paradise. It was almost criminal.

He peeled off the rest of their clothes, and his touch grew more intimate. A flush covered her body, and an overhead fan whirred a gentle breeze, cooling the heat, sensitizing her skin.

He scooped her into his arms once again and crossed through the French doors to the king-size bed.

"Tell me when to put you down," he said.

A shudder ran through her at his selfless memory. "Not yet."

She loved this. There was something about his strength, his caring, his bold masculinity that sent shivers to her core.

He smiled and kissed her lips. Then he kissed her eyelids and the tip of her nose. "You really like this," he teased.

"I really like this," she agreed.

"Gotta figure out what fantasy it is."

She grinned. "Caveman?"

"Viking."

Her body convulsed. "That's it."

His eyes turned stormy. And he sobered, covering her lips in a long, deep kiss as he gently laid her back on the bed. He brushed her hair from her eyes. "You're beautiful."

She felt beautiful. She felt desirable and wonderful.

He kissed his way up her body beginning with her ankle, then the bend of her knee, gently flexing her leg until he had access to her inner thigh. His days growth of beard gently abraded her tender skin, sending shivers of desire to her core. His lips nibbled and his tongue teased higher and higher while she gasped his name.

She tensed when he blew gently on her curls. But then she closed her eyes and bit down on her lip as sensation after sensation throbbed their way along her limbs.

This was Cole. She was safe. He wouldn't hurt her. He wouldn't hurt anyone.

Then his hand replaced his mouth, gently stretching and filling her as he moved on to kiss her stomach. Her hips came off the bed, and he murmured words of encouragement against her skin.

She grasped for his hair, her hands restless, needing something to do. He moved again and took one nipple into his mouth. She groaned, burying her fingers in his hair. Her entire body arched involuntarily, striving to get closer to the sensations that were driving her sweetly out of her mind.

She dug her fingernails into his shoulders, raking them down his back as he moved up to kiss her mouth.

She opened wide. Finally, finally. She wrapped her arms around his broad body, holding him tight against her breasts. She kissed his mouth, kissed his cheeks, kissed his eyelids, then buried her face in his neck and inhaled.

He kissed the top of her head, one hand stroking down her glistening body, coming to rest on her bottom. "Slow and you just don't go together, do they?" he gasped.

"Get over it, cowboy," she rumbled, reveling in the salty taste of his neck.

She felt his deep chuckle.

"I'll try," he promised, easing her thighs apart. "I'll try really, really hard."

He eased inside her inch by careful inch. She bit down hard on her bottom lip. Time was stopping again.

He did slow it down. Then he sped it up. Then slowed it down again, holding her shimmering until she was sure she'd cry out in desperation. He whispered her name over and over, until the city lights blurred and streamed together, melting into the hot, humid ground.

Hours later, the rising sun turned the edge of the ocean a pearly pink. The champagne bottle was three quarters empty. And the lazy ceiling fan pushed a breeze down on Cole's bare skin.

He dipped a fresh strawberry into the bowl of whipped cream on the bedside table and held it to Sydney's lips.

She bit down, smiling her appreciation of the delicacy.

He popped the other half into his own mouth, thinking he could happily stay here for the rest of his life.

"So," she continued around the berry. "Your great-great-granddaddy, the infamous and sexy Jarred Erickson—"

"I believe I take after him," said Cole, pushing himself into a sitting position, striking a pose among half a dozen plump, white pillows and a billowing comforter.

"The sexy part or the infamous part?" she asked, bend-ing her knees to cross her ankles in the air and resting her chin on her interlaced fingers.

Cole took in her tousled hair and her bare buttocks. Yep. Definitely forever. "I'm thinking both," he said.

She grinned and reached for her champagne flute. "So you're telling me Jarred decreed that the ranch should stay as one parcel into perpetuity?"

Cole nodded. "My ancestors were big on decrees. Every few generations, somebody comes up with something that wreaks havoc for a couple hundred years."

He figured most of them were lunatics, particularly those who had taken to piracy.

She took a sip of the champagne, and he had to curb an urge to kiss the sweetness from her mouth.

"And your solution is to come up with some new decrees?" she asked.

"Damn straight. It's my turn. I complied with theirs—"

Sydney coughed out a laugh.

"What?"

"You complied with *what,* exactly?"

"Passing on the Thunderbolt."

"Ha. You had to be railroaded into marriage."

That was unfair. He frowned at her. "It's completely voluntary."

"As a last resort."

He reached for his own champagne, leaning back against the birch headboard. "Point is, it'll get the job done."

"You're also splitting the ranch in half, in defiance of Great-great-granddaddy Jarred."

"That's just common sense. Keeping it intact was a stupid idea."

"Are you always this determined that you're right and everyone else is wrong?"

"Of course."

"Of course," she mimicked.

"Hey, if a man doesn't trust his own judgment, what's left?"

She laughed again, nearly spilling her champagne. Then she twisted into a sitting position, rearranging the comforter over her lap. "You know, whoever came up with the wenches and ale rule, sure had you Erickson men pegged."

"Wenches and ale?"

"Yeah. You know. The wenches and ale."

"I have no idea what you're talking about."

"Didn't your grandma tell you?"

Cole shook his head.

Sydney leaned across him, snagging another strawberry and dipping it in the cream. "That's why the women get the brooch." She popped the berry into her mouth. "Somebody back in the fourteenth century decided you guys might sell it for wenches and ale. You know, the Erickson of the day would change the tradition. And, poof, there would go the Thunderbolt."

Cole couldn't help but grin.

"What?" she asked.

"Who needs wenches and ale?" He lifted his flute in a mock toast. "I've got champagne and—"

"Watch it, cowboy."

He leaned forward and kissed her strawberry lips, taking the safe route. "A princess."

She pulled back. "A *princess?*"

Okay, too sappy. "A hot babe?"

She raised her eyebrows.

He decided to go with the truth. "A beautiful, intelligent, funny, gracious lady?"

"That's not bad."

He took the champagne from her hand and set both glasses down on the bedside table. "Come here," he said, needing to feel her all over again. He gathered her into his arms and they stretched out on the comforter.

She sighed and rested her head on his shoulder.

He stroked her hair, releasing its scent. "Wenches and ale. How is it you know more about my family than I do?"

"I'm nosey. I ask lots of questions."

He settled his arm more comfortably around her. Traffic sounds came to life on the street below, and the rising sun flashed its orange rays through the balcony doors.

"Let me ask *you* a question," he said, twirling a lock of her hair around his index finger.

"Fire away."

"You said you had foster parents."

She nodded. "I lost my parents in a house fire when I was five."

Cole tightened his arm around her, and the ceiling fan whooshed into the silence.

"My foster parents were friends of the family. Nanny Emma and Papa Hal raised me. But they were older. And they've both since passed away."

Cole's heart went out to her. He didn't know what he'd do without his family. "You must miss them all."

"Nanny and Papa, yes. But I don't really remember my parents at all. I have these vague images of them in my mind."

"What about pictures?"

"Burned in the fire. A few of the neighbors had shots of my father from a distance, but they tell me my mother was always behind the camera, not in front of it."

Cole's chest tightened at the injustice. Never to know what your mother looked like? At twenty, he'd ached for his mother. Sydney had been five.

Protective instincts welled up inside him. "What about newspapers? Her high school yearbook? Surely somebody—"

"It's okay." Sydney reached over and stroked her palm across his beard-stubbled cheek, comforting him, when he should have done it for her.

"What *do* you remember?" he asked, covering her small hand with his own.

"My mother's locket." Sydney relaxed against him again, smiling at what was obviously a touchstone memory. "It was silver, oval-shaped. It had a flower, I think it was a rose, etched into the front. I don't know whose picture was inside, but it would dangle down when she bent over to hug me. I distinctly remember reaching for it. Her hair was blond, and it sort of haloed around the locket."

"Where's the locket now?"

"Destroyed by the fire."

"Oh, Sydney."

"It's really okay."

He tucked her hair behind one ear and gently kissed the top of her head. "I guess that explains a lot."

She tipped her chin to look up at him, green eyes narrowing. "Explains what?"

"Your profession. Your burning desire to locate antiquities."

She pulled back. "I locate antiquities because I have a master's degree in art history."

"You have a master's degree because you've spent your life looking for the locket."

"That's silly. The locket was destroyed more than twenty years ago."

He touched her temple with his index finger. "Maybe in here." He placed his hand over her heart. "But not in here."

"Did you minor in psychology?"

"Computer science. With a major in agriscience."

"Then you're completely unqualified to analyze me."

"I supposed you're right," he said to appease her. But qualified or not, he knew hers was a personal search.

She stifled a yawn.

"We need to sleep," he said.

"It's morning already."

"Not quite."

He sidled down the bed, keeping her wrapped in his arms.

"We do need to sleep," she agreed. Then she smiled as she closed her eyes.

Cole sucked in a deep breath. Sleeping with Sydney in his arms. He could get used to this. He shouldn't. She had her career and he had his family.

Still, he could get used to this.

Eyes closed, Sydney waited until Cole's breathing was deep and even. Then she blinked away her fatigue and watched his profile in the gathering light. His tanned skin was stark against the white pillowcase, and she gave into an urge to run her fingertip along his rough chin. She wished she could be honest with him, take him with her, listen to his advice.

For a moment she considered waking him up and swearing him to secrecy. Then she could tell him all about his grandmother's problem, and they could solve it together.

But she couldn't do that. She wasn't even sure Cole would want her to do that. She had a feeling he'd consider a promise to any member of his family to be a sacred trust.

When she was sure he was sound asleep, she carefully inched out of the cradle of his hug and slipped from beneath the covers.

It was 8:00 a.m. in Miami, five in California and seven in Texas. She could only hope that Cole's late night and all those time zone changes would keep him unconscious a few more hours.

She tiptoed into the living room, carefully clicked the French door shut behind her and turned on a small lamp on the desktop. Then she opened her purse and retrieved the number for the Miami fashion show. Hopefully, they'd have contact information for Rupert Cowan.

She dialed the number, spoke to a show coordinator who had Rupert Cowan's business phone number and address. She jotted it down on the hotel notepad, peeled off the sheet and tucked the slip of paper into her purse.

She had no way of knowing if he was the right Rupert Cowan. Heading down there might be a waste of time. But she couldn't for the life of her come up with a way to broach the subject with him on the phone.

She had no choice but to approach him in person and keep her fingers crossed.

She might have one heck of a lot of explaining to do once she got back. But it was time to pull out all the stops. If Rupert Cowan did have the brooch, and if she could get her hands on it, Cole would probably be grateful enough not to question the details.

She unzipped her garment bag, retrieved a blazer and skirt that were only slightly wrinkled, then dressed and headed for the lobby.

When Cole woke up, Sydney was nowhere to be found. She wasn't in the suite. She wasn't in the hotel restaurant. And she wasn't in the lobby.

He knew he had to stop being suspicious of her, but it was unnerving to have her just up and disappear. They were supposed to be working together. Even though he'd promised to give her the benefit of the doubt, he couldn't help but wonder if she was up to something.

Okay, so there was every chance that she was investigating antique dealers, or maybe she'd just gone around the corner. She could easily show up any minute with coffee and bagels.

Still, he glanced around the suite, taking inventory. Her suitcase was open on the sofa. Her toiletries were in the main bathroom. She'd opened a bottle of water at the bar.

What else?

He glanced around for clues.

A pen lay haphazardly across the oak desk next to a hotel note pad. Nothing to say the housekeeping staff hadn't set them out crooked, but nothing to say Sydney hadn't used them, either.

Cole held the notepad up to the light, staring across the fibrous surface. There were a few indentations in the paper, so he took a trick from a television crime drama and shaded across them with a pencil.

Rupert Cowan—2713 Harper View Road. Didn't sound like a deli or a coffee shop to Cole.

Didn't sound like anything, he told himself. She could have a perfectly legitimate reason for writing that down and leaving.

After last night, he was giving her the benefit of the doubt if it killed him.

He crumpled the shaded paper in his fist.

It might even be left over from the last guest.

They'd probably laugh about it later.

He tossed the note into the wastepaper basket and sat down on the couch, bracing his fists on his knees.

He couldn't *wait* to laugh about it later.

Ten

Sydney stepped cautiously into 2713 Harper View Road. Unlike the other commercial businesses on the block, this one had a solid gray door that was tucked into an uninviting little alcove.

Inside, hanging fluorescent lights buzzed in the cavernous space. The shoes of unseen employees shuffled against the gritty concrete floor between rows of beige, Arborite countertops and fabric-filled shelving. A few voices sounded in the distance, and a lone man paged through sketch sheets a few counters back.

"Hello?" Sydney ventured.

The man glanced up, pushing his long, graying hair back from his forehead. "Hey there."

She took a couple steps toward him. "I'm looking for Rupert Cowan?"

The man straightened to about five feet seven. He wore

black slacks and a black, ribbed-knit turtleneck. "You found him."

Butterflies pirouetted in Sydney's stomach. "Oh, good."

He braced his hands against the countertop. "Something I can help you with?"

She moved forward and stretched out her hand. "I'm Sydney Wainsbrook."

He shook. His hand was pale and his grip noncommittal. "Nice to meet you, Sydney."

"I was wondering—" she glanced around, swallowing against her dry throat "—is there somewhere we can talk?"

He laced his fingers in front of his chest. "About?"

"It's a personal matter." Her heart rate was going up, and her palms were getting sweaty.

Thank goodness they'd already shaken hands.

"You looking for a job?" he asked.

Sydney shook her head. "It's… I'd feel better if we could sit down somewhere."

Rupert glanced at his watch. "Well, I'm a little—"

"Please?"

He hesitated. "We could go next door for coffee."

She nodded eagerly. "Perfect."

"Patrice?" Rupert called over his shoulder.

"Yeah?" came a woman's gruff voice from the back of the shop.

"I'm out for a bit. If the agency calls, tell them we'll need all ten girls there by Sunday for rehearsal."

"Okay," came the voice.

Rupert gestured to the door with an open palm.

Sydney gave him a shaky smile, then led the way outside and around the corner, into a small, glass-fronted coffee bar.

"Frappachino? Mochachino?" asked Rupert.

"Let me," said Sydney, pulling out her wallet.

Rupert addressed the clerk. "Small half-caf, two sugars, extra foam."

"Just black for me," said Sydney as she pulled out a few bills.

They took a corner table with a checkered plastic table-cloth and a metal napkin dispenser. The whine of the cof-fee machine filled the silence.

"Are we through being mysterious?" asked Rupert.

Sydney took a bracing breath. Then, making a firm de-cision, she opened her purse and took out the picture of the fake Thunderbolt.

"Do you recognize this?" she asked Rupert.

Rupert took the picture between his fingers and sat back in his red leather seat. "You must be one of the Ericksons."

Sydney's stomach bounced clear to the floor.

He *knew* about the Ericksons?

"So, you recognize it?" she asked, struggling to recraft her approach. She hadn't counted on him knowing the story. Did he know about Grandma? About his father? About his mother's extortion?

"It's the heirloom brooch," said Rupert, dropping it on the table top. "My mother warned me you'd come looking for it one day."

If he'd known about the Ericksons, why hadn't he come out of the woodwork before now?

"What, exactly, did she tell you?" asked Sydney.

He stroked his chin as if he'd once had a beard. "You know, you're not what I expected."

"What did you expect?"

The waitress set their coffee cups in front of them, and Rupert shrugged. "Someone a little less classy, a little more West Texas."

"I'm not an Erickson," said Sydney.

"Ah-hh."

She resented his tone. Cole had looked damn classy in his suit yesterday.

"I'm a...friend of the family," she offered. She wouldn't mention the Laurent if she could get away with it. If he thought there was interest from a museum, his price would probably go up.

"And you want the brooch."

She nodded. "I'm prepared to pay."

He shook his head. "Not for sale."

Damn. He was sentimental.

She kept a poker face. "You don't know how much I'm offering."

He propped his elbows on the table and rested his chin on his laced knuckles. "It's pretty valuable to me at the moment."

"For sentimental reasons?"

He let out a cold laugh. "Sentimental? Me? About them?"

"Then, why...?"

He leaned forward. "Ever heard of Thunder Women's Wear?"

Sydney shook her head.

"Don't worry. You will. We caused quite a stir in Miami last season, and we're scheduled for Milan in ten days."

She paused. "I don't understand."

"That little brooch? That stupid little brooch that my mother practically worshiped, is the centerpiece of my new line—the bold, crisp colors, the angular lines, the drama and majesty of it. We reproduced the jewel using embroidery thread and my final model wears the brooch itself in every show."

"A fashion line?"

He nodded. "Years, I've been slaving away in this fashion backwater. Then, one night, I'm hunting through the drawer for a pair of cuff links and out drops the brooch…"

Looking for a pair of cuff links? The man kept the Thunderbolt in his *dresser drawer?*

Sydney was going to have a heart attack right here and now.

He picked some lint from his sleeve. "So, you see. It may not have sentimental value, but it has business value to me."

Sydney took a sip of her coffee, searching her brain for a new tactic. She could blurt out a lucrative price—Grandma had arranged a line of credit. But instinct told her it was too soon to talk numbers.

"Did your mother ever tell you how she got the brooch?"

He cracked a knowing smile. "A gift from dear, old Dad. I figured it was hush money."

"Is that why you never contacted the Ericksons?"

Rupert tipped back his head and laughed. "That would presuppose I gave a damn about his reputation. I just figured those cowpokes would have no more interest in me than I have in them."

Sydney nodded. That was good. If Rupert didn't want anything to do with the family, all the better.

She took another drink of her coffee, choosing her words carefully. "You've probably guessed it has sentimental value to them."

Rupert sipped his frothy brew. "That would be why they sent you."

She nodded, toying with the handle of her mug. "I'm prepared to offer you a hundred thousand dollars."

Rupert didn't react. Not even a flicker.

Sydney swore silently. Maybe he'd had it appraised.

Unexpectedly, the chair beside her squeaked against the floor and a shadow loomed large.

"Whatever she just offered you," said Bradley, plunking himself down and crossing one ankle over the opposite knee. "I'll double it."

Sydney felt like she'd been sucker punched. "How did you…"

He cocked his head. "*Please*. Double-o-seven, you're not."

Sydney could have decked him.

Bradley picked up Sydney's coffee cup and took a deliberate swig. "I assume we're getting down to brass tacks?"

"Who are you?" asked Rupert.

Bradley stuck out his hand. "Bradley Slander. I deal in antiques."

"And I've got a bidding war?" asked Rupert with an impressive air of unconcern.

"If she makes another offer, I'll top that, too." Bradley took another defiant swig of her coffee and slanted her a cold look.

It was official. The man had no soul.

Grandma's line of credit went as high as three hundred thousand. Bradley could easily match that. Even if Sydney added her own savings, there was no way she'd beat him.

"Exciting as this is—" said Rupert, pushing his chair back from the table "—and much as I'd love to add six figures to my bank account today, the Thunderbolt is not for sale."

Sydney reached toward him. "But—"

He stared down his aquiline nose. "Sorry, Sydney."

"Four hundred thousand," said Bradley.

Rupert hesitated.

Sydney swallowed. Should she match it? It would take all of her savings…

"Sorry," said Rupert, taking another step.

Sydney jumped up, nearly knocking over the heavy chair.

She absolutely, positively could not let Rupert out the door without making a deal. Bradley wouldn't give up. He'd be on the phone to Oslo within the hour, upping the ante. He'd eventually win Rupert over, and Grandma would never see the brooch again.

"Really, Rupert—" Sydney began, trying not to gasp for air. "It's a family heirloom."

Rupert shook his head. "And I give a damn, because?"

Should she tell him the truth? That his mother was an extortionist? Put her cards on the table and betray Grandma?

Betraying Grandma would be better than losing the Thunderbolt forever. Wouldn't it?

Her heart was pounding and her palms were sweating. She needed time to think. Somewhere out of the heat, away from that infernal coffee grinder.

Rupert started for the door.

"Wait!" she called in a dry, hoarse voice.

He turned and gave her a salute. "I need it for Milan, Sydney. Milan and beyond."

The fake! The idea slammed into her brain with the force of an anvil.

"I can replace it," she blurted.

He paused with his hand on the knob.

She moved toward him. "I have a replica."

His brow furrowed.

"It's good," she assured him. "It's *very* good. Flawless diamonds, five-carat rubies. You could have the cash *and* the Thunderbolt."

"Half a million," drawled Bradley.

"I'd have to see it," Rupert said to Sydney.

"I'll have it here this afternoon."

Bradley stood up, clattering his chair against the floor. "For half a million you can make two fakes, and then some."

Rupert arched a brow. "Within the week?"

A muscle ticked in Bradley's jaw, and his eyes beaded down to brown dots.

Rupert shook a warning finger at Sydney. "I'll look at it, but it would have to be perfect."

"It's perfect," said Sydney, counting on the fact that the faceted diamonds were only a historical flaw.

He hesitated for a long minute. Then he nodded his head. "Here. Two o'clock. Right now, I have a conference call."

As soon as he disappeared, Sydney groped for her cell phone. Bradley pulled his out of his pocket and left the café. Calling Oslo no doubt. He'd be back with a higher offer this afternoon.

Never mind Norway, thought Sydney as she punched in Grandma's number.

By two o'clock, Cole was forced to face the fact that he'd been duped.

Sydney wasn't coming back. Whatever it was that had brought her flying to Miami must have been a damn good lead. She'd obviously decided she didn't need him anymore, and she'd had no compunction about ditching him.

Maybe she was going to sell the Thunderbolt on the black market. Maybe she'd decided that one big score was worth giving up her career. Maybe she'd never been from the Laurent Museum in the first place.

Lies upon lies upon lies.

Whatever it was she'd decided, it definitely included screwing him.

He stood up from the sofa and crossed the room to retrieve the address from the wastepaper basket. *Twenty-seven thirteen Harper View Road.* There wasn't an explanation in the world that would get her out of this one.

One of Joseph Neely's clerks personally delivered the fake Thunderbolt to the Miami airport. Sydney met him there and made it back to the café with less than five minutes to spare. Where, to her surprise, Rupert pulled out a jeweler's loupe and began inspecting the brooch.

Bradley sat next to her, drumming his fingers against the plastic tablecloth, all traces of his flirtatious persona gone.

"Five hundred and fifty thousand," he ventured, and she knew his profit margin was diminishing. He was going for pride now, pure and simple.

Sydney stared directly into Bradley's eyes. "Four hundred thousand, plus the replica."

Rupert paused, looking up from his inspection. "Will you two *stop*."

The muscle in Bradley's jaw began ticking again.

After an excruciating fifteen minutes, Rupert returned the loupe to his jacket pocket. He closed the case on the fake Thunderbolt, and Sydney held her breath.

Finally, he put his hand out to Sydney, palm up. "Four hundred thousand."

"A cashier's check?" she asked, her heart smacking against her rib cage.

Bradley swore, but Rupert silenced him with a glare.

"A cashier's check will be fine." He pulled a sheaf of papers from his breast pocket. "And you can sign here."

It was Sydney's turn to hold out her hand, palm up.

Rupert smiled his admiration, then he reached into the same pocket and pulled out a worn jewelry case.

She clicked it open, and her entire body shuddered in relief.

"May I?" she asked, pointing to the pocket that held the loupe.

He retrieved it. "Be my guest."

She checked the jewels, then she turned the brooch over to check the casting. A deep sense of satisfaction settled in the pit of her stomach. The Thunderbolt was going home.

She pulled out the envelope containing the two cashiers' checks—one from Grandma's line of credit, the other from Sydney's savings account.

Rupert handed her the pen.

Bradley smacked his fist down on the table.

The transaction was over with surprising speed, and all three of them stood.

"You need an escort to a taxi?" asked Rupert, slanting a glance at Bradley.

Sydney chuckled, enjoying the moment. Glad to have thwarted Bradley, excited about telling Cole, and absolutely thrilled for Grandma.

"I don't think he'll mug me," she answered.

"Man," muttered Bradley. "You're a freakin' lunatic," he said to Rupert.

"It was interesting to meet you, Sydney," said Rupert, ignoring Bradley's pithy comment and striding for the door.

Sydney zipped her purse securely shut and tucked it under her arm.

"Don't look so smug," said Bradley.

"I'm not smug," she returned as they paced for the exit. "I'm happy for the Erickson family."

"Don't you ever gag over all that syrupy sweetness you call a personality?"

Sydney opened the glass door and glanced back at him over her shoulder. "Been nice doing business with you, Bradley." Then she turned her head and took a step, walking straight into Cole's broad chest.

He grabbed her by the upper arms and put her away from him. "You lying, cheating, little—"

"Cole!"

He was dressed like Texas again. A denim shirt, his sleeves rolled up, with faded blue jeans riding low on his hips. His boots gave him an extra inch, and he looked truly dangerous.

He glared past her, eyes hardening on Bradley. "Looks like you changed your mind about slitting your wrists."

No. Oh, no.

Her stomach turned to a block of concrete. She had to explain. She had to make him understand. "It's not—"

Cole shut her up with a look of ice. "Don't even bother."

"But—"

"Do you actually think I'd listen to *anything* you have to say right now?"

Bradley made a move.

"Keep walking," Cole barked, squaring his shoulders and shifting himself between Sydney and Bradley.

Bradley hesitated for a split second. Then he held up his palms and took a step back. "Hey. Nothing to do with me. I've got bigger fish to fry." He turned to walk away.

"Hand it over," Cole demanded in a cold voice.

"You have to let me explain," she pleaded, searching her brain for something that would work as an explanation. She still couldn't give Grandma away.

"Explain?" He laughed coldly. "Explain why you ditched me in a hotel and bought the Thunderbolt for yourself."

"It's not for—"

"You've been stringing me along from the beginning."

"Will you *listen* to me?" What could she say? What would make sense? If only Bradley hadn't shown up. If only Cole had stayed back at the hotel.

He threw up his hands. "I can actually *see* you making up the lies."

"I'm not—" Okay, well, actually, she was.

He shook his head. Then he swiped his thumb across her bottom lip. "As far as I'm concerned, every word that comes out of your pretty little mouth is a lie."

"I never lied to you."

"Yeah? Then what the hell happened to 'Cole. I've got a lead on the brooch. I know who's got it. We can buy it back.' Did I miss that part? Was I not paying attention?"

"It's not that simple."

He folded his arms over his chest, gazing down at her with contempt. "It's *exactly* that simple. Now hand it over before I call the cops."

"You'd have me *arrested?*"

His blue eyes glittered like frozen sapphires. "Damn straight."

"What if—" What could she say? How could she explain it without betraying Grandma?

"You going to give me *another* logical story, Sydney? Been there. Done that." He held out his hand. "Give."

Sydney's shoulders drooped. It didn't matter what she said. It didn't matter what she did. "You've tried, convicted and executed me, haven't you?"

"I may be a little slow on the uptake, but I like to think I'm not a complete idiot."

Sydney yanked the purse from under her arm, fighting back a surge of stinging tears. At least Grandma would have the brooch, she told herself. And Cole would have his inheritance.

She dragged open the zipper. Maybe he would get married someday. Maybe some beautiful bride would give him beautiful children, and he'd pass all the traditions on to them.

She should be happy about that. But she just felt hollow and nauseous as she retrieved the jewel case.

"This the real one?" he asked with a derisive sneer.

She glared at him without speaking.

His voice dropped to a menacing growl as he clicked open the case. "If it's not, you know I'll come after you."

She wasn't about to dignify his accusation. "Tell Grandma…" She stuffed her purse back under her arm, squeezing it down tight. "Tell your grandmother I'm sorry."

His blue eyes hardened to stone in the bright sunshine, and he snapped the case shut. "I don't think so."

Sydney winced.

She'd lost the Thunderbolt. And she'd lost Cole.

Her body suddenly felt too heavy for her frame.

She searched his face, but there wasn't a crack of compassion, no sign of conciliation. Anything she said now would be a waste of breath.

She blinked once, then turned away. She took a couple of wooden steps toward the curb and put up her hand to hail a cab.

Cole didn't call her name, and she didn't look back.

Eleven

Cole wheeled his pickup into a wide spot in front of Grandma's house. The flowers were still blooming. The barns were still standing. And the horses still grazed in the fields.

He'd been to Heaven, then Hell, then home again, but the Texas landscape stuck to its own rhythm, not even missing his presence. He killed the engine, trying to shake the vacant feeling that had built up inside him, forcing himself to drum up some enthusiasm for the good news he was about to give his grandma.

He felt the breast pocket of his shirt for the hard, rectangular package, reassuring himself that the last four days hadn't been a dream—or a nightmare.

He kicked open the driver's door, snapping himself out of his mood. Nobody needed to know he'd been taken for a fool. They only needed to know the brooch was back.

He'd gloss over Sydney's betrayal and gloss over his own gullibility.

He crossed the dirt driveway and took the front stairs two at a time.

"Grandma?" he called as he opened the door.

She appeared in the foyer, wiping her hands on a dish towel. "I heard your truck. Do you have news?"

He forced himself to smile as he slipped the case out of his shirt pocket. "I have great news. I found it."

She searched his face for a moment. "And everything's okay?"

That wasn't exactly the reaction he was expecting. He smiled wider. "Of course it's okay. We have the Thunderbolt." He held the case out to her.

Her pale blue eyes shimmered with tears and she reached for the case, opening it carefully to gaze at the brooch. "Where's Sydney?" she asked, glancing to the open doorway behind him.

Cole inhaled, turning to close the door. "She's in New York."

Grandma stilled. "Why? Why didn't she come home?"

"She had things to do."

"What things?"

"Grandma…"

"What things? Cole Nathaniel? This is her triumph—"

Cole winced and bit back a sharp denial.

"—her achievement—"

He clenched his jaw tight to keep himself silent.

"She needs to be here with us to celebrate."

"Grandma."

"Don't you 'Grandma' me." She snapped the case shut. "She's gone."

"What did you do?"

"Sydney is not our friend," he said as gently as he could.

His grandmother glared up at him, waving the Thunderbolt case. "That's ridiculous. You're marrying her."

Cole ran a hand through his hair, gripping the base of his neck. He needed to get out of here. He needed some air. He needed *not* to be answering questions about Sydney right now. "No, I'm not marrying her."

"Oh, yes, you are." Grandma nodded. "I'm not letting you talk yourself out of this girl. It's time to grow up, Cole. It's time to take on your responsibilities."

"I'll marry someone else. I promise."

Grandma shook her head and clicked her cheeks.

Cole sucked in a breath, calming himself down. The sooner he got it over with, the better. "I didn't want to have to tell you this, Grandma."

"Tell me what? What did you do to that wonderful girl?"

That was it. Cole had had about enough. "That *wonderful girl* tried to *steal the Thunderbolt*."

"She did not."

Oh, great. Denial. That was helpful. "I watched her do it."

Grandma waved a dismissive hand. "Not possible."

"She's a stranger, Grandma. You can't have such blind faith in her." As Cole had done.

He'd been taken in by her sexy smile and her sultry voice. This was what happened when you started letting emotions mess around with your logic. Or maybe it was his libido that had messed around with his logic.

"She may be a stranger to you, Cole." Grandma tapped the case against Cole's chest. "But I know that woman. She did *not* betray us."

Sydney was amazing, a con artist of incredible talent. She probably duped old people all the time. Her and that partner, Bradley Slander.

"You do *not* know her," said Cole.

"Go get her."

Cole sputtered for a moment. "I will not go get her. Grandma, she ditched me in a hotel room to go and make a deal."

"I'm sure she had a perfectly logical explanation."

"Yeah. It was logical, all right. She wanted to steal the Thunderbolt out from under us."

Grandma waved away his words.

"I waited five hours," he explained. "I took the address from the trash bin. I followed her, and caught her and her partner red-handed, bribing some black market criminal."

The color drained from Grandma's face.

Cole was sorry to disillusion Grandma, but Sydney had to be stopped. She wasn't a good person. She was a thief. "I saw them through the window. The three of them."

"Cole." Grandma's voice turned to a hoarse whisper.

"I'm sorry, Grandma." Nobody wished more than Cole that things had turned out differently. The fake Sydney was one of the most compelling women he'd ever met. Even now, even after everything she'd done to him, he still remembered her laughing voice, her gentle caresses and her emerald-dark eyes. His stomach contracted with regret.

Grandma blinked at him. She gripped the jewel case against her chest. Then she squared her shoulders. "Sit down, Cole. There's something I have to tell you."

Perched on the couch, Cole listened with growing incredulity to his grandmother's confession.

His grandfather?

His *grandma?*

When she got to the part where she'd taken Sydney into her confidence, he jerked up and paced across the room.

With every word, with every passing second, his muscles tightened into harder balls of anger.

He didn't blame Grandma, and he didn't blame Sydney. He blamed his grandfather. And he blamed himself. It was their job to protect the family, to keep them safe.

"She bought it from your half-uncle," Grandma finished. "Then she didn't explain it to you, because I'd sworn her to secrecy. She kept my secret, Cole. She let you hate her, and she kept my secret."

Cole stopped in front of the fireplace mantel, fixing his furious gaze on the picture of his grandfather.

The man was grinning.

Grinning.

Before he was even aware of the impulse, Cole slammed his fist into the wood paneling next to the picture, cracking the veneer, putting four deep dents into the grain.

Strangely, he didn't feel the slightest pain.

"Did I miss something?" came Kyle's voice from the foyer.

A deafening silence swept the room.

"Cole and Sydney had an argument," said Grandma.

"You never punched a wall over Melanie," said Kyle.

As Cole stared at his grandfather, everything inside him turned to stone. Then his chest swelled with an ache, and his throat went raw.

He was just as bad as the old man.

He'd failed.

He wasn't there for Grandma, and he'd sent Sydney packing when he should have been down on his knees thanking her.

She'd done his job for him.

"Cole?" Kyle's voice seemed to come from a long way off. "Any news on the Thunderbolt?"

"It's here," said Grandma, holding out the case.

"Isn't that mission accomplished?" asked Kyle. "So what's wrong?"

What was wrong? Everything was wrong.

A family crisis had unfolded right under Cole's nose, and he hadn't even noticed. And he'd destroyed the woman of his dreams. She was back in New York right now, shutting down the Viking show and killing her career. She didn't deserve this. She'd stepped in to help, and what did she get in return?

He cringed remembering the insults he'd hurled at her on the sidewalk. He'd actually threatened to have her arrested.

And she hadn't said a thing. She'd kept his grandmother's confidence in spite of everything. Everything.

"Cole?" Kyle repeated, moving into the room, all humor gone from his tone.

Cole ignored his brother, slowly turning to meet Grandma's eyes.

When a man could no longer trust his own judgment, what was left? "I don't know what to do," he said.

Grandma took a step forward. "Give her the Thunderbolt."

He shook his head. It was too late. Sydney was canceling the show, and she'd never speak to him again.

"I thought you were marrying her," said Kyle, glancing from one to the other.

"They had a fight," said Grandma. "Get on the next plane, Cole. Go to New York and fix it."

"I can't fix it."

"Yes, you can."

Could he? Would an abject apology help at all? Would the Thunderbolt help, even now?

There was only one way to find out.

Cole straightened.

He filled his lungs.

"What the hell happened?" asked Kyle.

Cole turned on his heel and brushed past his brother. Grandma could tell Kyle, or not tell Kyle about the forgery. Cole would respect her decision. But right now, he had one thing to do, and one thing only.

He banged his way out the door and practically sprinted to the pickup truck.

In her cramped office on the mezzanine floor of the Laurent, Sydney hugged her arms around her chilled body.

"You fell for him, didn't you?" asked Gwen as she perched herself on the window ledge.

Sydney closed her eyes and nodded. At least there was one area where she could be honest with her friend. "I couldn't tell Cole what was really going on, either, and then Bradley showed up...."

"And Bradley's the reason Cole thinks you tried to steal his brooch?"

Sydney nodded again, struggling against the overwhelming weight of defeat. How had Cole found her? How in a city the size of Miami had he happened on that little coffee bar?

She'd thought she was home free. She would have come up with a story, any story. But when she placed the brooch in his hands, he would have known she was on his side.

Instead. Instead...

She groaned out loud. "I wish I could tell you more."

"Hey." Gwen gave a sad laugh. "It's really okay. I don't need to know. But what are you going to tell the boss? He's pretty upset, what with your promises and my promises..."

"That they wouldn't lend it to me, I guess." She shrugged. What did it matter? Her career was over. They were already scrambling to book another show for the front gallery.

Sydney had broken a cardinal rule. She'd made a promise she couldn't keep. She should have called her boss as soon as the brooch went missing. No. She should never have offered it in the first place.

She should never have offered up an item she didn't already have in her hand. But she'd trusted Cole. She knew that if he said he had the Thunderbolt, and he said he'd give her the Thunderbolt, it was as good as done.

Not quite, as it turned out. Not that it was Cole's fault. It was her fault. All her fault.

"Maybe we can replace the Thunderbolt," Gwen suggested. "Use one of the ruby necklaces."

"There's not enough public interest. It had to be a new piece. It had to be a fantastic piece."

"It's not fair that you should get hung out to dry."

Sydney gave a hollow laugh. "It's official. Life's not fair." She knew she should care a lot more about the demise of her career, but she couldn't seem to get past losing Cole.

Every time she closed her eyes, she saw him in the Miami hotel room—the sympathy in his blue eyes when she talked about Nanny and Papa, the twinkle when he fed her a strawberry, and the dark passion when he reached out to touch her hair and pull her in for a kiss.

Stop. She had to stop—

"For the record," came the voice that was haunting her brain, "I gave you the benefit of the doubt."

Gwen's eyes went wide. She quickly slipped down off the window ledge.

Sydney pivoted to see Cole, big as life, lounging against the jamb of her office door.

"I'll…uh…" Gwen quickly brushed past Cole to exit the room.

Sydney blinked, trying to adjust her focus to something that made sense.

"I waited five hours in that hotel room," he said. "It took me *five* hours to convince myself you actually had betrayed me."

"What are you doing here?" Her fingers curled convulsively into the palms of her hands. The Thunderbolt was genuine. He had no excuse to show up and torture her.

He took a couple of steps into the room, swinging the door shut behind him. "Grandma told me."

"Grandma told you what?"

"She told me the truth."

Sydney backed up, shaking her head. That couldn't be. They were home free. Grandma would never have given away her secret once she had the Thunderbolt back.

Sydney's butt came up against her small desk. "No," she whispered.

"Yes." Cole nodded. "Why didn't you tell me, Sydney?"

What kind of a question was that? "I gave her my word. My vow."

"I could have helped you."

"You were the one she was keeping it from."

"She's my responsibility," he snapped.

Sydney recoiled from the shout.

She wished she knew how to help him. This had to be hell on his pride. You took away what a man like Cole needed to protect, and he was lost.

He raked a hand through his hair. "I'm sorry."

"It's okay. I know you're upset."

He moved closer, shaking his head. "No. I'm not sorry I yelled. I mean, I *am* sorry I yelled." He stopped. "But I'm really sorry I mistrusted you. I'm sorry I treated you so badly. I'm sorry we…" His gaze drifted away from hers.

Some of the tension went out of Sydney. "Yeah? Well, I'm sorry about that part, too." They'd played with fire and they'd both been burned. She'd known all along that Cole was temporary, but she hadn't been able to resist him. And now any man she slept with from here on in was going to be held up to his standard.

Even now, his elusive scent teased her.

She shook herself. "Why are you here?"

He hesitated. "I'm here to give you the Thunderbolt."

Her throat went dry. "You can't do that."

"Oh, yes I can."

"But—"

He reached out and took both of her hands.

Her chest contracted with the touch.

"I'm proposing, Sydney."

Her heart skipped a beat. Proposing? For real?

"How do you mean?" she ventured, not daring to believe it could be true. She'd already had that dream crushed once.

"Just like we planned. You show the Thunderbolt. And then…" He shrugged his shoulders and glanced down at the floor.

The faint hope leeched out of her body. "A marriage of convenience, Cole?"

He nodded. "It is the only answer."

She'd once thought so, too. But she'd been wrong. Cole loving her was the only answer. Cole wanting to marry her and spend the rest of his life with her was the only answer she'd accept now.

He'd once asked her if she was ready to walk down the aisle in a white dress, promise to love him, then kiss him, throw a bouquet—and then go their separate ways.

She's been prepared to do it then. She couldn't do it now.

"I don't think it's the answer anymore," she told him, her throat aching with disappointment.

"You've earned it," he said.

She raised her hand to her lips to stifle a bitter laugh. "By lying to you? By sleeping with you?"

"Don't."

She shook her head. "Thanks for the offer, Cole. But I think I'll pass."

She couldn't show the Thunderbolt under these circumstances. And she wasn't even sure she wanted to show it. The brooch was exactly where it was supposed to be, safe with Grandma, safe with Cole, someday safe with Cole's real bride.

"I'm not taking no for an answer," he insisted. "You're the reason we found it. You're the reason we even knew where to look. You were there for Grandma when she couldn't trust me—"

"Oh, Cole." Sydney's heart instantly ached for him. "It wasn't a matter of trust."

"No?"

"She was embarrassed beyond belief. I was a stranger. She didn't care about my opinion the way she cared about yours."

"That's not how I see it."

"You're not thinking clearly."

"I'm thinking perfectly clearly. I want you to marry me. I want you to reap the professional benefits of showing the Thunderbolt. It's all I can offer to make up for..."

Sydney fought the chill that moved over her soul. "I don't want it." Did he think they could just erase the past two weeks? He'd shown her the moon and the stars, then he'd yanked it all away. She'd watched the way he'd treated his family, felt the way he loved them, felt the way life might be if he might have loved her. But he didn't, and he never would, and there was nothing she could do about that.

"You're lying."

"The answer is no, Cole."

"You'll break Grandma's heart."

"Low blow," she retorted, a weak smile cresting his lips.

"You ain't seen nothing yet." He clamped his jaw. "Marry me, or I'll fight dirty."

She folded her arms across her chest, not about to give an inch. "Go ahead. Give it your best shot."

"I'll call Bradley."

Sydney pulled back in horror.

"I'm sure he'll have some ideas about showing the Thunderbolt."

She shook her head. "Cole. No. You don't know what he'll—"

"I'll do it. Either you marry me, or I make a deal with Bradley."

"You're bluffing."

"I don't bluff."

"That man's evil."

"Then marry me."

"No."

He threw up his hands. "I'm not asking you to walk the plank. You only have to put up with me for an hour or two. Give me one little kiss, pretend you like me at the reception, then we each go our own way. You'll find reasons to be in New York. I'll find reasons to be on the ranch. And, after a decent interval, we tell everyone it didn't work out."

"Could a proposal get any less romantic?" she asked.

He glared at her.

"I mean, really, Cole. Is there anything you could add that would make a girl feel less desirable?"

He stared hard into her eyes. "My desire for you was never in question."

Familiar stirrings rose up in Sydney's chest. For a split second she considered saying yes and hauling him off on a real honeymoon. But she couldn't do that. It would only put off the heartbreak, maybe make the pain even worse.

"You're thinking about it," he said. "I can tell you're thinking about it."

She shook her head.

"Say yes, Sydney. You can do it."

Could she?

If she didn't get past her feelings for Cole, she'd go insane. She needed to focus on something else. And her career was the only reasonable distraction. And at least she'd have the satisfaction of thwarting Bradley.

She gazed into Cole's eyes, studied those flecks of storm-tossed gray for the last time.

"Fine," she said, suddenly tired of fighting, tired of feeling, tired of wishing for something he'd never be able to give her. "I'll marry you."

"Yeah?"

"Yeah." She tossed her hair behind her shoulders. "After all, it's the professional coup of a lifetime."

Twelve

Two weeks later Sydney was seriously rethinking her decision to marry Cole. But the Laurent was already poised for the Viking antique show, Grandma had already pinned the Thunderbolt to the bodice of Sydney's wedding gown and, most importantly, Sydney had already said "I do."

In the brand-new hay barn down the driveway from Cole's cabin, all eyes were on the bride and groom. The small band launched into the bridal waltz, and Cole pulled Sydney into his arms.

The floor was rough, and the walls were bare wood. But the acoustics were impressive, and they danced together like they made love together, every movement in sync, every breath in harmony. She could swear their heartbeats had synchronized.

"Relax," he whispered into her ear, gathering her close.

"I'm trying."

"Think about the Thunderbolt," he advised. "You're going to be a very famous woman."

"And so, I'm a success," she said on a forced laugh, fighting to keep it from turning into a tear.

His hand stroked up and down her back, just barely touching her exposed skin where the dress veed between her shoulder blades. Ironic that the very man who was tearing her heart out was also comforting her.

She subconsciously moved closer to the heat of his body, his scent taking her back days and weeks to the tiny bedroom on the shores of Blue Creek. She could almost hear the clock ticking as he messed with time.

He settled his arm more securely across the small of her back while the singer crooned his way through a wholly inappropriate Shania Twain tune.

"Are you remembering?" Cole whispered.

"No," she lied.

He bent closer to her ear, his breath puffing in warm bursts. "I sure am."

"Don't." Memories could kill her. They were killing her.

"No matter what happened," he rasped, swaying to the strains of promises and love for the rest of their lives. "No matter what I said and did that can never be fixed. I want you to know that you rocked my world."

"Cole," she moaned.

"For as long as I live, I'll see you in that billowing bed with strawberry-stained lips and tousled hair, sharing my secrets, looking out for my family."

"Please stop."

"I'm so sorry, Sydney."

She shook her head. "It's not you."

He gathered her closer still. "Well, it's sure as hell not you."

"Maybe it's us."

"Maybe it was circumstances."

She dared to look up at him. "Does it really matter anymore?"

It was over between them. Not that they'd ever had a chance. He was her ticket to the Thunderbolt, nothing more. That he was the lover of a lifetime had messed things up, and that she had to lie to him had messed things up. But even without the lies, without the lovemaking, the best she could have hoped for is exactly where they were now— going into a sham marriage to circumvent a will.

He sighed against the top her head. "I hate leaving things unsettled between us."

"We're settled." She was getting better and better at lying.

"No, we're not."

The band moved into the third chorus, and the lyrics all but pierced Sydney's heart.

"What do you need to settle it, Cole? To know that I'm sorry I lied to you?"

"No." He pulled back, cupping her face in his palms. "That's not what I meant."

To her surprise, he captured her lips in a long, soulful kiss.

Ridiculous hope fluttered to life as the song built to a crescendo of everlasting love.

She pulled back, intent on saving her sanity. "There are two hundred people watching us."

"Lucky them."

"Cole."

"Just tell me you forgive me."

"For what?"

He chuckled softly as the band held the final note. "Right."

"Seriously, Cole. What?"

He stared into her eyes.

The note faded to silence and the audience burst into applause.

Kyle appeared next to Cole's shoulder. "I believe it's the best man's turn."

Cole plucked an ice-cold beer from the bar in the corner of his new barn.

Sydney needed to forgive him for insulting her. She needed to forgive him for threatening to have her arrested. And she also needed to forgive him for not recognizing she was the most wonderful woman on the planet.

He'd picked that sappy song himself, hoping by some miracle she'd know he meant it.

She hadn't.

He briefly acknowledged the congratulations from one of his neighbors, but he didn't engage Clyde in conversation. He wanted to fade into the shadows and watch Sydney sway in Kyle's arms, since tonight might be the last time he saw her.

The song ended and he checked the impulse to rush back to her side.

She glanced around, then glided across the floor, her dress flowing softly around her ankles. A few people stopped her to exchange words, Cole's neighbors, Sydney's co-workers. Then a man cut in front of her, and Cole squinted. He didn't recognize the guest, but something prickled along his spine.

Her back was to him, but her shoulders tensed as the two began to speak. Cole ditched the beer bottle and headed across the floor.

Halfway there, he recognized Bradley Slander.

He swore under his breath and quickened his pace, shouldering his way between guests. He still couldn't see Sydney's expression, but Bradley was way too close.

When Cole got into range, he heard Bradley's tone dripping with malevolence. "—and so I'm wondering what it feels like to whore yourself for an antique."

Sydney recoiled, and something exploded inside Cole's brain. Instinct took over as he crossed the last few yards on a dead run. He grabbed Slander by the collar and slammed him up against the wood wall.

He held him there, nose to nose, forearm jammed against his sternum while Slander's face turned an interesting shade of maroon.

"I don't know how things work up in New York," stormed Cole. "But here in Texas, y'all 've got two choices. You can apologize to my wife and get the hell off my land. Or I can blow off your balls and feed them to the dogs."

Slander's mouth worked, but nothing came out except raspy squeaks.

"Cole?" came Kyle's warning voice.

Cole would have broken Slander's nose for good measure, but he'd already wasted too many minutes of his life on the man, and he needed to make sure Sydney was okay.

He jerked back and let Slander crumple to the floor. Then he turned to look for her.

She stood frozen, a few yards away, her eyes wide as a few people tried to engage her in conversation.

Cole marched to her side and wrapped an arm around her waist, pulling her away from the curious guests.

She was shaking.

Fortunately, the band hadn't seen the altercation, and they played on. He guided Sydney into the middle of the dance floor and gathered her into his arms.

Her glance went to the doorway where Kyle was escorting Slander outside.

Cole turned her so she wouldn't have to look.

Her voice quavered. "He—"

"He sends his apologies," said Cole.

She nodded against Cole's shoulder, her body stiff as a board.

"It's okay," he whispered, rubbing a hand up and down her back. "Relax. It's over. Just dance with me."

She shook her head against his chest. "He just said what they're all thinking."

"No, he didn't."

"That I married you for the brooch."

"They're all thinking you're a beautiful bride."

"They're wondering why you agreed to marry me. They're thinking I'm a mercenary."

"No, they're not."

"That's what Katie thought."

He tipped her chin up. "For a short time, maybe. But then she got to know you. She knows you're not a mercenary."

"But I am." There was a catch in her voice, and his heart ached.

"We both know the truth, and that's all that matters."

She shook her head once more.

He kissed the softness of her hair. "Stop. Just stop."

"But we don't, Cole."

"We don't what?"

She tilted her chin to look up, eyes glassy and tearful. "*You* don't know the truth."

He squinted at her. Oh, no.

"The truth is, I didn't marry you for the brooch."

A chill of fear iced Cole's spine. He couldn't take another one of her deceptions. Not here. Not now.

She bit her bottom lip, and her chest rose once, then fell. "I married you because I love you."

The fear in Cole's body plummeted through the floorboards. He gave his head a little shake. She couldn't have just said those words. It was his own wishful thinking.

"Say that again," he rasped, fighting the roaring in his ears.

"I love you, Cole," she repeated.

He squeezed her tight. "Oh, Sydney. I have loved you for…" He stroked his hand slowly over her fragrant hair, marveling that his dreams had actually come true. "Forever, I think."

Her voice lifted. "You do?"

He kissed her temple. "I do."

A soft sigh escaped from her, she seemed to melt against him.

"Oh, Cole.

"I know."

"We're married."

"I meant the song." He cradled her face in his hands. "For as long as I live. I meant every word."

"I meant my vows," she whispered.

"I will love you," he whispered back, "cherish you, honor and keep you."

"Till death do us part," she said, finding his hand with her own and twining their fingers together.

"Till death do us part," he repeated, pulling their joined hands between their bodies as the music swelled. The yellow lights shone through her hair and the scent of the wedding roses filled the new barn.

"I guess we'll be building that house now," said Cole, feathering light kisses down her cheek, heading for her soft lips.

"With the turret and the dormer windows." She sighed against him. "And a breakfast bar and some of those high stools with the curved backs."

He chuckled. "I guess if I'm going to be a patriarch, I'll need a big house."

"A patriarch?"

"Yeah."

"Oh, great. You're going to start issuing decrees now, aren't you?"

"You bet." He nodded. "Starting tonight, I'm whipping this family into shape."

"Kyle will never take the land."

"I know he won't." Cole smiled to himself. He'd been working on that one for a while.

"What?" Sydney prompted.

"I'm leaving it to his children."

"You're devious."

"That I am. But you love me, right?"

"I love you," she said.

"Say it again."

She pulled back and cupped his face between her soft hands. "I love you, Cole Erickson."

He sighed. He could listen to that all night long.

"Isn't there something you want to say to me?" she prompted.

He kissed her softly on the lips. "Hmm. Let me think."

She dug her elbow into his ribs.

"I love you Sydney…Erickson," he rumbled.

A funny expression flitted across her face.

"I guess we didn't talk about names, did we?" He wasn't going to insist. After all, traditions had to change sometime.

"Sydney Erickson." She rocked her head back and forth. "I think I like that." Her lips curved into a smile.

Cole grinned right back, smoothing her hair, kissing her again. They could have a real honeymoon now. He'd planned to hide out in Montana for a week, but he'd go wherever she wanted.

"Hey, Cole." Kyle danced up to them with Katie in his arms.

Cole nodded to his brother, hugging Sydney close.

"Who was that guy?" Katie asked Sydney.

"Antique vulture," Sydney answered, and Cole was proud of how quickly she'd recovered from the altercation.

"Won't *ever* be back to the Valley," said Kyle.

Cole nodded his thanks. He should've broken Slander's nose. But then the sheriff might have had to lock him up on his wedding night.

"Thought you two might like to know the wedding worked," said Katie with a wide smile.

"Sure did," said Cole, though he wasn't sure how Katie knew that already. He kissed Sydney's temple.

"Looks like along about April," said Katie.

Sydney let out a sudden squeal and pulled away from Cole's arms.

"What?" asked Cole as his wife embraced his sister-in-law.

"New little Erickson," said Kyle with wide, sappy grin.

Cole let out a whoop. He reached out and clapped Kyle on the shoulder. "That's fantastic! Congratulations, little brother."

"Thanks," said Kyle.

"Can we talk about splitting the land now?" asked Cole.

"No," said Kyle.

Cole smiled as he shook his head. "I'm going to win this one."

Someone tapped his shoulder and he turned.

"Hey, Grandma." He pulled Sydney back into his arms as Kyle danced off with Katie. "Don't you just love a good wedding?"

"You know I do," said Grandma. "And I have something for Sydney."

Sydney tipped her head questioningly. "For me?"

"This way," said Grandma with a mysterious wink. "Both of you."

They followed her through the crowd, past the band, toward the back of the barn where the light was dim and the air was a few degrees cooler.

Cole held Sydney's hand as they walked, unable to resist sending goofy smiles her way. He couldn't wait to get her alone.

Or maybe he could. It was fun to show her off. His wife. His *wife*. And tonight was the first of thousands together.

Yeah, he could wait.

He lifted her hand to his lips and kissed each of her knuckles. He was going to relish every single hour with this woman.

Grandma came to a stop at a back table, rattling something out of a paper bag.

She turned to face Sydney with a very serious expression on her face. "Sydney Erickson."

Cole squeezed Sydney's hand. He loved her new name.

"It is my honor," said Grandma, "to present you with the providence and chronicles of the Thunderbolt of the North." She handed Sydney a large, leather-bound book.

Sydney's forearms sagged with the weight of the dark, heavy volume. Cole started to take it from her, then checked the impulse. Her eyes were wide with wonder as she stared down.

Cole blinked in amazement as well. He hadn't even known such a thing existed.

"It was translated in the mid-1700s," said Grandma, patting her hand gently on the cover. "I've never been sure if it was taken from a written account, or if Sigrid wrote down the oral history. In any event, it's all here. The life and times of the Thunderbolt."

Sydney ran her fingers over the embossed cover. "This is absolutely amazing," she whispered, glancing up at Cole. "It's priceless."

Grandma smiled with obvious satisfaction. "And it's your turn to continue the saga."

Sydney's jaw dropped open.

"And I suggest you start with the Thunderbolt's latest adventure."

"Are you sure?" asked Sydney. "The *entire* adventure?"

Grandma patted the book again. "Yes. The whole adventure. The diary deserves no less than the truth."

Cole wrapped an arm around his grandmother's thin shoulders and gave her an affectionate squeeze. "Thank you, Grandma."

Her eyes shimmered bright as she smiled up at him.

"For everything," he said.

"I was right about Sydney, wasn't I?"

"You were absolutely right about Sydney."

"Good. Well, I'll leave you two alone now," she said with a quick smile.

"I can't believe it," said Sydney, her voice hoarse with awe.

"It couldn't be in better hands," said Cole, loving her more by the second.

She shook her head, and her eyes shimmered jewel-bright under the lights. Then she pressed the big book more tightly against her chest. "I never thought it could happen," she whispered. "But you did it, Cole."

"I did what?" He searched her eyes. "I fell in love with you?"

She shook her head. "That, too." Then she reached up

and stroked her soft palm against his cheek. "What I meant was, you found my silver locket."

Ah. His gaze went to the brooch, nestled against the beaded fabric of her wedding dress. "The Thunderbolt."

She shook her head again. "No. It was never the jewelry." She smiled. "It was never the things."

"Then…"

"It was the heritage, the home. I finally realized." She swayed toward him, and his arms automatically wrapped around her.

"I was searching for the family I never had. And you gave it to me."

His chest expanded almost painfully.

She was his. She was here forever.

"Welcome home, Sydney," he whispered against her hair. "We've been waiting for you all along."

* * * * *

Queens of Romance

Uncertain Summer

Serena gave up hope of getting married when her fiancé
jilted her. Then Gijs suggested that she marry him instead.
She liked Gijs very much, and she knew he was fond of her –
that seemed as good a basis as any for marriage. But it
turned out Gijs was in love…

Small Slice of Summer

Letitia Marsden had decided that men were not to be trusted,
until she met Doctor Jason Mourik van Nie. This time, Letitia
vowed, there would be a happy ending. Then Jason got the
wrong idea about one of her male friends. Surely a simple
misunderstanding couldn't stand in the way of true love?

Available 1st August 2008

Collect all 10 superb books in the collection!

0908/25/MB157

Queens of Romance

Bedding His Virgin Mistress

Ricardo Salvatore planned to take over Carly's company, so why not have her as well? But Ricardo was stunned when in the heat of passion he learned of Carly's innocence…

Expecting the Playboy's Heir

American billionaire and heir to an earldom, Silas Carter is one of the world's most eligible men. Beautiful Julia Fellowes is perfect wife material. And she's pregnant!

Blackmailing the Society Bride

When millionaire banker Marcus Canning decides it's time to get an heir, debt-ridden Lucy becomes a convenient wife. Their sexual chemistry is purely a bonus…

Available 5th September 2008

Collect all 10 superb books in the collection!

Queens of Romance

Mackenzie's Magic
Maris Mackenzie woke up to sexy stranger
Alex MacNeil in her bed – and she'd lost all recollection
of their night together…

Heartbreaker
Michelle was deeply in debt to sexy John Rafferty, the
tough-talking, hard-loving rancher. Yet out of self-
preservation she still refused to become his mistress!

Overload
Stranded with him in a Dallas skyscraper during a power cut,
Elizabeth Major thought Tom Quinlan was too much for
her to handle. So now he was changing her mind…

Available 3rd October 2008

Collect all 10 superb books in the collection!

Queens of Romance

The Baby Bonding
Midwife Molly Hammond had once carried a child for
surgeon Sam Gregory and his wife. But now he's a single
father and feels his son should get to know Molly.

The Pregnant Tycoon
Rich and successful, Izzy Brooke meets gorgeous single
dad Will Thompson, the boyfriend she had as a teenager,
and she's suddenly accidentally pregnant…

The Baby From Nowhere
Handsome James Sutherland is Maisie McDowell's new
neighbour…and her new GP! And then he tells her
she is pregnant…

Available 7th November 2008

Collect all 10 superb books in the collection!

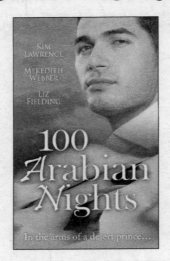

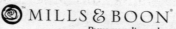

FREE!

2 Books
and a surprise gift!

We would like to take this opportunity to thank you for reading this Mills & Boon® book by offering you the chance to take TWO more specially selected titles from the Desire™ series absolutely FREE! We're also making this offer to introduce you to the benefits of the Mills & Boon® Reader Service™—

- ★ FREE home delivery
- ★ FREE gifts and competitions
- ★ FREE monthly Newsletter
- ★ Exclusive Reader Service offers
- ★ Books available before they're in the shops

Accepting these FREE books and gift places you under no obligation to buy. you may cancel at any time. even after receiving your free shipment. Simply complete your details below and return the entire page to the address below. You don't even need a stamp!

YES! Please send me 2 free Desire books and a surprise gift. I understand that unless you hear from me. I will receive 3 superb new titles every month for just £4.99 each. postage and packing free. I am under no obligation to purchase any books and may cancel my subscription at any time. The free books and gift will be mine to keep in any case.

D8ZEF

Ms/Mrs/Miss/Mr ....Initials...................................
                                                                            BLOCK CAPITALS PLEASE
Surname...
Address..

....Postcode..........................

Send this whole page to:
UK: FREEPOST CN81, Croydon, CR9 3WZ